I0675049

Dear Walt

A novel by

R. D. Frazier

A
WordSpresso
Publication

Dear Walt
by R.D. Frazier

www.DearWalt.com

Copyright © 2008 by R.D. Frazier

All rights reserved

This book or parts thereof may not be reproduced in any form, stored in a retrieval system, or transmitted in any form by any means — electronic, mechanical, photocopy, recording or otherwise — without prior written permission from the publisher, except as permitted by United States of America copyright law.

"Dear Walt" is a novel based purely on fictional characters. No actual person or event is portrayed in this book. However, the dog named Bronson is a close approximation of our now departed and much loved canine companion.

The setting is the state of Colorado, primarily in and around Platteville, Glenwood Springs and Grand Junction, but the details of these locales may be (and probably are) inaccurate.

Published by Knowing Him Press
10087 League Line Road
Conroe, Texas 77304

A WordSpresso Publication
www.WordSpresso.com

International Standard Book Number 978-0-9768824-9-7

Printed in the United States of America

Main Players:

ANDY – It was 2 a.m. when Andy pulled the wrinkled note from his pocket. Not a good time to call Aunt Margaret, so he curled up on the bus station bench and slept. When the groan of bus brakes awakened him, his duffle bag and everything he owned was gone. The harmonica his Daddy had given him was really the only thing he would miss. An uncertain future lay ahead, but there was no turning back now.

JOHNNY – Johnny limped a good bit and seemed to rest a lot sometimes. He looked for a check in the mail every month, and was stressed if it didn't come on time. The near-fatal injuries he suffered in Viet Nam had almost shattered his life, requiring multiple operations on his heart and lungs, and leaving him with an artificial leg. Viet Nam was not the last time he sacrificed personal safety for others.

AUNT MARGARET – Her infectious smile and zest for life helped Andy through one of the worst times in his young life. She gave him grape sodas, combed his hair into place after mussing it in fun, and talked about eight-year-old things … for a while he didn't have to think about anything but her hugs and boisterous laughter.

Acknowledgements

On a Sunday morning as I sat listening to Pastor Dan tell the story of Moses' self-imposed exile from Egypt to Midian ... because Egypt was "a place he could no longer live" ... I was stirred to begin writing the opening letter for "Dear Walt." His inspired message was a driving force that very afternoon that would not be denied. Without Dan's constant support, inspirational conversation and brotherhood along the way, "Dear Walt" would have languished. Thank you, Dan, for your encouragement and unbounded confidence.

And Grace, you, along with Barbara and Dan endured reviewing the manuscript at all stages. Your enthusiasm for "Dear Walt" played a key role in staying the course.

Of course my wife, Barbara, has been continually involved in the process with great insight into characters and events, as well as providing her considerable editing and proofreading talent. Thank you, Barbara for your patience, endurance and loving hand which contributed immeasurably to this first fledgling effort.

Cover design by R.D. Frazier.
Photo Copyright © 1981 by R.D. Frazier

Contents

For the exiles

A Deepening Dark

They have not imagined the weight

of their sin: that it makes a knot

in their hearts, cages the mind's wings.

Their trouble is only the trouble anyone,

all of us, know: exchange the truth

about God for a lie,

live in a deepening dark.

In a world brittle, seamed with cracks,

ready to shatter, comes a certain slant

of light, a love-blazing fire into the

sensuous night. Found identity

causes their voices to rise in their

throats. From broken hearts, now mended,

like good bone, uprises a spirit-song.

Dan Schiel

Exile

Dear Walt,

Tragedy struck two months ago. I was walking through Denver on my way home and heard sirens. When I turned a corner I could see blood along the curb beneath the paramedics working frantically on a man lying at the edge of the sidewalk. A small crowd had gathered and the police were holding them back from the drama unfolding before them.

I crossed the narrow street to avoid the confusion, continuing my walk toward the lot where I had parked. But a haunting pall came over me when I saw the shoes of the man on the sidewalk.

I knew those shoes!

I stopped.

I froze.

I listened.

The police were taking statements from two young women on the street as the life-blood dripped over the curb and the paramedics suddenly slumped in horrible disappointment and exhaustion. They covered his face ...

8:47 p.m. the same day

... I can't write any more now! There's just too much to say ... too much to put in a letter without more thought, more reflection. I need to find just the right words to explain it all to him. Could he have any inkling of what I need to say, after a lifetime has passed?

How did I become so involved with his past?

Now as I sit in silence, staring at my computer, this unfinished letter mocks me more with every passing minute.

Should I call him instead? I haven't actually heard Walt's voice in decades. What if I choke on the phone?

I stare out the window of our Denver home. I can see the mountains to the west ... not much snow on the peaks this time of year.

My first night in Denver had been so bleak and frightening. The bus had come in at night. I remember seeing snow on the road in the headlights over thirty years ago...

... *Denver* — January 1976

I was new in town. I was fourteen, confused and scared. I was a long way from Texas, a long way from the settled life I had known there — white porch rail, Saturday matinee movies with hot dogs and buttered popcorn, Sunday school the next morning and later Mama's fried chicken on the dinner table — fading memories from what seemed another lifetime, another world.

It was bitter cold on the streets of Denver and my blanket lined denim jacket just didn't cut it as the Colorado wind bit through my Texas winter coat. I had spent all but twenty dollars on the bus ticket, and this was the end of the line. The $20 hadn't gone as far as I'd thought for grilled cheese sandwiches and Cokes in bus depot diners. I'd have to hitch from here, not a welcome thought with only my thin denim jacket between me and the cold while I dragged Daddy's heavy old duffle bag. At least it wasn't snowing again ... yet.

I pulled the wrinkled note with my great Aunt Margaret's phone number from my pocket. It was 2 a.m. I curled up on the bus station bench with my coat over my shoulders. I slept. The groan of bus brakes and the smell of diesel colored my dreams as the snow melted in my imagination and I dreamed fitful dreams of eighteen wheelers on a Texas Interstate. When I woke up my duffle bag was gone. It had everything I owned inside, except the clothes on my back. What I would miss most was the harmonica Daddy gave me the year before he died at the wheel of his truck on a Houston overpass six years ago.

It was 7:32 a.m. by the bus station clock when I pulled out my last $1.67 in change from my front jeans pocket and headed for the phone.

Two months after Mama died too I had taken all I could carry and hit the road. I just couldn't face living with Aunt Flora and Uncle Ted in Corpus in the same house with those snotty little kids and their sniveling voices. Worst of all was that Aunt Flora was Mama's identical twin sister ... I couldn't stand the thought of seeing Mama's face in hers every day.

I was about seven or eight years old the last time I saw Aunt Margaret, but I still remember her infectious smile and zest for life. She came to be with Mama after Daddy's funeral. That summer in Brownsville Aunt Margaret worked her way into my heart forever because she was more like a forty-year-old kid at times than my mother's favorite aunt. Her boisterous greetings of hugs, laughter and hair mussing had made me giggle every time. Then she'd give me a grape soda to drink while she combed my hair back into place and we talked about eight-year-old things ... for a little while I didn't have to think about Daddy's face in that coffin or Mama's sad red eyes.

That summer Aunt Margaret told me stories about when she lived in Brownsville as a kid before Mama was even born. She told me about standing on the side of the road with her school friends and catching cucumbers the farm workers threw to them from the trucks. What a treat! They ate them just like they were candy. In 1942 sugar was scarce because of the war, and candy was even more scarce.

She took me to a few Saturday afternoon movies and made sure we had hot dogs and buttered popcorn like Mama sometimes did when Daddy was on the road. She took me to church and listened patiently as I told her all about baby Moses we learned about in Sunday school. We spent the next few weeks talking more about Moses, the Ten Commandments, and crossing the desert to the Promised Land. Sometimes she read from Exodus to me so I could hear more about Moses from "The Good Book."

After school started that year, somebody from Denver called Aunt Margaret on the phone. She didn't smile that night while she was packing to go home. She told me she had to go home to take care of Johnny now, so she wanted me to take her place helping Mama since Daddy was gone.

I asked her when Johnny came home from Viet Nam. She said he wasn't home yet, but she had to go home and wait for him to get there. He was coming home from the war for good. Her eyes looked like Mama's the day of Daddy's funeral. I was scared. I asked her if Johnny was OK. She said "He's still alive, but I don't know if he's OK. I need to go home to see him, but I'll keep you and your Mama in my prayers. I love you Andy."

She took the bus to Denver the next morning at 3. That was the last time I saw her. And now here I am in the Denver bus station by myself.

I picked up the pay phone on the corner outside the bus station and called her number. Johnny answered. When I asked for Aunt Margaret he seemed confused about who I was.

"Your Aunt Margaret isn't home now. She's in Denver for her treatment this morning and she won't be home 'til after noon. Who is this?"

"I'm Andy, her great nephew from Brownsville ... Nora's boy."

"Whatcha doin' up here in the snow, boy ... sorry. We heard about your Ma. Are you OK? You say you're at the bus station?"

"Yeah, I came in last night, but I didn't want to wake

anybody up, so I waited 'til now to call. All I have is
your phone number, so I don't know how to get to your
place."

"Who's with you? Do they have a Colorado Map?
We're a few miles out of Denver."

"I'm by myself. I couldn't stay at Aunt Flora's
anymore ... I just couldn't ... so I left."

"So Flora doesn't know where you are?"

"No"

"You just stay put! I'll be down to get you in about
an hour and a half. These roads are a little slow with the
snow and all."

I wondered what Johnny looked like. I took a walk
outside the station while I waited for him and remembered
the last time I heard his name or thought about him much.
It was just before Aunt Margaret left Texas on the bus to
come back and take care of him. I thought about how
she must have spent those same long hours on the bus
wondering about Johnny. At least he was still alive, not
like Mama and Daddy.

When Johnny picked me up we went to a little coffee
shop for breakfast not far from the bus station. We talked
until he was satisfied I was okay, then we left for their
house in Platteville. The sun bouncing off the snow was
so bright you could hardly see sometimes. We arrived
a few minutes before the church van brought Aunt
Margaret home about noon.

After the required hugs and hair-mussing we sat
down at the kitchen table and talked about why I was
here alone and how far I had come alone. I told Aunt
Margaret I had gotten some money for my birthday a
couple of weeks ago, so after Aunt Flora moved me to
Corpus, I bought a bus ticket to come to Denver. I told
her why I couldn't stay in Corpus. Aunt Margaret called

Flora to tell her where I was and that everything was fine. She looked very tired. Johnny fixed lunch and later we had leftovers for supper.

You could see the mountains in the distance from here. Nothing around here was green. It was bitter cold. It was a long way from Texas.

Aunt Margaret talked to Flora on the phone again that evening and they agreed to let me stay here for a while and go to school. I settled in on the closed-in porch behind the kitchen. The snow was bright in the full moon. The window was frosty and the two homemade quilts Johnny gave me to keep warm made me feel secure. I thought about Mama the last time I saw her alive. I cried under the covers so nobody would hear me.

I slept.

Saturday Aunt Margaret dragged me around to a few of her friend's houses and rounded up some clothes and a real winter coat to fit me, since everything I had brought from Brownsville was in my duffle bag when it was stolen. My feet were wet from the snow by the time we got back to her house Saturday night, so she made me take off my shoes and socks so they could dry before Sunday school the next morning.

I told her I wasn't going to Sunday school or church again.

She asked why. I refused to answer. She said "Andy, I want to know why you don't want to go to church any more."

"What good is it?"

"What do you mean, what good is it?"

"First Daddy died, and Mama told me we had to go to church and pray, even if we didn't feel like it anymore. We kept going and I was even baptized when I was twelve. Mama was already getting sick sometimes then.

I hoped I could pray better for her after that. Mr. Johnson prayed for her when I had to stay at his house sometimes while she was in the hospital and he listened to me pray for her when I asked the blessing before supper at his house. Even after all that church and praying Mama still got sicker and sicker. And now she's dead. What good did it do? I'm not going."

"Yes you are! I'm not leaving you in this house alone tomorrow. You're going with us to church whether you like it or not. I know we had lots of fun when I was in Brownsville that time, but this is different. I'm taking care of you now, and if you want to stay here you're going to listen to me, just like you did your Mama. Go on to bed now, it's been a long day for both of us. I love you Andy. Good night."

We ate breakfast in time to go to Sunday school the next morning. My shoes were mostly dry, but they felt stiff when I first put them on because they dried out in front of the gas heater in my room. I was glad to have clean dry socks to wear.

The Sunday school room was still cold, and the metal folding chairs made it seem worse than it was. I looked out the window toward the distant mountains and squirmed a lot. Later when Aunt Margaret asked me what the Sunday school lesson was about I couldn't remember. She asked me if I had made some new friends and I told her no, I just met some other kids but I couldn't remember any of their names. Her eyes looked sad and when she stroked my head she didn't muss my hair or say anything more about it. We just walked into the sanctuary and took a seat four rows from the back. It was warmer in here by now, so I took off my newly acquired winter coat and sat down between her and Johnny.

The windows didn't have the pretty colored stained glass like the ones in our church in Brownsville. I could see the cold, white snow outside stretching across the flat land all the way to the mountains on the western horizon. I heard my name when the preacher prayed, but that's all I remember from that day. When he preached I just looked at the snow and thought about Mama and how all the people had told me she was in heaven now. Did they have snow in heaven? If they did was it this cold, too? If it was this cold how could it be so nice there? Daddy didn't like the snow. Were he and Mama really together there now?

So many questions flood my head about them now. Why did they have to leave me? I didn't hear anything the preacher said that Sunday or any Sunday for a long time.

I was mad at God. I was numb to the world around me.

School was boring. I worked just hard enough to keep Aunt Margaret off my back and didn't make any real friends.

It was a long cold winter in Platteville, Colorado.

When spring came everything that had been so white turned to mud, the rivers ran high and turned ugly brown for a while. We had a few more cold days, but mostly it was just mud and then things started turning green.

School and church, school and church, that's about all I did for a long time. I heard my name in the preacher's prayers on Sunday for a while, then not so much as spring came.

Aunt Margaret was not as much fun as I remembered her from that summer in Brownsville, but I knew she cared about me. She seemed tired a lot and she continued to make her twice-weekly trips to Denver for a while, then once-weekly for a while. Johnny did the cooking most of the time, except when she felt up to it.

I thought about Mama before she died and how tired she was when she was home from the hospital. I had learned to make grilled cheese sandwiches for my lunch and sometimes I cooked breakfast for Mama. She usually just wanted coffee and toast. The third time she was in the hospital she never came home again.

Aunt Margaret had been in the hospital one time for surgery already. I was scared for her. I wrote a letter to my old Sunday school teacher in Brownsville, Mr. Johnson, to let him know I was doing okay. I told him about my solo trip to Denver, my new home and how much I missed Mama. I told him I was mad at God for not answering my prayers and healing Mama. And for the first time I told him thanks for letting me stay with them while Mama was in the hospital and that I would always remember how they helped me through that time. It helped a little to tell him that. I know Mama would have wanted me to. I also told him about Aunt Margaret's chemo treatments and how scared I was about that.

He wrote me back to let me know that he and the rest of the church would be praying for me and Aunt Margaret. When I read that they were praying for us, I couldn't write him again for a long time.

Six months later
... June 1976 — Platteville

Life here is different except for Aunt Margaret's fried chicken on Sundays. It tastes a lot like Mama's. The mashed potatoes are never quite lumpy enough for me, but she tries to make it seem like home, even when she can't eat any of the chicken herself because fried stuff makes her sick when she's on the chemo. We pray every meal, even breakfast. I think to myself, "What's the point?"

Johnny seems like a big brother now. He said he was going to Cheyenne this Sunday afternoon to get someone and take them to Denver and asked if I wanted to come along for the ride. I said "Sure."

After church we took Aunt Margaret home and turned north on highway 85 to Greeley. Johnny said we'd take the "scenic" route to Cheyenne on the way up and the interstate coming back. Our 4-wheel drive Blazer was more at home on the back roads than the freeway anyway. We rode mostly in silence through Evans and on into Greeley. Johnny didn't talk much, but in Greeley we passed by a building with a huge American flag out front and he told me how beautiful it looked and how when he was in the Marines he raised the flag outside the barracks sometimes while the bugler played Reveille. He told me how Taps made him feel sad on the days he lowered the flag at sunset after he came back from his first tour in Viet Nam. He didn't say any more about why it made him feel sad. We drove on in silence for a few more miles.

In the months since my arrival Johnny never had what you'd call a steady job. He worked for different people at odd jobs like fixing windows, painting and so forth, but that was only when someone needed an extra pair of hands. He limped a good bit, and I supposed that was why he didn't chop much wood for the fireplace, except for small stuff like kindling, or work all day in the fields on a farm. He looked for a check in the mail every month and was a little stressed if it didn't come on time. He seemed to rest a lot sometimes. But once a month he would make a trip into Denver to the VA hospital to get his "meds" and stock up on things we couldn't find in the stores in Platteville.

After we were out of Greeley for a few miles I got up the nerve to ask him about his limp. He didn't answer at first, and I didn't press it. Just north of Eaton he started to talk.

"It was on my second tour in 'Nam. Do you remember seeing the news about the war? ... so many died.

My buddy George was walking just in front of me when he stepped on a mine. I don't remember much after that, except for a guy in the helicopter telling me I was going to be OK just as he gave me a shot in my arm and I passed out again. I woke up in the hospital. A couple of days later I was heading back to the states in a military transport. George was from Pelahatchie, Mississippi. I saw the flags over the coffins coming off another plane when we arrived back in the states and wondered if George was among them"

He pulled the Blazer off the road in a parking lot of an abandoned gas station and we stepped out. He said "I wound up with this." He pulled up his left pants leg and showed me his artificial leg attached just below the knee. I was shocked. Then he took off his shirt and showed me the scars on his chest from the shrapnel and multiple surgeries to fix his lungs and heart. He told me his lungs and heart wouldn't let him do heavy work any more. He just had to stop working when he was tired and if he got too tired all at once it would take a few days to recuperate.

Johnny changed in my eyes that day. Standing in that parking lot I suddenly realized why Aunt Margaret had left Brownsville to come back and take care of him that year. I could see her red eyes again and hear the shake in her voice as she must have been dealing with the news of Johnny's near-fatal wounds. It all made sense to me now.

We drove on to Cheyenne and followed the directions and map Johnny had to a church. The building out back had a sign by the door that said "Counseling."

Johnny went inside for a few minutes and came back out with a suitcase. He put it in the back of the Blazer and went back inside. When he came out again he was with an older woman and a pretty girl who looked about 15 or 16 and very scared. Johnny told me to move to the back seat and leave the door open. He reassured the girl with a firm hand leading her down the stairs and out to the front seat of the truck. He introduced her as Gloria. She had red hair and a hint of freckles on her cheeks. She looked too young to be "expecting," probably only a little older than me. I could hear him tell her that Margaret's friend had a room ready for her in Denver.

We pulled away from the church and headed toward the interstate. As we drove down the street we saw a woman walking a Great Dane as big as she was. We wondered about whether she or the dog decided which direction and how fast to walk. All of us chuckled a little at that then Johnny began to talk, "Hey Andy, do you like dogs?"

"Yea, Sure"

"Mother and I were talking the other day about getting one to watch the house on the days when we go into Denver. We thought about a good size dog if we could find one at the shelter or something, one that would make a thief think twice before he stopped at our house. What do you think?

"It's okay by me, I like big dogs."

"How about you, Gloria. Do you like dogs?"

You could barely hear her timid voice as she spoke:

"I love them. We've always had a dog at our house, ever since I was little."

As we headed west toward the interstate Johnny turned and headed toward a building with a tin roof. It was the local animal shelter. The sign on the door said they were closed for adoption on Sunday, but we could see through the chain-link cages from the fence. I turned around to go back to the truck, but stopped in my tracks.

Outside the fence there was a large, skinny white dog watching me. He must have come to the shelter thinking he might get some of the food he could smell, or maybe he just wanted some company from the other dogs in there. He turned and trotted away from me a few steps when he saw me looking at him. I knelt down to his level and spoke calmly to him. He kept watching me. I called him in a low voice and offered him my hand, palm up. He took a couple of steps toward me and stopped when he saw Gloria move inside the truck. Johnny tossed me half a ham sandwich we had left over from our picnic lunch and I tore it in three pieces. I tossed the smallest one toward the dog. He flinched a little, but the prospect of food overcame his fear and he ate it in one big bite. I continued to talk to him and gently tossed a second piece of the sandwich in his direction, but closer to me than before. He looked doubtful, but approached it with more confidence this time. After he ate it I offered the last bite from my hand and he approached carefully, but he seemed to be more trusting. As he took the last and biggest bite I began to scratch his ear while he chewed. He sat down in front of me and licked the last bit of flavor from my hand.

Gloria was watching with a big smile on her face when I turned around to see their reaction. Johnny was now standing in front of the Blazer with his hands on his hips. He spoke calmly to me.

"Well, pardner, it looks like you made a friend. Let's see if he likes anybody else."

I stood up slowly and walked toward the truck, the dog followed, but stopped as I got closer to Johnny. I put out my hand toward Johnny so we could shake hands. I spoke to Johnny so the dog could hear me and then invited the dog to come closer. Johnny knelt down to his level and put out his hand, palm up like I had. The dog looked at me for reassurance and I put my hand on Johnny's shoulder. In a couple of minutes Johnny was scratching his ear too.

Gloria had gotten out of the truck quietly and was standing behind Johnny now. She joined in welcoming that big, white, skinny dog to our little group. By the grace of God, we had our dog and the shelter wasn't even open!

It appeared he had been running the highways for weeks or months. His toenails were worn almost to the quick and he had tar between his toes. We poured water from a plastic jug into the top of the lunch pail and he drank all of it without stopping. It didn't take much coaxing to get him in the Blazer for the trip to Denver. We stopped at the first grocery store we found to buy him a bag of food and a bowl. Gloria stayed in the truck with him while we went in the store. She said he worried about us the whole time we were in the store. He welcomed us back to the truck like we had been gone for days. About fifteen minutes into the trip down the interstate that dog was sound asleep in the back seat beside me. The rest of the trip to Denver was one long conversation about what to name him, speculation about where he had been before we found him, and how many miles he had covered on his own.

There had been a couple of Charles Bronson tough

guy movies on TV last week and we decided that since he was going to protect our house, we'd name him Bronson. We guessed he'd probably weigh over 100 pounds when he filled out to his normal weight.

We arrived in Denver about 5 p.m. Aunt Margaret had a friend with a place for Gloria to stay over the next few months, so we followed the directions to the house. An older couple met Johnny and Gloria at the door while I stayed with Bronson near the truck. I sneaked him a few bites of food and walked him down the block a little. He would not get far from me. I wondered why Johnny had brought Gloria here.

On the trip back to Platteville we talked about why Gloria had gone to Denver. Johnny said that she had some things to think through and it would be easier for her to do that away from Cheyenne. The folks in Denver were just kind enough to give her a place to stay that was close to the "Center for Hope" that Aunt Margaret helped start when she was a young mother. It was a place for girls who were about to be young mothers themselves to think, talk to people who care, and learn a little about "The Good Book."

We made it home around 6:30 and Margaret had supper ready for us. She hadn't had chemo for a few weeks, so her appetite was back and we had our fried chicken Sunday dinner for supper. We put Bronson out in my room because the door to the kitchen still had a screen door attached and he could look through it to the kitchen while we ate. Aunt Margaret saved the chicken neck just for him.

Bronson slept on the floor beside my bed. The next morning he woke me up with a cold, wet nose on my cheek. I climbed out of bed and let him out in the back yard.

Over the summer Aunt Margaret's trips to Denver came around about once or twice a week to the Center, and her trips to the doctor were just for monthly blood tests. The chemo was over for now. Prayers of thanks for Margaret's healing joined the prayers for God's will to be done in the lives of the young mothers and mothers-to-be at the Center. All the while I was thinking "what's the point." Prayer didn't save Mama, but I didn't say anything to Aunt Margaret or Johnny.

Bronson became my steadfast companion night and day. He put on weight every week. The two of us learned the streets of Platteville by heart over the summer. We walked and ran so much I had to get new soles put on my shoes. I talked to Bronson about Mama and Daddy sometimes. He seemed to understand better than anybody else what it was like to be on your own traveling away from a place where you could no longer live, to a place you knew nothing about, like Moses running to Midian after he killed the Egyptian. The two of us sat on the rocks outside town and looked toward the snow capped mountains.

Rebellion

Four years later
... Platteville - January 1980

Our old '69 Blazer is hard to start when the temperature drops to around 10° overnight. Record snowfall this year has made getting around town pretty tough and sometimes the snowdrifts in the front yard almost touch the edge of the roof if the wind is high while it's coming down. Bronson loves it. He'll run down the path we've shoveled to the front door and dive head-first into a drift. The shy white dog we picked up outside the shelter has turned into a free spirited companion, fiercely loyal to the family. Just ask the guy who came one day to install the T.V. cable. Bronson took a chunk out of his tool belt when he moved toward the door a little too quickly. Aunt Margaret was on the couch by the door and Bronson made sure she was safe. After that the cable guy asked her to put him out so she put him in my room and just closed the old screen door. Bronson watched him through the screen door without blinking. I think the cable guy didn't trust that old screen door to stop a 100 pound dog, so he finished quietly and left as soon as he could ... minus one chunk of leather on his tool belt.

The new preacher stopped by Friday. I could hear him talking to Aunt Margaret while I was finishing up in the bathroom. I had a date for the basketball game and wanted to look sharp. The preacher introduced himself as Brother Denton when I came into the living room and asked me what I was all spruced up for. I told him I had a date for the basketball game.

He said, "You should bring her to church Sunday."

"I think she goes to church somewhere else Brother Denton."

"Where's that, there aren't that many churches around here?"

"She goes to St. Anne's."

There was silence for a few seconds while Brother Denton considered his reply.

"Have you thought this through, son?" he said.

"Thought what through?"

"Courting a Catholic girl."

"What do you mean, Brother Denton?"

"Well ... I've counseled marriages in deep trouble because of mixed faiths. It can lead to conflicts down the line."

I stood there for a minute trying to understand what I had just heard. Marriage? It was our second date and we were in high school. Where did he get marriage? The longer I considered what he said the hotter I became. I looked at Aunt Margaret. She knew I was angry.

"Marriage! Are you crazy! I met you two minutes ago and you're telling me who I should or should not take to a basketball game! It's only our second date and Johnny's driving us! Do you want me to call you for permission to kiss her good night, too?!!"

Johnny stepped in front of me, put his hands on my arms and told me to go outside and he'd be out there in a minute. I slammed the front door on the way out.

I couldn't hear what they were saying inside, but Johnny was doing most of the talking. When he came outside to drive me to the game, he just tossed me the keys instead and said, "It's all yours for tonight. I'm staying here. Be careful driving on the snow and have a good time. Back by midnight!"

Nothing else was said about that night. I didn't go

back to church while Brother Denton was in the pulpit and Aunt Margaret never asked me to. As it turned out that was the last date I had with that girl, but it had nothing to do with her religion. She fell in love with a basketball player.

The rest of my senior year I dated a few times and spent most of my spare time working and looking forward to a full time job after graduation.

Six Months Later
... Platteville — June 13, 1980

I'm eighteen now. Aunt Margaret told me yesterday that she'll be starting chemo again soon. I was so upset by that news that I had to apologize to her later for storming out of the room.

With my job at the feed store I manage to buy an old used car and fix it up a little. Platteville never quite feels like home. I still gaze at those mountains. I told my boss I'd be leaving at the end of next week, but please don't tell anyone else. The world beckons, and I don't want to listen to any more prayers for Aunt Margaret.

Platteville — June 20, 1980

Bronson watches through the screen door with a puzzled look as I close the front door and walk away without him. I left a note on the kitchen table:

> *Dear Aunt Margaret,*
> *I need to leave here for now. You and Johnny were here when I needed you. I'll always remember that. You are both very special to me, but I need to find my own way now. I don't know exactly where I'm*

*going, but it's somewhere west toward the
mountains.*

*I'll be in touch when I get an address, so
don't worry if you don't hear from me for a
while.*

*Explain it to Bronson for me. I wish I
could take him with me, but you need him
here, and he's seen enough of the road I
think.*

Andy

My old Falcon was ready to go with my clothes out
of sight in the trunk. I had saved $112 from my job for
gas and meals. The sign at the bank flashed 3:15/52° as I
drove out of Platteville before dawn.

Glenwood Springs, Colorado — June 23, 1980

A "HELP WANTED" sign in the screen door of the
office is the only sign of life at the old motel except for
the two cars in front of a couple of the rooms. I walk
around to the side of the office and see an old man sitting
on a stool painting the trim on a window.

"Hello?"

He doesn't react, so I walk closer and call to him
again.

"Hello!"

He looks at me calmly and says, "I heard you the first
time."

I asked him who I needed to see about the job. He
said, "You're lookin at him."

He just kept painting without saying anything, and
I kept standing waiting for him to say something else.
He calmly finished painting the trim on that one window

over the next few minutes, meticulously keeping the paint off the brick and the window glass. He cleaned two spots of paint from the glass with a rag. After he was satisfied with his work he put the paint brush down on the can and turned toward me, still not saying another word.

He sized me up for a minute, then asked, "Can you paint?"

I said yes and he pressed the point. "Can you paint the window trim without paintin' the brick?"

I said, "I don't know. I never painted anything but a wooden shed before, but I'll give it a try."

"Here's the brush, there's the paint. Do the window by the back door, so if you mess it up nobody will see it much. I'll fix some coffee. Come on in the back door when you're through."

I hadn't painted anything before but the shed behind Aunt Margaret's house. The window was small and looked like it had been painted many times before. Only a few small white spots of paint were on the dark red brick around it. The window glass was spotless. For some reason I was nervous. It took me almost an hour to paint the trim on that one small window.

I carefully inspected my work and wiped a couple of white spots from the glass like the old man had done. When I was satisfied, I carefully cleaned the brush, cleaned and recapped the paint can and went in the back door.

The old man was at a small table drinking his coffee. It was clear that he had been watching me through the kitchen window on the other side of the building. As I sat down he poured me a cup of coffee, then went outside to inspect my work. When he came back in he said, "You're a little slow at it, but you did okay. So many kids your age now would just slop it on and call it good. You live around here?"

"Not yet. I drove into town this morning. I'm looking for a job and a place to stay. I was driving down the street and saw your sign in the window."

"Where you from?"

"Platteville, over by Denver."

"I know where that is … flat land. I like the mountains myself. How old are you?"

"Almost nineteen."

"Any relatives around here or can anybody around here vouch for you?"

"No. I just drove into town today."

"You think you could do some paintin' for me if the price was right?"

"Probably. What's the price?"

"Depends on whether you want a room in the deal. Can't pay much if you want a room too."

"The sign says you have rooms with kitchenettes. I need the room too if we can work it out so I can make enough to buy some groceries and gas."

We sat down and haggled out a deal for me to paint all the white trim on the buildings and all the carports next to the rooms along with some other chores around the property. He'd provide a room with a kitchenette for a month and pay enough to buy a few groceries. We'd try it for a couple of weeks and see how things worked out. He showed me where he kept the paint, brushes and ladder and we agreed I could settle in and start in the morning. He told me to take the help wanted sign down.

His name was Martin Reed and I guessed him to be about 75 or 80 years old.

The Springs Motor Lodge sits back a couple of blocks off the main road toward Carbondale, so there is not much traffic. I guessed that they had changed the path of the main highway quite a while back before the latest commercial development, and the motel had struggled since then. Most travelers stay in newer places along the main roads, so the people who stay here are usually local or temporary workers and rent by the month.

I unloaded my clothes and went inside. Everything looked clean. It had a small kitchen stove and refrigerator, a cabinet with a few essential dishes and cookware, a shower stall and a double bed. A small wooden dining table with two chairs by the window was the only other furniture in the room except for the T.V. on a small dresser in the corner. I remembered the old neon sign out front which had proudly announced "Color T.V." under the vacancy sign. The local grocery store had all I needed for meals and other essentials for the next couple of days, but the prices in this resort town were a lot higher than Platteville. I wasn't sure my deal with Martin was enough money to buy groceries and gas around here.

The well kept grounds of the motel had several large trees including one big beautiful blue spruce by the road. I guessed it to be fifty or sixty feet tall. There were large, white painted rocks lining the gravel driveways. All the trim on the red brick buildings was white.

After supper I walked back to the office and bought two post cards from the rack on the counter so I could mail them to Aunt Margaret and Johnny the next day. I put my hanging clothes in the curtained off area with the closet bar. I opened the top drawer of the dresser to put my socks and underwear away and stopped. There was a Gideon Bible in the drawer. I shoved it to the back and dumped in my things. I had no need of it.

It was lonely in the room when I wasn't watching television and after I turned out the light I didn't hear Bronson settling in on the floor beside me.

It took a long time to go to sleep.

I thought about that first night in Platteville, crying under the quilts so nobody would hear me. I thought about life in Brownsville when Aunt Margaret was there after Daddy's funeral. I remembered the Sunday school lessons about Moses, the matinee movies with buttered popcorn, and the phone call from Denver for Aunt Margaret the day before she left. I remembered her red eyes and the change in the tone of her voice when she told me about Johnny coming home from Viet Nam. I couldn't get Mama's tired face out of my mind from the last days she was home. It didn't look like the face I remembered from the coffin. I remembered all the futile prayers for Mama over those last two years ... I remembered being mad at God about those wasted prayers.

I finished the trim around the office Tuesday and three duplex room units by Friday. When I went to my room Friday afternoon I found cash in an envelope for four days work on my dining table. I stopped by the office that night and Martin told me I could knock off until Monday.

Brownsville, Texas — July 1980

Mr. Johnson picks up the letter opener on the table to work on that stack of bills he'd been putting off for a couple of days. One of the envelopes is hand written, obviously not a bill. He must have put it in this stack by mistake. The return address reads Platteville Colorado.

> *Dear Wally,*
> *Andy moved out of the house a few*
> *weeks ago. He didn't say anything before he*
> *left, but he left a note on the kitchen table*
> *so we wouldn't worry. A few days later we*
> *got a post card from him with a Glenwood*

Springs return address. He told us he had
a job and a room there and everything was
alright. I thought you should know since you
were the only one he wrote while he lived
here.

He was with Johnny and me for about
four and a half years. I remember that
summer in Brownsville when he so enjoyed
your teaching him about Moses in Sunday
school. It really helped him get his mind off
what was going on around him. I want to
thank you for that time, that teaching, that
caring love in his time of need and then
again while his mother was so ill her last
two years. After his mother passed away
he seemed to change and he never got past
it. I still pray for him to regain that sparkle
in his eye. He doesn't pray anymore unless
we ask him to say the blessing and then
his prayers are short and cold. Maybe you
could write him, I know he'd like to hear
from you.

It's been a long time since our school
days in Brownsville. I hope you are doing
well. I know your faith has stood you well
over the years. The last time Andy heard
from you I mentioned that you and I had
graduated from high school together and he
asked me all kinds of questions about it.

Johnny and I still have our work at the
Center to keep us hopping, such as we are
able. So many young girls need help. Keep

*them in your thoughts and prayers as you
are in ours.*

*As Always,
Maggie*

*P.S. I've started chemo treatments again.
Remember me in your prayers.*

He sat down in the recliner to read the letter again
... the decades rolled away as he remembered that last
summer of high school before Maggie went away with
no explanation. It hadn't made any sense then ... it still
doesn't. After all, they had talked about marriage once,
but had decided to wait until he had a good job. He hadn't
seen her again until Glenn, Andy's dad, was killed. Then
they really hadn't had time to talk about anything except
the funeral or Andy's Sunday school class. It had seemed
strange not to have her run up and hug him, even after all
those years apart, but he understood and had let it pass
without comment.

Why had she left Brownsville?

After Maggie quit answering his calls, he had met
Shirley and suddenly life changed. They were married
within four months. Within a couple of years his career
at the insurance agency took off and they started their
family. He seldom thought about Maggie after that.

The door opened and startled him out of his thoughts.
"Hello, honey. Are you home?" It was Shirley.

... After dinner he sat down to write Andy. He
wasn't sure where to start. An hour passed, then another.
He said good night to Shirley and told her he needed to
sort some things out about Andy. He'd be coming to bed

later. Instead of writing, he picked up his bible. He read long into the night. A light kiss on the cheek woke him at 2 a.m. Shirley offered him her hand and led him to bed. Sunday morning came too early.

Ten eight-year-old boys waited noisily for him to start the lesson. After the customary greetings he asked Tommy to open the Sunday school lesson with prayer.

"Dear Lord, thank you for the sunshine today. Thank you for our parents, our friends in this room and for Mr. Johnson. We pray for all the sick people and the sad people so you'll make them feel better. And thank you for Jesus. Amen."

For the lesson that day he just read to them from the bible and they talked about what he read. Their curious young minds were so eager, so full of innocent belief. He thought about Maggie's letter and Andy's cold prayers. What had happened?

Sunday afternoon was full of questions ... Andy questions, Maggie questions, WHY questions. The blank page mocked his efforts to write. How could he write without answers? At six o'clock Shirley wrapped her arms around his shoulders and neck from behind and whispered in his ear that it was almost time for evening service. Suddenly he remembered that it was a business meeting and he hadn't even started his financial report.

When they called on him for his report he stood silently for a moment, then began simply to pray ...

Glenwood Springs — September 1980

The painting job at the motel is almost finished and I know that the mowing and such won't pay enough to keep the room and buy groceries. I told Martin I needed to look for more work, but I'd like to keep the room, so we agreed on a rental price. He said he'd keep his eyes open for something if I wanted him to. After all he needed to keep the room rented.

Martin didn't say much, but you could depend on what he said, and when he did talk, it paid you to listen … and sometimes watch.

In my two months at the motel, there had been only a few guests, but many personal visitors for Martin. I didn't speak with many of them, but I watched from a distance as I continued my work. He had at least two or three visitors a week, all sorts of people, young, old, rich, or poor. He'd offer them a cup of coffee and they'd sit and talk quietly outside under the trees or in his little kitchen. He'd always greet them with a warm, inviting handshake, or sometimes an understanding hug. Occasionally they'd spend one or two nights here.

On Sunday mornings he left early for church and didn't come home until after eight at night. He'd invited me to go with him the first couple of weeks, but didn't press it after that. I just waved to him from my window as he left.

Late one Saturday afternoon, a woman drove up in a new Lincoln pulling a small closed trailer and started yelling in a loud, raspy voice as she got out.

"Brother Martin, it's great to see you … are you still knockin' around here in this old motel? I figured you'd have had enough of this by now … you know you've got a standing invitation to marry me! We could set this part of the country on fire!"

Martin yelled back, "Hey, Annie … you still kickin' those cowboy's butts around the ranch? … How 'ya doin?!!"

I watched from a distance as they greeted each other with an old-friends hug and walked arm-in-arm through the door and into his kitchen. It was completely out of character for Martin. All his other visitors had been subdued and he had been obviously respectful of them, as they were of him. About an hour later they came outside laughing and he showed her to one of the rooms, unhitched the trailer and parked her car under the carport adjacent to the room ... then he started my way.

"Andy! Put your tools away and get yourself a shower ... we're going out for dinner tonight! Put on your Sunday best!"

In the time I had been there, we had never socialized much, other than an occasional cup of coffee when he laid out different jobs to do around the place. He had always treated me well on my wages and time and we were building a friendship based on mutual respect ... the kind of friendship I'd not had since I was a kid in Brownsville. I'd never seen him this keyed up before and I couldn't resist his contagious, assumptive invitation.

On the way to the car he introduced me to his long-time friend Annie as the orneriest woman he'd ever known. It seems they had known each other for over sixty years. In the car they reminisced about their days on the "ranch" and I had no choice but to listen as we drove downtown and stopped at what appeared to be the most expensive restaurant in Glenwood Springs. Martin and I sat down at the table and Annie went over to talk to the manager. Annie let us know that she was buying, and we could have two of anything on the menu.

As the waitress approached the table, Annie got up and gave her a big hug and introduced her to Martin and me as her granddaughter, Piper. She looked to be in her early twenties and a little embarrassed about the public introductions.

"Grandma! ... I work here! Can I just take your order?"

"Okay, honey, I'll leave you alone. Just call me sometime. I miss you at the ranch."

Annie ordered a t-bone, baked potato and Caesar salad. Martin ordered grilled rainbow trout, broccoli and rice pilaf. I stuck with Annie's lead and ordered the t-bone.

The conversation changed over the meal from old-times to Annie's questions about how I wound up at Martin's place. I told her about coming from Platteville after graduation, but left out anything about the reason I had been in Platteville in the first place. After all, I hadn't even had that conversation with Martin yet.

Annie and I each topped off the meal with a big piece of Dutch apple pie alamode while Martin had sherbet. Annie said she "liked my style" and put the keys to the Lincoln on the table in front of me for the drive home. She said she wasn't sure she could trust Martin's judgment any more after calling a single scoop of sherbet "dessert."

As we left, Annie went over to Piper and pressed something quietly in her hand as she paid for dinner at the register. Piper looked in her hand, realized that we had seen what had happened, and quietly slipped whatever was there in her pocket. She rang up the meal without a word and went into the back of the restaurant without telling us goodbye. Annie had embarrassed her again.

The drive back to the motel was quiet. Annie's mood had changed.

When we got back to the motel I went back to my room and left Martin and Annie talking quietly outside at the picnic table by the big blue spruce. I left the curtains open. About nine-fifteen Annie drove away alone and Martin walked around the grounds for a while with his hands in his pockets, shivering in the cool September evening air. He had something on his mind he couldn't quite shake.

The next morning he hitched up the trailer to his old pickup before leaving for church. He came home early that afternoon without the trailer.

The mail came late on Monday. I saw Martin visiting with the mailman for a minute, and then stopping to sort through the mail on his way back to the office. I was at the opposite end of the property when I saw him walk to my room and slide an envelope into the mail slot. I figured it was from Aunt Margaret or Johnny, since they usually wrote once a month or so. I finished painting the carport trim and knocked off at around 5:30.

Postmark: Brownsville, Texas … return address, Walter Johnson? How did he know I was here?

Dear Andy,

You're probably wondering how I knew your address. Your Aunt Maggie wrote me a couple of months ago that you had left Platteville and moved to Glenwood Springs.

It was good to hear from her. We hadn't talked since your father's funeral, and even then there was no real time to visit. She told me you had talked with her about my going to high school with her. I guess you and I are both learning that special connections with people like your Aunt Maggie are God's business. You never know when He may connect you again, or for what purpose.

Maggie was concerned when you went away, and seemed hurt that you left so suddenly. I'm glad you're keeping in touch

*with her. She's a wonderful person, but you
probably already know that, after all, she
took you in as her own with no reservations,
and no thought of how much it would
complicate her own life. But that's typical
Maggie.*

*You've been on my mind since she
wrote me and the Lord has kept both you
and Maggie in my prayers ever since. Did
you know she had started chemo treatments
again? She could really use your support
now ... and your prayers.*

*Write when you get a chance.
Remember, you are loved by more people
than you realize. Your old Sunday school
classmates were thrilled when I told them
I was writing to you. All of them are still
coming to church here, except Eddie and
Monte. So you see, you're still connected to
them too.*

*The peace of the Lord,
Walt*

I hadn't thought about Mr. Johnson since I arrived
in Glenwood Springs. It was the first time he had signed
a letter "Walt." Our relationship had moved perceptibly
from Sunday school lessons to life lessons. The letter
brought up old scars and re-opened an unresolved issue
— Aunt Margaret's cancer.

"Cancer." Until now I had avoided even thinking
that word. It had taken Mama away from me and I had
run away from Aunt Margaret's house, as soon as I was
able, at the mere mention of another round of chemo.

Walt's words about her needing my support and prayers stung me. I realized that even though my belief in prayer had vanished, hers hadn't. It suddenly came home to me that I needed to talk with her again, even if it was from a distance.

I was relieved that I didn't feel the need to pray with her over the phone that night because she told me about the success of the treatments and how she was in remission. She sounded strong. This had been a completely different type of cancer than her first time years back. I was ashamed that I had never asked about that before I left Platteville. Her prognosis was good. She subtly changed the course of the conversation around to my life in Glenwood Springs. She was thirsty to know if I was truly happy. I told her about painting for Martin and our foray with Annie into town last week. She enjoyed the story about the "sherbet" dessert and said it was good to hear me laugh. I told her I'd make a trip to Platteville when I could save enough money and afford the time from whatever new job I might get around here.

Glenwood Springs — December 1980

Heavy snow tonight. My Falcon's old tires, cursed by gravity and eight inches of snow, need help getting untracked. Tomorrow I'll park facing downhill. On the next tire-spinning attempt I get some unexpected help from two heavily bundled bodies pushing from behind as I steer toward the cleared part of the street. Safely freed from the deep curbside snow, I stop and get out to thank my anonymous rescuers and see them already headed downhill toward the restaurant where I work. I yell "THANKS" to them and they signal with mittens waving a shivering "you're welcome." It was two women wearing heavy winter coats!

My old Falcon and I tiptoe along the slippery streets toward the motel. I'm grateful for the timing of my Thanksgiving trip back to Platteville two weekends ago. The weather had been perfect, and the visit warm and wonderful.

Aunt Margaret and Johnny were both doing well and in good spirits about the Center. She had prepared a full Thanksgiving meal for fifteen people including some from the church and several who worked at the Center. I was thankful she had the strength to do that. Mama's last Thanksgiving had been difficult for her because of waning strength. We had gone to Aunt Flora's house that year.

Bronson was the hit of the Thanksgiving party when he walked by the main dinner table sporting a whipped cream beard ... he had been seduced by the smell of chocolate cream pie resting on a coffee table and had succumbed to temptation. Nobody saw him take that bite, but his fluffy white beard gave him away. Johnny nearly fell off his stool laughing about it. Bronson spent the rest of the day peering through that screen door from my old bedroom, or out in the yard separated from the food ... except for the turkey neck and some other rather meaty tidbits I saw him eating as Johnny sneaked back into the house.

The spoken prayers of thanks from so many for Aunt Margaret's recovery echoed through my head. They were a bittersweet blessing. I loved Aunt Margaret, but why had God chosen her to recover instead of Mama? After all, we had prayed for Mama too. How did God choose?

Thanksgiving night I was too tired from the trip and the lively party to think about it anymore. I fell asleep to the reassuring sounds of Bronson curling up on the floor beside my bed. That night after Thanksgiving was over was the best night's sleep in months. I headed back to Glenwood Springs early Sunday morning to avoid my required attendance at Aunt Margaret's church in Platteville.

As I turn the last corner toward the motel, flashing lights shake my wandering memory about Thanksgiving into a hard reality of the immediate present. An ambulance pulls away from the driveway just as I arrive. Mrs. Gary, one of our semi-permanent residents, told me it was Martin. I didn't even get out of the car. The trip to the local hospital was a very long ten minutes. I arrived at 11:37 p.m. Since I wasn't family they wouldn't tell me anything about his condition. I took up residence for the night in a waiting room chair hoping to hear something. Intermittent bad dreams assaulted me as I dozed in the discomfort of the waiting room chair and later the dying screams of a siren arriving from a highway accident scene hammered me back into consciousness at 2:43 a.m.

Again, I drift into fitful sleep.

Dawn silence arrives in sharp contrast to the noisy, unsettled night and 7 a.m. finds me in the hospital cafeteria with a cup of coffee and a cheese Danish on the table. On leaving I hear a loud, familiar voice wafting down the hall:

"I know I'm not a relative, but I'm the one they call in case of emergency, doesn't that count?!!"

"Are you Ann Caldwell?"

"You got it, honey!"

"I'm sorry Ms. Caldwell, I didn't realize you were on the list. He's had a heart episode, and his condition at the moment is guarded, but he's responding well to treatment. You'll be able to see him as soon as they get him into a room. Just wait in there, I'll let you know."

"Thank you, darlin'. I'll be here"

When she turned around I could see how tired she looked through that strained smile.

"Andy?"

"Hello Annie. I've been trying to get a report on him all night, but they wouldn't tell me anything. How did you know he was here?"

"We've been the 'notify in case of emergency' contact for each other since Olivia died almost twenty years ago."

"Was Olivia his wife?"

"Yes she was. I thought you'd know that the way Martin seemed to have adopted you the time we went to dinner."

"We never talked about that kind of thing. I just work for him at the motel and we have a cup of coffee sometimes."

"He tells me about you every time we talk. In fact, he told me you had a job working downtown at some restaurant now."

"Yeah. I've been there since September. I still work for Martin when he needs me, though."

"Your being here has really perked him up, it's been good for him. But don't tell him I told you that or he'll scratch me off his Christmas list. Just keep being here."

Annie's comments surprised me. I had lived there for over six months and he and I had never had dinner together, except for the night out with Annie. I realized that I had never told him about how Mama died, or how I got to Platteville in the first place. He had respected my unwillingness to talk every time there had been an opportunity, and I was grateful.

I had a long conversation with Annie while we waited. She told me about Martin's history of heart problems, and a little bit about how they had known each other since they lived on the same ranch in Wyoming as kids. Martin was about ten years older, but she looked up to him like an older brother. They had lost track of each other after he graduated from college, but re-connected at a home-town funeral some thirty years later.

The nurse took her into his room around 10:15.

That sherbet dessert made more sense now.

As soon as Annie came out of his room I went in to see him for a few minutes and promised to keep an eye on the place until he got back. He told me Annie had volunteered to stay a few days and work the desk and we could close the office early this time of year anyway. No one mentioned I had been there all night.

The motel office was locked when I got there. Someone had put a homemade sign in the office screen door. It read "Office Closed Until Further Notice." It must have been Mrs. Gary who put the sign up, because her phone number was on the sign as an emergency contact. I went to my room, showered and slept for a couple of hours before I went to work at the restaurant busing tables and washing dishes. The work was a relief compared to sleeping in a chair.

Annie took up temporary residence in her favorite room at the motel, even though she could afford any place in town. She liked it because the front window allowed her a perfect view of Martin's front door. When I told Martin about her room choice he told me she could probably BUY any hotel in town if she wanted to, since her late husband had owned half the oil wells in Wyoming.

Over the next few days I met a few people from Martin's church on my daily visits to see him. I was surprised to find out that most of them knew who I was even though I had never met them, except for Pastor Bernard. I had met him when he visited Martin at the motel a couple of times. Martin called him Frank.

Martin came home the next week complaining about the expense of another new miracle drug to keep him alive, but generally okay as long as he took it easy. No more coffee except 'decaf,' though. And driving was out of the question for a month or so until they got the medicine regulated. Annie came home with a wide selection of herb teas and such for Martin. I didn't say anything about it, but thought it might be interesting to hear their conversation about what to drink tomorrow at breakfast.

Annie and I came to a silent understanding about the role each of us took around the motel. I did the physical stuff and she took care of Martin and the office. His job was to behave on his diet and new recovery exercise routine … walking around the block once a day if he felt up to it.

My job at the restaurant progressed from busboy/dishwasher to waiter trainee and I was beginning to make a little extra on tips. The restaurant was across the street from the old Denver Hotel and the skiers who stayed there in the winter season usually gave fair tips if the service and food were good.

Between the motel and restaurant, I didn't have much time for a social life, but Terri, a new waitress at the restaurant had definitely gotten my attention. The sparkle in her eyes when she laughed was intoxicating. Our afternoon napkin/silverware wrapping sessions took as long as I could stretch them.

Glenwood Springs — February 1981

Breakfast in Martin's kitchen provides a perfect view of the window trim I had painted for him in my audition for the "Help Wanted" job last summer. It seemed an eternity had passed since then. Even the decaf coffee with him this morning had become routine, along with Annie's twice-weekly telephone interrogation about his recovery. When the phone rang he said he'd get it … no sense in my answering Annie's call because she always wanted to hear his voice for her long-distance voice-strength diagnosis of how he was really feeling. He took the call in the office to give me a few minutes peace.

Over the winter I had come to share his unbridled enthusiasm for the mountains as we gazed at the snow blanketed peaks bathed in every imaginable winter light from noon radiance to full-moon mystique. On clear days the daylight color cycled through white and gold, blending into a wash of orange, lavender and blue — and the splendor was so thick you could almost hear it. It was more than Bronson I could have imagined from Platteville. But then, Bronson may have been born in these mountains for all I knew. He may have been remembering days of his youth inside his silent western gaze. I could certainly never have imagined these winter mountain landscapes from Texas.

For a few minutes I was back there, remembering winter flatland sunset colors in an endless Texas sky behind the bare silhouette of a February cottonwood tree, Mama calling me in from the cool winter evening for supper. And Daddy was home. His favorite "first day home from the road dinner" was chicken-fried steak with mashed potatoes, cream gravy, and green beans. We had homemade chocolate cake with real fudge icing for dessert later, along with a glass of cold milk to wash it down.

Texas loomed bittersweet, like a pleasant dream with a bad ending.

"Are you okay?"

"Yeah. I was just thinking about some things."

"You didn't seem to know I was here for the last few minutes."

"Sorry Martin. I've never told you I was born in Texas … Brownsville. It doesn't seem real anymore."

"I knew that accent wasn't pure Colorado."

"Accent?!!"

"Yes, ACCENT! When you live in a tourist town you recognize who's local and who's not after about three words. I figured you for Texas, but I didn't want to say anything about it when you told me you were from Platteville. You seemed kind of quiet, like you had a lot on your mind, so I gave you some space."

"Thank you for that. Some things aren't easy to talk about."

I recognized the same caring attitude in him that I had seen in Aunt Margaret and Johnny. I couldn't explain it, but I knew now that it had been there all the time, from painting that first window until our decaffeinated breakfast this morning.

Martin absorbed my story as it came in a torrent. I told him about Daddy's accident, leaving Texas on that bus after Mama's funeral and Aunt Margaret's scheduled chemo treatments the week before I left Platteville. The words seemed to take on a life of their own as I rambled on about unanswered prayers, Johnny's leg, Sunday school lessons about Moses running to Midian after the murder, and how we got Bronson and how Colorado was like Midian to me … then silence. My entire life was exposed.

Martin's demeanor changed from that playful

character complaining about Annie's mothering him to an anxious friend who didn't know how to respond.

"There are no easy answers Andy. Death is hard, especially when it's someone you can't imagine being without."

Martin poured me another cup of coffee and we sat quietly for a while watching the colors change on the mountains to the south. Then he put on his coat, stopped for a moment to look at a picture on the fireplace and went outside for a slow walk by himself, hands in his pockets, eyes on the sidewalk.

After he left I looked at the picture on the mantle in his living room. Annie's words came back to me. In the photo a young Martin and a beautiful woman were playfully posing for the camera in front of a rushing mountain stream. It must have been Olivia, Martin's wife who died over twenty years ago. On the back of the frame, the words "Our honeymoon, May, 1931" explained it all. This year would have been their fiftieth anniversary.

I could only wonder what had happened to her, since Martin didn't talk about her. But we did talk about the mountains. He had worked as a civil engineer for the National Forest Service right out of college until his retirement for health reasons five years ago. These mountains were his passion. According to Martin they were a place where "creation and mankind converge in a dance orchestrated by God."

During January, I drove Martin to church but now he drives himself, returning shortly after noon — no more exhausting all day Sunday sessions. The visitors at the motel are less frequent since his return home from the hospital. Others at the church have temporarily taken his role as the elder overseeing the benevolence fund. The reasons for all those unexplained visitors here during the first few months were clear now … the long confidential conversations, the selfless concern for others.

Those few weeks taking Martin to church had been difficult for me as I sat in the congregation beside him with my arms folded in defiance of the God who had failed to answer earnest prayer. It was a relief for him to be well enough to drive himself.

Saturday morning Martin stopped by for a visit as I was finishing breakfast. He told me he'd had his wife Olivia and their daughter Patricia on his mind since our conversation.

"Twenty one years ago today they were on their way to Denver for a wedding. A truck with no brakes on a long downhill grade hit them from behind. The state troopers said they were knocked off the road on a curve, then rolled down the embankment about a hundred feet onto the rocks below. They were killed instantly and my life was destroyed. It took years for me to find my way again. I still have no answers about why the two most important people in my life had to die. They were my purpose for life, the reason I was on this earth. Even now it makes no sense to me and I struggle when their death takes over my thoughts. My only solace is to go to the mountains and thank God for those years we did have together. I couldn't do that in the beginning because all I could see was the tragedy and all I knew was my own loss. I know what it's like to withdraw from everyone around you, to shun God and deal with the pain alone.

No one can handle it alone. I'm here for you Andy. Annie is here for you. Your Aunt Margaret and Johnnie are here for you. And God is here for you when the time is right and you're ready to respond.

When you're ready to acknowledge him he'll hear

your cry. Listen to his voice when it comes. You'll recognize it."

I sat silently, staring at my coffee, unable to look at Martin's face or reply. I wasn't ready to deal with God yet.

After a few minutes of silence, Martin got up and walked toward the door.

"We're here for you Andy. Reach out when you're ready."

Glenwood Springs, May 1981

Terri's 21st birthday party is getting a little wild for me. People keep showing up with more liquor and it's getting louder by the minute.

About 10 o'clock a couple came in. He'd already had too much to drink and I got an uneasy feeling about him. He looked pretty rough and treated her like he owned her. It didn't take him long to ignore her and start flirting with any girl who'd listen. She looked familiar, but I couldn't remember where I had seen the girl he was with. Then Terri introduced her:

"Piper, this is Andy. Who's your date, Piper?"

"Oh, that's Jeff. He's back in town for a while. He's working on the road crew in the canyon."

The last people left the party a little after midnight. I helped Terri clean up the glasses and plates around her apartment.

"I remember where I met Piper. She was the waitress who served Martin, Annie and me when we went to dinner in town last year, not long after I started working for him. She's Annie's granddaughter."

"You know her grandmother?"

"Yea, she's quite a lady. She's known Martin since she was a little girl on a ranch somewhere near Laramie. She's also rich."

"That guy Piper was with is a jerk. I think he's the same one she was with last summer when she was having such a bad time. She wound up in the hospital once."

I remembered Annie's pressing something into Piper's hand that night and Annie's long conversation with Martin after we got back to the motel. I didn't tell Terri about it.

Terri softened the lights and music. We were finally alone. I didn't get back to my room until almost noon the next day.

Martin watched me through the window as I drove in. The note on the door said that my pay for the week was in the office. He had also left a small list of jobs he needed me to do around the place. I picked up a newspaper in the office and took it back to my room to look for a better paying job than the restaurant.

"Construction helpers wanted. Good pay, hard work. Apply in person."

The address they gave was somewhere east of town in the canyon. I figured it must be helping build that new section of I-70 I'd heard about. It turned out I was right. The office was a trailer house set up in a wide spot beside the old highway. I went in the door marked "Construction Supervisor."

The guy I interviewed with said it was tough work. I needed to be able to follow orders and carry lumber and materials for the carpenters building forms for concrete. It would be eight hours a day, six days a week to start, everything over forty hours was time and a half. Standard hours were 7 to 3:30 with a half hour lunch.

He said, "I don't need any panty-waists. Think you can handle it kid?"

"I can handle it. I just need a few days notice for my old job. Can I start a week from Monday?"

"You got it. Fill out the necessary papers on the way out so you'll be ready to roll first thing that morning. You'll need some steel-toe shoes, leather gloves and your own hammer. And bring your lunch, there's no place close enough to buy it around here. See you then!"

It only took about twenty minutes from the time I walked in the door until I was hired and had all the paperwork finished. I was back in Glenwood Springs in less than an hour.

On the way back to the motel I decided I could still do most of what Martin needed me to do for him after work, so I'd let him know about my new schedule and we could work it out. I'd let the restaurant people know I was leaving when I went to work tonight.

I went back to the motel and told Martin about my new job. We talked it over and agreed I could probably handle the lawn mowing and the other odd jobs around the place in a couple of hours a day when I got home and we'd call it even on the room rent. It was a good deal for both of us. He said he didn't envy me my new job, but he was glad to see me get it.

The guy wasn't kidding about the work being tough. Carrying full sheets of ¾" marine grade plywood from a stack to where they were building the forms was no fun, especially with the wind whistling through the canyon. The first week I was the target of some good-natured "new-kid" ribbing and a couple of practical jokes, but it was just part of the process. It wasn't long before I was "one of the guys" like everybody else. The first month passed quickly. I found out what it meant to be bone tired every day and still have the chores to do for Martin after work. But the pay was good.

Martin and I didn't visit as much as we had when he first came home from the hospital. Most Sundays I took Terri to breakfast somewhere and we spent the day together. Martin invited us to Sunday dinner a couple of times, but everyone seemed uneasy. He was like a parent who didn't approve of my staying overnight at her apartment some Saturdays.

Johnny wrote that he wanted to come to Glenwood Springs for a visit and asked about getting a room at the motel for a few days over the 4th of July weekend. He said he'd like to drive in on Thursday and go back Tuesday morning so he could miss most of the heavy traffic. He also wanted to bring Bronson if it was okay, since Aunt Margaret was flying back to Brownsville to see family.

I called to tell him it was fine, and Martin said he and Bronson could stay for free since they were "family." Johnny sounded good on the phone. He seemed excited about my new job. I told him how to find the place, and that I'd be at work when he got there, but Martin could settle him and Bronson in. I told him I had to work Friday, but they were letting us off at 1:00, so I'd be home early.

Glenwood Springs, Thursday July 2, 1981

Johnny parks in front of the office and puts Bronson on a leash for a much needed "walk." Martin yells from across the yard to him, "Are you Johnny?"

"Yes! I guess you must be Martin. It's good to meet you."

"It's good to meet you too. Andy thinks the world of you, you know."

"I hope it's okay to let Bronson do his business here. It's been a long drive today. I've got a scooper in the truck."

"Don't worry about it. We'll let Andy take care of it when he gets here, he won't mind. Come over here to the picnic table and sit down, I'll get us some coffee or something cold if you'd prefer?"

"Cold sounds good. Ice water is fine!"

"You can let him off the leash if you think he'll stay close. Andy's anxious to see him too. He should be home in a couple of hours."

They spent the next hour or so getting to know each other, talking about the town, the motel and how beautiful the drive in had been except for the road construction. Eventually the conversation turned to Andy and how he was getting along. Martin told him it was a blessing to have Andy here taking care of the work he couldn't do anymore. They talked about their military service, Martin in the Navy in WWII and Johnny in the Marine Corps in Viet Nam.

"Andy told me about your injuries in Viet Nam. I want to thank you for your personal sacrifice for this nation. It means a lot to me. I served in the Navy, but I stayed pretty safe for most of the war and I didn't get hurt."

"Thank you. The real sacrifices were guys who didn't come back from either war. A flag draped coffin is my last memory of my best friend George. Flag waving holidays are tough sometimes."

Martin got them settled in a room next to the fenced common area so Bronson could have easy access when he needed it. Bronson had already accepted Martin as "family" and talked him out of a few snacks by the time I got back to my room around 4:15. After the requisite greeting Bronson invited me out on the grass to play a little Frisbee-catch-and-slobber ... just like old times.

We bought some KFC for supper and ate outside at the picnic table. Bronson even got to chase a couple of squirrels up the blue spruce during dinner. About 6:30

Annie drove in for a surprise visit to check up on Martin. She ate the leftover chicken and adopted Bronson for the evening. It seems she knew just the right spot to scratch on his ear to make him lie down beside her lawn chair next to me. I'm sure her "dropped" biscuit had nothing to do with it.

Annie was surprised and pleased to hear that I had met Piper again at Terri's birthday party. I went into my room to call Terri and find out what her work schedule was for the holiday weekend. She was working Friday, Saturday, and Sunday nights, but was free for lunches Saturday and Sunday. I told her she'd get to meet Annie then and asked her if she'd seen Piper lately. She said she hadn't seen her since the party. When I came back to the table Annie and Martin were talking privately in the office and Johnny was cleaning up after our picnic supper.

Johnny and I took Bronson back to my room and had a good conversation. He said Aunt Margaret was doing well and the doctors had given him a new prescription which seemed to make him feel better and have more energy. I told him I'd introduce him to Terri Saturday and showed him her picture. He shook his head and told me "She's too good lookin' for a guy like you." We talked until about 10 p.m.

When Johnny left the lights were still on in Martin's kitchen and I could see Annie's silhouette on the shade. She left for her room a few minutes later.

Bronson decided to stay with me for the night.

It felt good to hear him settle in after the lights went out. I asked him if the mountains were like we imagined from Platteville. As he stretched out on the cool concrete floor he replied with a sigh which I could almost imagine meant "I told you it would be beautiful."

I knocked on Johnny's door Friday morning at 6:15 and let Bronson inside his room before I went to work.

On Friday afternoon Annie took Martin out for dinner and Johnny and I drove south on Highway 82 toward Aspen along the river. We could see some of the mountains Martin and I had watched during the daily changing light of winter on the snow covered peaks. There was still snow in spots, but only small patches were visible from the highway. We stopped for an overpriced burger in Snowmass for dinner. Sunset over the mountains was incredible with high altitude neon lighted clouds above silhouettes of 13,000 ft. peaks. Johnny commented about God's fireworks on July 3rd being more spectacular than the fireworks we'd see tomorrow night in town.

We met Martin and Annie in his kitchen about nine that evening and made plans for Saturday, but Annie didn't have her usual bubbly personality and you could tell Martin had something on his mind.

Saturday morning Bronson spoiled my plans to "sleep in until 7:30 or 8." He couldn't resist putting that cold nose on my arm at daylight. I knew that meant only one thing … he needed to go outside. He danced by the door while I put on enough clothes to go outside for a minute. Johnny called Bronson from across the yard and I waved to him as I went back inside to sleep a little while longer. I finally woke up again at nine. What a luxury!

Terri came over about noon. It was love at first sight.

"What a beautiful dog! Is that Bronson?!!"

It took less than thirty seconds for Terri to have Bronson chasing that Frisbee. I warned her about the slobber, but she just ignored me and kept on throwing.

After a few minutes Johnny and Annie came out of the office applauding after Bronson caught a high one over his shoulder. Terri threw up her hands like a football official signaling a touchdown. I lost complete control of the introductions as the three of them introduced themselves while Bronson took a water break.

Johnny and Martin fired up the charcoal grill for burgers and hot dogs while Annie and Terri brought out all the fixings. I put the watermelons on ice.

Martin had invited everyone staying at the motel to join us along with some friends from church, about thirty people all together. Bronson made quite a few new friends and Terri beat Annie at the dart board three times in a row before she had to leave for work that afternoon.

Andy's room, Sunday September 6, 1981

The phone jolts me to consciousness at 2 a.m.

"Hello Andy."

It's Annie. Her voice sounds shaky.

"Sorry to wake you at this hour, but I was hoping you could help me out. Piper's in trouble. She's at the sheriff's department. They picked her up when they came in to get her boyfriend Jeff on a drug warrant. She's not under arrest, but they have her in for questioning and I won't be able to get there from Laramie until late tomorrow. When she called I told her I'd talk to someone about picking her up. Could you help me out and give her a ride home. I didn't want to call Martin for something like this and she's pretty scared."

"Uh — sure Annie. That's here in Glenwood Springs?"

"Yes. The Sheriff's deputies would take her back to her apartment, but she needs someone to talk to, I think. I know you don't know her very well, but at least you are a familiar face."

"I'll call Terri and see if she can ride over with me. She knows her better than I do."

"That would be good. I really appreciate it. Call me if you need anything. I won't be flying out of here until I take care of a few things here at the ranch in the morning."

Terri and I arrived at the sheriff's office at around 3:15 a.m.. As we entered the building we saw Piper sitting in a hall next to a detective's office door with her head in her hands. Terri sat down in the chair next to her. I stayed by the door and let them talk. After a few minutes Terri signaled to me to come over to them.

The officers had knocked on Piper's door about 10 o'clock the night before with a warrant for Jeff's arrest along with a search warrant for drugs. They arrested Jeff without incident, but took Piper in for questioning. They hadn't charged her with anything, but told her not to leave the county until she was completely cleared. She told us she didn't want to go back to her apartment yet, so we took her to Terri's place.

Martin was at church when I got back to my room Sunday morning. I called Annie to tell her what was happening. Piper had already called her grandmother to let her know she was okay and told her not to fly down. She slept at Terri's place for several hours Sunday. Piper asked if she could stay with Terri until they knew what was happening with Jeff.

Annie was still concerned.

"Tell me Andy, do you think it's better if I don't come down right now?"

"I don't know Annie. Piper seemed to settle down after she talked to Terri and me for a while. I don't think she was involved in anything. Jeff was probably using her apartment as a base of operations for his drug business. They didn't find any drugs in her apartment but they tore the place up looking for them and kept him in jail for arraignment."

"Can you and Terri keep tabs on her for me. I'd rather not trouble Martin for something like this just yet. I've talked to him about Piper a few times, but this could be a lot of stress on him with the drugs and all. He knows she was having some boyfriend problems, but I've never told him Jeff's name or any details. We've also prayed together for Piper since she left the ranch after her mother ran away with a man to Utah."

"I'll call you if I hear anything more Annie. I think she appreciates Terri's concern.

"Thank you Andy. And thank Terri for me, will you. I feel better now that Piper has the two of you to talk to about things."

Martin and I talked Sunday afternoon and I told him Terri and I had helped Piper with some boyfriend problems the night before. It was hard to respect Annie's request to keep the details quiet with Martin, but I figured Annie was the one who should tell him about Jeff in her own way.

Within two weeks we learned that Jeff had made a plea bargain and been sent to the state prison for 3 to 5 years. Piper decided to move back to her apartment when she was sure Jeff wasn't coming back. After a week or so, Annie came to visit, but this time she stayed at Piper's place for a couple of days before she moved to her usual room at the motel.

Work on the highway wasn't getting any easier for me. I was assigned to the crew building the big concrete support columns for the highway. The plywood for the forms was delivered to us by crane, several sheets at a time and, at times the work was dangerous as we leaned out to guide the stack into position to release it. High winds through the canyon complicated our jobs and safety harnesses were mandatory when the column reached over twenty feet in height. By October I had gained about fifteen pounds of pure muscle from handling heavy loads day in and day out. Some weeks we worked seven 10-hour days to stay on schedule. We never worked less than six days a week.

With the extra money I replaced my old Falcon with a '76 Mustang. I considered moving from the motel to a better apartment or maybe a rental house, but I wanted to help Martin out when he needed it. That was easier to do from my old room because I could see what needed to be done most of the time before he asked me. We continued the arrangement to trade my part-time help for the rent.

The significant snows started in October and work began to slow down because of the weather. We were told that the crews would totally shut down for the winter with the next big snowfall and wouldn't start up again until spring. We would be on-call for the spring startup if we wanted, but there was no guaranteed date. They understood if we needed to move on.

I knew about the seasonal shutdown plans when they hired me, so I'd saved some money for the winter. I had already decided to stay at Martin's place until spring and maybe get a temporary job at a ski resort or something. Fate had other plans.

Charlie

One month later
Glenwood Springs November 1981

Two days after the first big snowfall Terri called me. She seemed shaken and asked me to meet her at the restaurant at five before her 6 o'clock work shift, but wouldn't tell me over the phone what she wanted. I wondered why we were meeting at the restaurant instead of her apartment. When I got there she was pacing the sidewalk out front and we decided to go to the hotel lobby across the street.

"I just came from the hospital. My dad was there. They admitted him last night after a man found him in the snow behind a bar here in Glenwood Springs. Witnesses said he was so drunk he could barely walk when he left the bar. They found him unconscious in the alley. My name and address were in his wallet and they called me from the hospital after the ambulance arrived there."

"Is he going to be okay?"

"They said he's out of danger now, but he collapsed from alcohol poisoning. Andy, I don't know why he was in town. I haven't seen him in over four years, and now this. He came to my high school graduation smelling like booze … thank God he didn't stay long that night. I told Mother not to ever give him my address. The last I heard he was in Pueblo selling cars. Mother's not coming to see him. She said she stopped worrying about him the last time he hit her in a drunken rage. She told me not to let him talk me into getting involved helping him, but he asked me to let him stay with me for a few days when he gets out of the hospital.

He can't stay with me Andy!"

We talked until time for her work shift and she told me about her father's escapades when she was growing up. It seems he was a smooth talking salesman who did quite well until he fell off the wagon and started losing time from work. Her mother finally threw him out when Terri was in high school because he had become physically abusive. She divorced him after the second time the police were involved.

After I left Terri at the restaurant I took a short drive on the ridge above town and stopped at a turnout to look at the town with the snow and the lights of early evening. From here the town was the dominant landscape feature along with a single mountain peak on the southern horizon and Glenwood Canyon to the east. Twilight covered everything except for the one pink sunbeam on the peak, the street lights on the snow, and the neon lights of the store fronts. I was far enough away from the city bustle to imagine complete silence as I gazed over the scene from the car.

Her father was the problem. My own father's return from the road had always been a celebration. I hadn't thought about him in a long time. It seemed an eternity since he brought that harmonica home to me from Memphis. I don't remember his ever taking a drink of alcohol or using any bad language like the guys I worked with on the construction crew. Mama tried hard to keep everything normal while he was on the road, but she was always excited when he came home from a long trip. If he was home on Sunday he always wore a tie to church, even in the summer. He had borrowed money to buy his own truck so he could make more money on the road than driving for someone else. That was the truck he died in. My father had never been a problem like Terri's. I was thankful for that. I resented that her drunken father was still alive and Daddy was dead. We never prayed for Daddy the way we did for Mama because he was never sick, but we prayed for God to keep him safe and he didn't.

Headlights coming around the corner shine in my eyes and bring me back to the moment. I need to talk to Martin.

I knock on his door about 6:30 and find him finishing supper.

"Hello Andy. Come in!"

"Thanks. I need to talk to you about something."

"Okay. Have you eaten?"

"Not yet, but I've got groceries at my place."

"If you're up to eating my cooking I've got some baked chicken and green beans if you want. There's plenty and you're welcome to eat. I can use the company."

"Sounds good. I was planning on a T.V. dinner."

"Martin, Terri's father is in the hospital here in town. It seems he collapsed outside a bar from alcohol poisoning and almost died. Terri's only seen him for a few minutes since he woke up, but he's already asked her if he can stay with her when he gets out of the hospital. Terri doesn't know what to do about him. She hasn't seen him in the four years since her mother threw him out because of his drinking and abuse, and she sure doesn't want him to stay with her. She's afraid of him and I can't let him stay there either. Can I pay you for a room for him to stay here until he can leave town?"

"You know he may have a rough time for a while if he's an alcoholic. And more than likely he'll continue the drinking that put him in the hospital in the first place."

"He told Terri he was going to quit drinking, but she knows better than that. That's why she's scared to be around him. She's heard that promise before."

"Okay, Andy. He can stay here for a few days if it will help Terri out of a tough spot, but what he needs is more than we can give him here. He needs to check himself into a rehab hospital set up for dealing with that. He can stay here in the short term. Tell Terri it's okay."

After supper I went back to my room to relax before meeting Terri. There was a preacher on television reading from Exodus. I remembered talking about Moses and the burning bush with Aunt Margaret in the park after Sunday school and the innocent faith of an eight-year-old in the aftermath of a family tragedy. Where had this God of the burning bush been in my time of need? Could he part the Red Sea for the Israelites and not be able or compassionate enough to answer the earnest prayers of an innocent boy?

Terri and I met at her apartment after her work shift to discuss things. I told her Martin had agreed to let her father stay in one of the motel rooms for a few days after he was released, but we'd have to see how things worked out after that. She seemed relieved. She had called the hospital and they told her they would release him tomorrow before noon. They also recommended he check into a rehab center as soon as possible, but no one could force him to check in. We discussed things until about 1 a.m. and I told her I'd go with her tomorrow to pick him up and take him to his room at the motel.

The next morning I picked Terri up around 10:30 and we headed for the hospital.

When we arrived, he was packing the last few things in his suitcase so he could leave and mumbling about the "snakes" in the financial office having him "sign his soul away" to promise to pay the bill before he could leave. When he realized we were there, he stopped mumbling and stood up straighter than he probably should have, he still looked wobbly.

"Hello, honey. Thanks for coming to get me. I'm really glad to see you. Can we get out of here, these bloodsuckers want to bill me for every minute I'm here. I'll buy you two a burger on the way to your place."

"You can't stay with me, especially since you're drinking again. You have to go someplace else!"

"I don't have any place to go tonight."

"Andy has found a place for you tonight. It's all set."

"Is that his name? 'Andy?' you didn't introduce us."

"Okay, I'm sorry, this is Andy King. Andy, this is my dad, Charles Anderson."

He stuck out his hand toward me.

"Call me Charlie."

"Okay, Charlie."

"Andy has a room for you at the motel where he works. It's all arranged."

"Okay Terri, I hear you. I'll go if you can give me a ride over there, but can we just catch up on things a little. We haven't really even said hello yet. Can I at least have a hug?"

Terri gave in and hugged him as she looked toward me shaking her head. After we left the hospital we stopped for lunch. Terri and I ate, but Charlie said he didn't have his appetite back yet, so he just had a cup of coffee. Despite his promise to buy our lunch, Charlie never put a finger on the check when it came.

I left the tip on the table and picked up the check.

He told Terri he had been in Pueblo selling cars until things went sour for him. When he looked through his wallet he found Terri's address he'd gotten from her mother the last time he was in Grand Junction. The first bus brought him to Glenwood Springs. He had stopped at the bar beside the bus station and intended to take a cab to her apartment. The next thing he knew he woke up in the hospital and they told him they had contacted Terri. He said we knew the rest. Then he asked how she had been and if she'd talked to her mother lately.

Terri called one of her friends to pick her up from the restaurant. When Charlie was in the restroom she told me she had called them because she didn't want Charlie to see where she lived. Terri and Charlie talked for about an hour before Charlie and I left for the motel and Terri's friend picked her up.

"You and Terri seem comfortable together. Have you been seeing her long?"

"A while."

"Are you two serious?"

I didn't answer for a few seconds. I had never thought about us as 'serious.'

"I wouldn't call it serious. We see each other pretty often."

"I thought so. Don't hurt her like I did her mother. I'm sorry for that. I can never take it back. I still love her mother you know."

He looked exhausted and depressed. We drove in silence to the motel and went into his room. Everything he owned was in two medium sized suitcases.

"Terri looks like she's doing okay. I'm glad to see it, even if she doesn't want me around anymore. I'm tired. I need to lie down for awhile. They told me to take it easy for a couple of days. Thanks for the ride, Andy."

I left him alone the rest of the day.

That night I woke up from a fitful sleep and looked out the window of my room. I could see Charlie across the yard standing and smoking a cigarette. He looked down as he paced slowly in the driveway, his shoulders burdened with bad memories from a misspent life. He smoked two more cigarettes before going back inside. It was 2 a.m.

The next morning I found Martin at the breakfast table finishing an omelet while Charlie was busy cooking another one.

"Morning, Andy. Sit down and have some breakfast. Charlie does a great omelet. It's the first one I've had since I left the hospital. It sure beats whole wheat toast!"

"Hi, Andy. How do you like your eggs? I walked down to the store and bought some for Martin and me this morning. He told me he hadn't had an egg in months!"

"Just scrambled."

"That's easy. Are you sure you don't want an omelet?"

"No, just coffee and some eggs will be fine Charlie. I see you two have met already."

"Yeah, Martin and I have been up for about an hour. We didn't want to wake you until you were ready to get up."

The subject of why Charlie was here in the first place never came up during breakfast. We made small talk and I was beginning to see what Terri had meant about Charlie's 'deceitful charming self.' I decided to let it go for now and talk privately with Martin after Charlie left. After breakfast I went back to my room to check the newspaper for winter jobs in the area.

Later Charlie knocked on my door and asked if he could come in for a minute.

"Thanks for helping me out with the room and everything. It kind of smoothed things over with Terri I think."

"That's okay Charlie. I did it for Terri."

"I know, but it really helped me out. I want to pay you back for the room rent when I can. Do you think you could see your way clear to put me up here for another day or two until I can get a job around here. I'll pay you back as soon as I can."

"I don't know if it's a good idea for you to stay in town. Terri's not comfortable with you here."

"I hear you Andy, but I need to make things up to Terri and I can't do that if I never see her. I'm going to try to find work around here and straighten my act up."

"No, I can't be a part of that by loaning you money for the room. I think we both know you need to get out of Glenwood Springs and check into a rehab clinic somewhere."

"You seem like a pretty good guy, Andy and I can tell Terri thinks a lot of you, but it's not your choice or Terri's whether I stay in town or get rehab. I'm going to try to make a go of it here if I can. I've started over before; I can do it again."

"Terri told me all about your sweet talking ways between binges. Don't show up drunk on her doorstep. I won't be so accommodating next time. There won't be time to sober up, I'll just call the cops and they'll take you downtown. The only thing I'll believe from you is what you do, not what you tell me you're going to do. You made a bad start with me. It'll take a long time to make up for that."

"I'm sorry about upsetting Terri. I was just so nervous about finding Terri I had to have a drink and it got out of hand, but I'm staying around if I have to sleep under a bridge. It will just be easier to stay sober if I have a real place to stay. I won't bother you or Terri again until I'm straight. Martin said it was okay with him if you agreed. He said you had already told him all about me. I have nothing more to hide. Give me a week to find a job and stay sober. If I can't do it, I'm gone."

Charlie put out his hand like a salesman doing the "assumptive close" for a big sale, assuming, of course, I'd say yes. I hesitated, skeptical as I remembered what Terri had told me about his sweet talking ways.

I looked him straight in the eye.

"No booze, and you have a paying job, not a 'commission only' scam job that's nothing but a sham?"

His hand was still extended.

"Agreed!"

"Only one week, Charlie, no excuses. If I even smell booze it's over and you're on the next bus out. I'll buy the ticket?"

"Agreed!"

"Terri probably won't want to see you at all, so you only see Terri when she wants to see you and you don't show up at her place at all unless you are invited?"

"Agreed!"

I hesitatingly shook his still outstretched hand and reinforced that this was between him and me. Terri didn't know about it and had not agreed to it. It told him I was doing it because I didn't want his frozen carcass on my conscience after they found him under that bridge. I also told him that I was going to confirm what he said about Martin agreeing to this and if he hadn't really agreed, that was the end of it. I wasn't sure if I was helping Charlie out or if I had just been conned.

As Charlie walked back to his room he looked like a different man than the one I had seen last night smoking cigarettes and pacing the driveway. I hoped it was real. I took note that it was 9:37 Saturday morning. We'd see how things looked next Saturday morning at 9:38.

Later Saturday morning I picked up Terri and took her to the restaurant to work the lunch/afternoon shift. We had already made plans for me to pick her up after work and go out for the evening.

When I told her about my conversation with Charlie, she nearly came unglued and told me I'd be sorry and she wanted nothing to do with it. When I explained that he was planning to stay under a bridge if I hadn't agreed to it, she said she had warned me about listening to him. He knew how to wheedle anybody into anything.

It was a very cold date that night. She didn't say much of anything during dinner or after the movie. I took her home around 11:30. When I got back to my room I couldn't sleep, so I decided to write Mr. Johnson — make that Walt now:

Dear Walt,

It doesn't come easily to call you Walt after all these years calling you Mr. Johnson, but that's how you sign your letters to me now. Let me know if I'm being presumptuous.

I need to ask you some things. You always seem to know how to talk to me when I have something on my mind, and I'm hoping you can shed some light on this for me.

The father of a girl I've been seeing is an alcoholic. He showed up a couple of days ago in the hospital here after a near fatal binge. She's afraid to have him around because of his history with alcohol and wanted him to leave town. I found him

*a place to stay and the next day he talked
me into helping him stay around here until
he could straighten his life up. Terri, his
daughter, says he's conning me like he
always does and she won't help him at all.*

*I've agreed to loan him the money for a
week's rent as long as he keeps straight and
sober and gets a paying job. He's agreed to
leave after that if he can't do it.*

*Terri makes me feel that I have betrayed
her by doing this, but I can't stop thinking
about the look of relief on his face when we
shook hands on the deal.*

*We'll see how it works out after a week,
but I wanted to ask your opinion about this.
Did I really betray Terri by agreeing to
this with her father? Is it wrong to agree to
help someone begging for another chance
after they have failed for years to keep their
promises to stop drinking?*

*I know it's hard to give advice on the
basis of a brief letter, but I know your heart
for others and I trust your judgment on
things like this.*

Sincerely, Andy

Sunday morning I took the letter to the corner
mailbox, walked back to the motel and knocked on
Charlie's door. There was no answer. I wondered if
Terri was right and he'd already fallen off the wagon. I
knocked harder ... still nothing. I used my master key to
open the door. There were three empty beer bottles in the
trash and Charlie was gone!

My mind went crazy with all kinds of fears and explanations. I went for a walk around the neighborhood. After half an hour I went back to my room and called the police station to see if they had picked him up. No, they hadn't. Where was he?

A few inches of snow had fallen overnight, so I decided to work off some nervous energy. I started the snow blower and cleared the sidewalks in front of the motel along with the main driveway and parking area in front of the office. It took until noon to finish and I decided to walk to the shopping center three blocks away for a sandwich at Blimpies. As I was finishing my lunch I saw Martin's truck drive by toward town with two people inside. I figured it was someone from church with him.

Martin called me late Sunday afternoon to tell me that Charlie was with him and invited me to meet them at his place around 8:15. I told him Charlie had been gone all day and asked him what was going on. He said we'd talk about it tonight.

"Hello Andy. Come sit down."

"Okay Martin. What's up?"

"Saturday was a rough night for Charlie and we got a few things straight before it was over. Charlie and I have been together all day. He told me everything about how he'd lost his wife and family because of his drinking. He tells me he's finally ready to change things. I've agreed to help him as long as he stays sober. I told him I know how hard it is because I've been there ... but that's another story. Right now Charlie has the tough road and I'm here for him when he needs me."

"Terri told me about how many times he claimed he wouldn't drink again. What makes you think it will work now?"

"We don't know if it will. That's why we prayed together about it and asked the other elders at church to keep us in their prayers as well. Only Jesus can provide the grace for something like this to work over the long haul."

"You know how much faith I have in prayer, Martin. It's never helped me. It didn't keep Mama alive."

"This is not about you Andy. You'll have to deal with God yourself when your time comes. Right now Charlie has shared with us that it's his time to repent and begin a new life in Christ. We can only take him at his word and we are bound by faith to give him every opportunity to turn things around."

Tomorrow morning I'm driving him to a rehab center in Grand Junction. He's agreed to stay as long as it takes. We've found a benefactor who has agreed to pick up all the cost until he can pay it back. As soon as he's released, he'll come back here and work for one of the members of our congregation. He will make enough to pay for his room and meals with me here. I've agreed to take him to and from work for a while and Charlie and I will be spending some time together after that."

Martin's words came over me in waves. Had they forgotten about Terri's fears when they planned for him to come back to Glenwood Springs after rehab? Did Martin really believe they could pull this off? Who's paying for all this?

All day, with Charlie missing, I had believed the worst and couldn't shake the feeling. Martin's explanations weren't enough for me, or I suspected for Terri.

Charlie sat quietly listening, watching Martin and me.

He saw my doubt.

I saw a tear in the corner of his eye as he left to go back to his room without a word.

Watching through that small window I had painted for Martin on that first day at the motel, I saw Charlie close the door to his room behind him. He didn't turn on the light.

War & Peace

Thanksgiving 1981
... Platteville Colorado

Johnny opens the front door to let Bronson out as I drive up. At first he barks because he doesn't recognize the car, but figures out who I am before I can get my feet firmly on the ice-covered driveway and we go tumbling. Johnny can't stop laughing.

From the ground I looked up to see Aunt Margaret smiling and waving through the kitchen window with a flour-covered hand. For the first time since Texas I knew I was really "home."

On Friday morning Johnny and I are fixing breakfast. Aunt Margaret says it's a good tradition, especially since she fixed an entire Thanksgiving dinner the day before. She and one of her long-time friends visiting from Denver are in the living room waiting for us to call them to breakfast.

"Johnny, I want to ask you something ... would you believe an alcoholic if he told you he was going to get straight and stay in the same town as the daughter who witnessed him hitting her mother while he was in a drunken rage?"

"Wow! Where did that come from?"

"Terri's father showed up in the hospital there in town a couple of weeks ago almost dead from alcohol poisoning. He asked Terri to let him stay with her for a while. She was really shaken up and adamant about not letting him stay with her, or even in Glenwood Springs for that matter. We worked it out for him to stay at the motel instead, but Martin convinced him to go to a rehab center in Grand Junction. He's planning to come back to Glenwood Springs when he gets out and Martin's going to help him get started again there. I don't like it!"

"Martin is a good Christian man, Andy. Don't you trust his judgment?"

"Not this time. He and Charlie prayed together about it and Charlie is 'repenting' for real this time. I don't buy it and I can't let him hurt Terri again."

"I understand that you want to protect Terri, but it's not up to you to decide how other people's lives work out. Martin and I got to know each other pretty well this summer. Follow his lead. He's dealt with this kind of thing before and his brothers at the church are there for counsel and prayer in the tough spots. Be there for Terri, she's bound to need someone to lean on if Charlie stays around, no matter what the outcome of the rehab. And trust God. Remember He's always there to call on."

"Hey you guys, are we going to have breakfast today"

"We were just waiting on the biscuits … come and get it!"

"We'll talk later, Andy."

Saturday morning Aunt Margaret took her friend back to Denver. Johnny and I were alone in the house and Bronson was taking advantage of the warm spot in front of the heater to stretch out for a nap. Johnny started to talk.

"I spoke with Martin last night while you were out with your old friends from school. He filled me in on what was happening with Charlie. Martin said you were pretty upset about the turn of events after you found those empty beer bottles in his room. He said your main concern was for Terri and you seemed bent on protecting her from her dad's problems no matter what.

I can understand that, especially since I know where you came from and how hurt you were when you got here. What I can't abide is your hostility for a man Martin has committed to help. Have you forgotten your words to me: "Martin has become my best friend outside of you and Aunt Margaret. We don't talk much, but I know I can rely on him and I'll do whatever I can to help him when he needs it."

You said those exact words to me the day I left Glenwood Springs last summer. Has something changed since then? Martin needs your help now as much as Terri does. He is bound by his faith to help Charlie with this thing and it's not going to be easy. Martin is convinced that Charlie is sincere about his repentance and is engaged in a life and death struggle. Only time will confirm the validity of his confession, but as a Christian brother Martin has committed to give him every chance. Martin truly believes Charlie is one who has fallen into the hopelessness of alcoholism as a prerequisite to the ultimate hope of a life in Jesus.

I've never really told you the story of how I arrived here in Platteville. You see, I didn't grow up here. Mother and I lived in Denver during my school years. I was certainly no saint as a kid and I caused Mother a lot of grief sometimes because of my minor scrapes with the law and I had some pretty rough friends. A couple of those guys are in prison now, and one is dead from a drug overdose. The last time the cops picked me up for questioning about one of my friends I got fed up with Denver life and joined the Marines.

That was 1965, and I was about your age, a little older I guess. Boot Camp in San Diego was a lot tougher than I had ever imagined and I found out I wasn't as tough as I thought. I saw and experienced things in those two months I still have a hard time describing to anyone who hasn't been through it. The process of making potential killers out of boys is not pretty, even if it is necessary. There is no second place in a hand-to-hand encounter with a killer enemy.

Viet Nam was coming into its full horrible reality about then and almost everybody in boot camp expected to go sooner or later. The drill instructor's job was to break us mentally to a point just this side of hopelessness, a place of vulnerability where the 'weak sisters,' as he put it, would drop out and they could discharge them and 'send them back to mommy.' Only survivors were mentally or physically able to become experts in the deadly skills of war. We learned how to rip a man open with the single powerful thrust and slash motion of a bayonet; hesitation was not an option unless we had a death wish. They taught marksmanship to the point of deciding in a split second whether to take the easy main torso vital organ shot or to go for the 'clean' death shot to the head. Then we drilled for days on how to break a man's neck from behind with one swift move, no sound no weapon, no blood, just instant death.

Mental toughness was mandatory to survive insane platoon wide punishments for the failures of just one man. Platoon punishments ranged from an extra five miles of double-time on a hot, dusty road carrying packs and rifles, to 100 push-ups in mud so deep you'd drown if you collapsed. Teamwork became a survival skill to avoid the wrath of what we saw as an out-of-control D.I.

But in those sixty days they transformed us from arrogant kids into lethal weapons capable of incredible teamwork, loyalty, and potential heroism. Unfortunately for many of us, just the fact that we survived it gave us justification for the return of our lost arrogance.

About six months after boot camp I got my first set of orders for 'Nam. I was a 'grunt,' — the Marine term for infantryman — in the middle of the war. I had no idea how appropriate that name was until I got into the field. Suddenly the next three and a half years of my enlistment looked like an eternity. Mud, heat, cold, filth, death and dysentery were constant companions. Boredom interrupted by brief heart-pounding forays into enemy territory set the rhythm of life.

Two of the twelve guys I shipped over with came home in body bags. My reaction to their deaths was not to fear for my own life, but to kill as many as possible in retaliation for the sneak attack of that lone sniper who picked them off like melons on a fence. We never caught him, but I brought home the two empty rounds he left in his sniper nest. The fire fights we had after that were never successful unless we chalked up at least two 'confirmed kills' that I could notch into those shell casings with a file. I didn't get hit in my first 13 month tour but I was changed forever.

When my enlistment was up, I wanted more revenge so I reenlisted and volunteered for a second tour in 'Nam. Then I went one step further and volunteered to train for and join Force Recon, or Marine Special Forces. Their operations are often secret and known for covert but deadly force in extracting friendly forces from impossible situations. Force Recon's casualty rates are high because of the high risk missions that are its trademark.

Our five-man team had gone behind enemy lines to recover a downed pilot. We drew fire shortly after we recovered him, so we formed a perimeter around the pilot to protect him. I signaled Perry that I was going "freelancing." That meant I would silently outflank the enemy position while the rest of my team kept them occupied by exchanging fire.

There was a half-moon with scattered blowing clouds, so I was able to move while the moon was behind the clouds and observe when the moon was bright. I could see four shooters spread out about ten yards apart behind trees. My team was doing a good job distracting them with fire away from my approach angle. I slipped behind the nearest shooter. He was kneeling between two trees with a clear field of fire toward my team. I took him from behind, snapping his neck with one move as I let surprise and the weight of his body do the work. The only sound was from breaking vertebrae. I let his body down silently to the ground and double-checked his pulse to be sure he was dead. From this position I had a clear shot at two of the remaining shooters. I pictured their heads like the "melons on a fence" my buddies must have been for that sniper two years before. I fired two quick head shots, knowing that the remaining shooter would not realize that the shots were mine and not theirs. I moved quickly behind the last shooter who was still occupied firing at my team's position. I'll never forget his silhouette in the moonlight as I approached silently from behind. He must have heard me at the last second, because he tried to turn and face me with his rifle, but I was too close and was able to hit him hard with my rifle butt. Before he could recover I ran my bayonet through his chest and kicked his weapon away. In the moonlight I could see desperation in the whites of his eyes as his life slipped away in the blood pooling on his chest, his left hand twitching toward his weapon. It was the first time I had actually witnessed a man's face as he realized death, a death I had personally dealt. He looked to be about 16 or 17 years old and his blood was still on my bayonet blade.

I signaled the team that it was clear and felt queasy as I turned to leave. I vomited in the bushes on the way back to the team, then jammed my bayonet blade into the ground a half-dozen times to clean off his teenage blood.

I rejoined the team after a few minutes by myself to get my head straight. We then proceeded to rendezvous with a black-ops helicopter to carry our rescued pilot back to the field hospital. It was, by necessity, a small chopper, too small to carry the team. We were on our own to get back.

The team set a perimeter and the chopper landed. As soon as the downed pilot was aboard I signaled the rescue chopper pilot he was cleared for takeoff, exchanged a thumbs-up smile with the rescued pilot and closed the chopper door.

I watched from the grass as the chopper rose about 100 feet and began to turn toward home. Out of nowhere we heard machine gun fire and instantly the chopper exploded. They must have hit the fuel tank with the first round or two. We watched helplessly as the wreckage hit the ground only a few meters from where it had taken off.

In recovering from my death-dealing encounter I had misjudged the situation. We thought the area was clear of hostiles. The chopper was a sitting duck. That rescued pilot's thumbs-up smile still haunts me.

No one spoke as we quickly exited the rendezvous point, knowing another larger enemy unit must have arrived and spotted the chopper as it took off. We headed back to base using only hand signals to coordinate silently. Those hand signals took on a morbid character in the dark, deadly silence of the moon as we navigated on foot back through the dense Viet Cong jungle. As the sun came up shots rang out from our left flank and Perry, the radio man, fell in front of me. I dragged him behind a tree and began firing back. The fire fight took only about two or three minutes before the shooting stopped. Perry had his hand over the leg wound and I could see the blood seeping between his fingers. I ripped open a medi-pack and tied a tourniquet around his thigh. The other three guys cleared the area and signaled it was okay to proceed. We had orders not to break radio silence for another two kilometers, so I handed my weapon to Marvin, put Perry over my back and we headed back as fast as I could travel. We rotated carrying him between the four of us.

The minute we could radio in, we called for a rescue chopper for Perry and changed course for a known landing zone to rendezvous. We got there a few minutes before the chopper and laid low waiting for chopper sounds. The other three covered our backs while I carried Perry to the chopper. I loaded Perry on board and looked back to signal the rest of the team to board. As Marvin started to move a mortar round landed right beside him and he went down. George and Ralph were about 50 yards away from him, so I ran back to help Marvin. I threw him over my back and started for the chopper with George right in front of me. They must have known we'd use this clearing for a landing zone, because George took about ten steps and stepped on an anti-personnel mine about 3 feet in front of me. The next thing I remember is the medic on another chopper telling me I was going to be okay as he gave me a shot. I remember feeling something very wrong below my knee and bloody bandages across my chest. When Ralph came to visit in the hospital he told me Perry made it okay, but George and Marvin didn't. A few days later I was on a medical transport plane bound for the states.

In two days I had gone from invincible Marine Recon team leader to a crippled failure. Forty percent of my team was dead and I felt guilty about killing the enemy. I was at the bottom of the pit with endless hours to second guess that signal for the chopper to take off ... to remember that thumbs-up smile of the rescued pilot ... to doubt the decision to bring Perry to that clearing instead of going the extra kilometer toward home before breaking radio silence ... possibly tipping off that Viet Cong mortar team to fire the round that took Marvin. And I had the rest of my life to deal with all of it along with the loss of a leg and a damaged heart and lung. And there was George, killed by the mine that nearly killed me. Nightmares frustrated sleep as the eyes of that teenage boy I had so savagely killed laughed at the fallen faces of my team. Hopelessness dominated my life ... I flirted with thoughts of suicide.

As I lay on my back in that hospital bed an endless parade of doctors, nurses and orderlies monitored my entire existence. Tubes, bandages, bedpans, sponge baths and prognoses replaced weapons, revenge, strategies, codenames and military objectives. Instead of routing the enemy, I was ringing the nurses for more pain killers. I couldn't even walk across the room.

They notified Mother I was coming home to a military hospital in the states and she got there only hours after I arrived. In the next few months I had five separate surgeries to repair three major wounds. They officially discharged me from both the navy hospital and the Marines. My career as an elite fighting man was over and we were heading back to Denver in mother's car. My world had collapsed.

Months went by with life centered around rehab sessions at the VA hospital and dozing in the living room in front of the TV. Bitterness and self-pity shaped every conversation. One day I found myself staring at Mother's tears and hearing my own voice screaming at her about turning the TV off while I was out of the room for a minute. It was as if I wasn't really in the room, I was just watching a bad program on the idiot box. I stopped yelling and left the room on my crutches, then sat on the porch as darkness gathered around me and I stared into the approaching night. Hours later I heard Mother close the door to her bedroom. Standing with my crutches, I carefully maneuvered down the steps to the sidewalk and then around the block, stopping to rest at the bus stop. When I returned to the house I found supper on the table with a note beside the plate:

"I hope this is enough supper for you, wake me up if you need anything else. I'll see you in the morning for breakfast.

Love, Mother"

As I passed her room I could see her shadow from the moonlight under the closed door. She was listening from the other side. I went to bed. The image of her tears hounded me and the faces of my fallen team members invaded the darkness under the cold stare of those dying teenage eyes. I was ashamed for how I had treated her, for my mistakes on that mission, for the revenge that fueled my military career, and for my failure to survive as a viable man.

Daylight found me still awake. I struggled to put on my prosthesis, stood without crutches and quietly dressed. As I went toward the kitchen I found Mother in her robe, asleep in the living room chair, her bible open under the still burning lamp.

I'll never forget that picture. It was the only Sunday morning she missed going to church in all the time I had been home. It suddenly dawned on me that it was not just my life that changed; Mother's life was altered forever as well ... and I was a selfish ass.

About 12:30 p.m. the phone rang and I could hear the conversation from the other room. She told them she was not sick, she just needed to stay home with me. Then she asked them to pray for me.

I've never told her I heard her say that. That afternoon I called Jim, my oldest friend. I had known him since we were six years old in Sunday school together, but as a teenager I got too "tough" for church and for his crowd. I hadn't seen or talked to him since just before I left to enlist. As a draftee, he had spent one tour in Viet Nam during his two years in the Army. He knew the horrors of war and how difficult much of it could be to talk about openly.

Jim and I met frequently over the next few days and weeks, mostly in the park or in coffee shops. There was no dramatic talk about what happened in Viet Nam, my dead buddies, or that slain teenager's eyes I continued to see in my dreams; Jim was just there to connect me to the reality of a normal life ... and we both knew it. He simply lived his life before me as a Christian brother ready to hear my cry if it ever came, ready to treat me as a fellow human being who had lost his way and needed assurance that he still mattered. My dramatic cry never came audibly, but the Lord heard my cry of repentance in the dark on one long, sleepless night. Over time I regained my life and discovered a new hope and fulfilling life in Jesus. Those prayers Mother had asked for that Sunday were answered, no thanks to me.

That's what Martin is doing for Charlie. Alcoholism is Charlie's Viet Nam and Martin is the Christian brother walking the long road beside him.

Charlie deserves the same second chance I was given. Would you be the one to deny him that?"

I couldn't answer Johnny's question. There was too much to absorb, too much to ponder.

"I don't know what to say Johnny. I need to take a walk."

Bronson and I wandered the streets of Platteville while I thought about my first days here. The cold Sunday school room, the prayers from the pulpit on that first Sunday morning as I stared at the snow beyond the church window. I couldn't say that those early prayers for me weren't answered. I only knew that my prayers for Mama had done nothing. I was alternately confused and angry. Bronson and I found our private boulder on the edge of town and stared at the now familiar mountains. It was late afternoon when we got back to the house.

It took a long time to go to sleep that night. I left for Glenwood Springs early Sunday morning. There was much on my mind as I drove. I was anxious to see Terri.

I drove out of Platteville at 6 a.m. Sunday.

On the trip back to Glenwood Springs I was still dealing with Johnny's revelations about the war. I could still see Aunt Margaret's red eyes the night she told me about Johnny coming home from Viet Nam and how she needed to go back to Denver to be there with him because she wasn't sure he would be okay. At the time I had no idea what she and Johnny were going through, or what war was really about. Johnny must have been on that mission half a world away around the time Daddy died in Texas. At the time, all my eight-year-old mind could understand was that Aunt Margaret was leaving and she was sad. My world was not the only one turned upside down in those weeks and months to follow. When Johnny picked me up at the Denver bus station, he had been back from the war a little over six years and he must have still been dealing with the after-effects of that deadly raid. In all the time I lived in Platteville he had never talked about the war except on that trip to Cheyenne when we saw the big flag and he showed me his leg and chest.

When I went to Terri's Sunday evening, I couldn't talk about my conversation with Johnny. I still had too many unanswered questions, too many things to sort out. Terri had gone to visit her mother over Thanksgiving and I encouraged the conversation about that and her speculation about what would happen if Charlie came back to Glenwood Springs in a few weeks. I got back to the motel about 1 a.m. It was another almost sleepless night as I tried to sort things out.

Rocker Seven

The Following Day
... Glenwood Springs, Andy's Room

Monday morning about seven I could see Martin through the window having his decaffeinated breakfast, so I decided to join him for a cup of coffee.

"Good morning Martin, how was your Thanksgiving?"

"It was good Andy. Annie came down for a surprise visit, checking on me I think, but she denies it as usual."

"That's our Annie."

"A friend of mine called me while you were in Platteville and asked if I knew anybody who was dependable and needed a job for a few months. He's the head foreman on a ranch just outside of town and needs someone to keep the snow off their ranch roads and access roads the county can't get to soon enough to suit him. I told him about you, but let him know that I didn't know if you would be interested. He said the pay is pretty good for a temporary job."

He handed me a piece of paper with his name and phone number as I sat down at the table. Martin started a separate coffee maker with, as he put it, 'the real stuff' for me.

"He's been a friend of mine for quite a few years. I met him when we both worked for the Forest Service. He said he needs all his regular hands to tend livestock when it snows and they need the roads clear so they have access to all the barns and stockyards. It sounds like a good job for somebody who can handle the odd hours in bad weather. A single guy is who he needs. Give him a call if you're interested. He needs to hire somebody before the Wednesday, because they are predicting a winter storm in a couple of days."

"I'll call him after breakfast."

We had a quiet breakfast. I didn't talk about my conversation with Johnny that morning. I went back to my room around nine.

"Hello, Mr. Patterson? This is Andy King, Martin's friend."

"Oh, good, I was hoping you'd call this morning. Did he tell you what we need out here?"

"Yes, he said you need somebody to clear the roads when it snows. I haven't done anything like that before, but I learned to handle some of the smaller heavy equipment moving loads around on road construction this summer."

"Martin told me you had done a little of that. Can you come out here to see me this morning? We're south of town toward Carbondale to the turn off for the ranch."

"I can be there."

"Good. You'll see the sign for the Rocker 7 ranch on the highway. It's just under eleven miles from the Glenwood Springs city limit sign. Turn right and go about five miles on a gravel road until you come to the main complex. My office is in a log cabin on the right across from the equipment barns. I'll be expecting you about noon if that's okay for you. We can eat lunch in the bunkhouse dining room and discuss it."

"Sounds good. I'll be there!"

It was a welcome relief from the last few days to think about a new job as I drove to the Rocker 7. As I turned off the highway on the ranch road I could see that I was already on the ranch itself from the occasional small signs along the wide, well maintained gravel road. Most of the snow from our first major snowfall of the year had melted in the valley, but the road was climbing steadily and snowdrifts on the mountainsides became more prevalent with every turn. I crossed a small stream with a wooden bridge, and later crossed a longer bridge over a narrow canyon where it appeared water ran violently at times. As I crested a small saddle between two peaks the road suddenly dropped and I could see the ranch complex made up of some steel buildings and a couple of large log cabins.

The building on the right was smaller than the other one, but it had large plate glass windows and double glass doors facing the large front porch. The sign over the door read "Ranch Foreman."

I parked and went inside. As I opened the door a man came out of the front office door and offered me his hand.

"The name is Stony, Stony Patterson. Are you Andy?"

"Yes."

"Come on inside for a minute. Sit down while I finish up a couple of things and we'll get some lunch."

He was a small wiry man with a strong, working man's handshake and gravel in his voice. He picked up the phone he had placed on hold to greet me and continued a conversation with a feed supplier about a delivery before the predicted mid-week winter storm.

"Okay Andy, let's eat. We've got pretty good grub around here. The cook on duty today used to be a chef at a high dollar restaurant in town. You never know what he'll concoct, but it's usually better'n the average ranch mess cook can manage."

I had to push a little to keep up with Stony as we

crossed the yard toward the three-story log bunkhouse. By the time we got there Stony had pointed out the equipment barns and told me that he had a short crew this winter and couldn't spare anybody to take off from stock work to clear the roads. He said he needed someone to be here anytime it looked like snow. He was throwing words so quickly I had to hurry to listen.

There were about ten hands eating when we sat down. I heard a voice in the kitchen yell.

"Stony! You want the barbecued chicken or the pork chops and gravy?"

"What's good, Hank?"

"I'd go with the chops. How many you want, they're small?"

"Make it three for me with some potatoes and some of those green beans from last night if you've got 'em, and Andy here is eating too."

The same voice came from the kitchen, "Andy, what's your pleasure?

"The chops sound good to me too. Ditto on Stony's order."

"You've gotta eat well when you can around here. You never know if the rest of the day includes food."

Those "small" pork chops were almost an inch thick and the mound of mashed potatoes was covered with cream gravy. I wasn't sure if I could eat it all. Fortunately I didn't have to talk much because Stony was busy telling me about the ranch and snow clearing duties for the winter. Despite his constant conversation, he cleaned his plate before I did. As I was finishing my last bite of potatoes he asked me if I was interested.

"Don't you need to know a little more about me? You just met me."

"You look solid to me and Martin told me you were a

good hand and know how to handle a forklift and backhoe. I've known him for over thirty years. A recommendation like that from him is like money in the bank. It's up to you, and I need somebody now, if you're up for it. We can start showing you the ropes this afternoon — that storm's picking up speed and I need all the hands I've got to tend the herd."

"Wow! You don't give a guy much time to think about it! Yeah, I guess it sounds good to me. Where do I start?"

"If you're finished with lunch I'll introduce you to Kelly at the equipment barn and he can show you how to handle the snow rigs. We've got all the cold weather gear you'll need to stay warm, so don't worry about that."

"Okay Stony, let's do it!"

I spent the rest of the afternoon learning how to handle the truck with the snow plow mounted on the front and getting familiar with the maps I'd need for the job. There were a lot more miles of ranch road than I imagined, but Kelly showed me the ones that weren't used in the winter much when all the cattle were gathered in to their protected pastures. He said sometimes the county needed help clearing area roads, but that wouldn't likely happen until I was settled into the job for a while. He said he'd take me out the first night or two, but he'd be needed for the stock after that since they were short handed.

Kelly told me to get a good night's rest and be back to the equipment barn by eight in the morning to fill the bed of the dump truck snow plow with sand for the bridges.

By the time I left a while after dark, my head was spinning with new information.

At the motel there was a letter on the floor beneath the mail slot in my room. It was from Walt.

Dear Andy,

You are a man now Andy, you have been for a while now. Of course you can call me Walt. It's always good to hear from you. We've been through a lot together, both in Texas when you were a kid and now as Christian brothers across the years and miles.

Do you remember when they suspended Monte from school because he kept getting into fights? The principal couldn't get Monte to tell him what was going on to make him want to start fights. When his mother called me, she told me his big brother had been killed recently and he had been too quiet at home since then. I was surprised that he hadn't mentioned it to us at church. I tried to talk to him about things, but he wouldn't say much, and things didn't change at school, so he was suspended again for the rest of the semester.

That was just before you came to stay with us while your mother was in the hospital. While you were there, you and Monte became friends. In the weeks following I saw a change in Monte, and in you. I don't know what you talked about, but I sensed that he knew that the pain of losing your father helped you relate to his loss of his brother. As you and Monte became closer, I heard Monte pray for your mother's recovery in Sunday school and watched as his heart changed over the months. By focusing on the pain of a friend he found purpose. I watched two young boys naturally discover, cultivate and live out the lessons Jesus taught the apostles in the daily life he lived with them and subsequent building of the early church by those same apostles. At the age of twelve, Monte and you learned the gospel truth that giving your life for others is more rewarding than inwardly turned self pity. It was a lesson I've never forgotten; the value of simply walking beside our troubled brother in his time of need, whatever that need may be. Both of you came through that time with not only a lifelong friend, but the strength to survive moment to moment in the tough times.

I see that strength in you now in your desire to help Terri, but I also see a little bit of the Andy I saw with Monte in your reaching out to her dad.

From here, I can't tell you to pick a side. I can only bring your thoughts back to that special relationship with Monte and the way you helped him weather his conflicts at school. When you see Terri's father remember that if he is to overcome his alcohol demons, he'll need all the help he can get from the Lord and anyone willing to walk beside him. The same is true for Terri in fighting her demons of distrust for her own father.

It seems the Lord has given you a place in both their lives. If I have a word for you in this, it is that there is no side to pick, only a path to walk and love to share. Then watch

what unfolds as the Lord works in lives as
you pray your heart's true desire for both of
them. Seek his guidance both in prayer and
in the reactions of those you have learned to
trust, just as you have with me.

   As always in this, and all your life, you
are in our thoughts and prayers.

Your Brother in Christ,
Walt

I hadn't thought about Monte and those critical months in my young life for years. Walt's letter unleashed another wave of streaming thoughts, memories, and doubts about what to do. I knew I had a heart to help Terri, but how could I "walk a path" beside her alcoholic father when he was the cause of her troubles? How could I pray about this when I could not feel those prayers within me?

I called Terri to let her know about the uncertainty of my schedule for the next few days and that I wouldn't be able to make our lunch date for Tuesday. We talked for a long time and I carefully didn't mention the letter from Walt.

It was the third near-sleepless night in a row for me, and I had a new job to start. I hadn't taken Kelly's advice to "get a good night's rest."

Thankfully the activities of the next day completely occupied me. There was no room for lingering questions and speculations. Kelly rode with me as we drove around what he called the "main" ranch roads to get me oriented, pointing out major landmarks and intersections while marking our position on the map. He said we'd learn about the outlying spreads later. He told me the total acreage owned by the ranch was over 15,000 acres

plus leased land of nearly a quarter that. I was relieved
when he told me I probably wouldn't need to worry about
anything but the "main" ranch property.

We checked the weather from the office before I
left work about a half hour after sundown. They were
predicting heavy snow starting about noon Wednesday.
Kelly said I needed to be at the ranch about then to make
sure I could get there in my car before the roads got bad.
I could sleep in the bunkhouse until the job was done ...
whenever that was!

The next ten days was a confusing jumble of days,
nights, exhaustion and boredom as two windy snow
storms came through. They weren't extreme, but the
work kept me on the ranch more than I was in town.
Dinners with Terri were only a memory and I hadn't
shared a decaffeinated breakfast since I started the job.

After that I found out that clearing the snow on the
roads was only part of the job. I had also inherited the
job of pulling trucks and equipment out of the mud with
a tractor equipped with a heavy duty winch, changing
tractor tires that went flat and any other disagreeable job
the "experienced cattle hands" couldn't take the time to
do. Odd jobs around the ranch kept me busy for another
couple of weeks before the next snowfall.

That "free time between snowfalls" I had envisioned
somehow got buried in the mud, covered with sweat and
then washed off in the bunkhouse showers at bed time.

Blowing snow was all that was visible through the
window this Sunday morning as Hank put out Belgian
waffles, eggs and bacon on the serving line about 9
o'clock. No point in starting the road clearing again until
the snow slows down.

After breakfast I continued to watch the snow and
wondered if Aunt Margaret and Johnny were in church

yet, and if they ever looked out those windows toward the mountains like I had that first Sunday in Platteville. I thought about Bronson and how much he would love it out here on the ranch with plenty of room to run and plenty of snow for romping. The radio weatherman says the snow will quit in the next couple of hours. I headed toward the truck, coffee thermos and lunch box in hand. The clouds seemed lighter as I started her up.

Sunday, December 20, 1981 — Glenwood Springs

For two days and nights I had been repeatedly clearing the same drifts caused by high winds and dry snow, but now it looked like there was an extended break in the winds and snow. Just before dawn I decided to go back into town instead of staying in the bunkhouse.

I was feeling guilty about leaving Martin to hire somebody to clear the snow at the motel instead of doing it myself. As I pulled into the parking lot I saw the snow had been cleared off the parking lot and sidewalks. I knew Martin hadn't done it but must have hired someone from his church or a local kid. The newspapers and mail on my dining table let me know that Martin had been keeping an eye on my room for me. Just before sunrise I turned up the thermostat and went to bed, exhausted.

I woke up a little after 2 p.m. and took a shower. The newspaper confirmed the forecast for clear, calm weather for the next few days and I was grateful.

As I picked up the phone to call Terri I saw Charlie going into his room. I hadn't expected that. He must be back from rehab. I stopped dialing and hung up.

Walt's letter stared at me from the table. He and Johnny had said the same thing ... that Charlie deserved the chance to turn things around and needed someone to help him find his way in that. I knew it couldn't be me, and I knew Terri wouldn't be happy about Charlie staying in town. I had to think! I needed to talk to Martin.

"Hello, Andy! You've been pretty scarce around here lately. How's Stony treating you out there?"

"Okay, I guess. I haven't seen him much between the snow, the mud and the roads."

"Sit down! You want some "real" coffee? The doctor said I could have a cup every couple of days. I might even have a piece of pie to go along with it."

"Sounds good to me!"

"Stony called here the other day to let me know you were working out as a pretty good hand. I figured you'd do alright."

"You didn't do all the snow clearing around here did you? Annie wouldn't like that!"

"Charlie did that for me this time, right after he got off the bus from Grand Junction. The last couple of weeks I had a kid down the street clear it for me."

"Do you need anything else done around here while I have a few days off?"

"Charlie has agreed to help out around here while you're out at the ranch and I think it'll be good for him to stay busy right now."

"Does Terri know her dad is back?"

"No. She called last week while he was still in Grand Junction, but Charlie asked me to let him call her when he was ready to talk. I think he wants to wait awhile."

"That's probably a good idea."

For the next few days I was careful to keep Terri away from the motel and I called Aunt Margaret and Johnny to let them know I couldn't come for Christmas because I was on call at the ranch.

Annie showed up in her new Lincoln the afternoon of

December 23rd with a trunk full of presents and a trailer full of loaded ice chests. She informed Martin, Charlie and me that we were going for lunch Christmas Eve at her favorite restaurant. So, what were all the loaded ice chests about?

Christmas Eve, 1981

She tossed me the keys and winked while Martin was unhitching her trailer. At lunch we suffered through Annie's routine that we could order two of anything on the menu because she was buying. Charlie looked a little skeptical about Annie. I guess Martin hadn't warned him about Annie's bigger than life persona.

After a few minutes Piper joined us … at the table this time instead of as our waitress. She looked a lot more relaxed than she was the last time I saw her at Terri's apartment a couple of months ago. After the main course, Annie ordered dessert for everybody, including a scoop of sherbet for Martin, and announced a Christmas Day proposition for all of us.

"I know Andy's curious about all those loaded iced chests I brought down from the ranch, so I guess I'd better come clean. Last Christmas Martin was a little under the weather after his hospital stay, so some other folks at the church took over the annual Christmas Dinner he'd been ramrodding for the past decade. This year we're going to help him get back on that horse, that is, if you're willing. I've already drafted Piper here.

There are seven needy households here in Garfield County that Martin's church has been helping out this year who've accepted an invitation for Christmas Dinner at the church. And while we're here eating this wonderful lunch, volunteers are taking the food from those coolers to their own kitchens to prepare alongside their own family

Christmas Dinners. Tomorrow morning I'm looking for volunteers to work the kitchen when our guests arrive and allow a few of those church volunteers to either stay home for Christmas dinner with their families, or sit down with our guests and get to know them while they enjoy a genuinely home-cooked dinner. Any takers?"

I had to hand it to Annie. Here we were, satiated and defenseless against her cunning, benevolent plea. Martin had pushed his chair back from the table and let her have center stage, a knowing smile growing on his lips as Annie deftly suckered us in.

Charlie didn't say anything at first, he just looked at me, the only other one at the table who had been in the dark about this, smiled and shrugged his shoulders. He knew as well as I did that we'd been had.

I jokingly told Annie that I had "snowplow duty tomorrow" and then looked out the window at the bright winter sunshine.

"So Andy, if it doesn't snow tomorrow can we count on you?"

She knew full well that there was no chance of snow for the next few days, and Terri had gone to her Mother's house for Christmas.

"Yea, I guess so, Annie. Martin didn't tell me how devious you could be."

Annie feigned innocence about setting us up while letting us know we'd be expected at the church kitchen by eight o'clock Christmas Morning to receive the food and be ready to serve by noon.

We headed back to the motel and enjoyed Christmas Eve until about 9:30 when Annie declared that she needed her "beauty sleep" before the big day tomorrow.

I went back to my room and decided to write a letter:

Dear Johnny,

I had no idea about how tough it must have been for you after Viet Nam. I still remember Aunt Margaret's red eyes and sad face the night she told me about going home to Denver to take care of you.

Those years in Platteville must have been my very own "selfish ass" period and I apologize for that. I couldn't see anything but my own grief and I guess I ignored everybody's needs but my own.

Thinking back now I can see how you and Aunt Margaret sacrificed a part of your lives to meet my needs.

Charlie, Terri's dad, just completed a rehab session and is now staying in a room here at the motel. He seems subdued and a little anxious about things. Martin is committed to give him every chance the way Jim did with you. Only time will give us an answer about Charlie's turnaround.

Annie drafted us for Christmas dinner kitchen duty at the church, so I need to get some sleep now because I'll be getting up early. Leave it to Annie for the unexpected!

Martin said he filled you in about my job at the ranch. It's challenging sometimes, but I like it, even with the unpredictability and hard, messy work pulling vehicles out of the mud.

I probably won't be able to get away from here until spring to see you and Aunt

Margaret, so give her my love,
Andy

Christmas Day, 1981
... Martin's church

It was a large inviting room with well kept, but aging hardwood floors and drapes, big enough to hold the church fellowship meals of about a hundred people. The tables, some round, some rectangle were set family style, each with a different color table cloth, homemade Christmas center pieces, and the rest of the table left open for a turkey platter, food dishes and the individual place settings. Each of the seven tables was set with enough chairs for a guest family, their sponsoring family and an extra place or two for anyone else who happened to show up. Warm sunlight streamed past the edges of the drawn drapes from the two large windows on the far south side, opposite the kitchen. There were four couches and various mismatched, overstuffed chairs around three large area rugs near the windows. That area was arranged something like an oversized living room with a large Christmas tree in the corner covered with silver icicles, hand-made decorations and old-style Christmas lights like the ones I remembered from the Christmases before Daddy died. There must have been over a hundred small, hand wrapped packages beneath it.

Home cooked food began arriving at the kitchen door around 8:30, each labeled for a specific table and bearing handwritten heating, or other special instructions for final preparation just before serving. Annie assigned me to keep track of the food for the Bristol family, one of the smaller tables with only eight place settings. Charlie, Annie's other "victim" was also assigned to a family table and Piper was in charge of keeping the turkeys hot until serving time without burning them up. I was puzzled when I saw Martin leave in Annie's car about 11:15, but I was too busy with food preparation to wonder about it.

Frank (Pastor Bernard) worked by checking details and greeting the families as they arrived one at a time, each with their sponsoring family from the church. No one appeared "dressed up" for the occasion, especially the sponsoring families. Hugs and warm greetings were the order of the day as I watched through the kitchen door. As the numbers grew, the sounds of the room graduated from individual voices to the warm bustling timbre of an assembled fellowship.

Martin came in just before noon with three people I didn't recognize; he must be their sponsor. He brought them in my direction, so I wiped my hands on a towel and met them just outside the kitchen door.

"Sally Bristol, this is Andy King, your table host for today. Just tell him if you need anything and he'll take care of you."

"Hello, Andy, it's nice to meet you. This is Mark, my second oldest, he's fourteen, and Alicia, my daughter, she's eleven. Say hello to Andy, you two!"

Sally looked to be a very tired 40-to-45-years old and a little uncomfortable. Both kids were shy and seemed overwhelmed by the size of the room and all the activity, but Mark soon recognized a friend across the room and ran over to say hello. Alicia just stayed with her mother, clinging to her hand as the Pastor called the group to prayer before the meal and asked everyone to find their tables. We already had most of the side dishes on the tables and brought out the turkeys for each table after everyone was seated. Martin carved the turkey for our table and Annie, as usual, kept the discussion going at a lively pace. The sounds of a meal merged with across-the-table conversation as the focus changed from greetings to earnest fellowship around Christmas Dinner.

No mention was made of the difficult family circumstances which brought this congregation together with these particular families. All the children, guests and sponsors alike, speculated with a common anticipation about the gifts under the tree. There were no grand gestures of the rich giving to the poor, or the fortunate caring for the unfortunate, only people sharing a Christmas Day, together in a single room, the circumstances of their differences set aside as they walk on the common ground of faith, each person calling the other by name.

The cleanup later was another time for fellowship as we stacked the dirty dishes in the church's commercial dishwasher and took the tables down. We all sat on the couches for a while, listening to the sounds of the dishwasher running and talked about the day's experience. Later we ate leftover turkey and dressing, cranberry sauce and pumpkin pie while we good-naturedly argued about who would take out the rest of the trash. Charlie and I lost the argument.

Two months later
4:15 a.m. February 22, 1982, Rocker 7 ranch

The hypnotic motion of the wiper blades makes fighting sleep a chore, so I reach over for the thermos in the seat as I raise the snow blade and pull to the side of the road. I've been working since nine o'clock last night clearing the roads to all seven primary winter stockyards on the ranch so the cattle trucks will have reliable access later this morning. From the top of this ridge I can see the bunkhouse lights in the distance. Before long Hank will be serving breakfast to the hands so they can follow the trucks to the yards before daybreak. If I hurry I can get a bite to eat before I hit the sack.

"Rocker 7 base to Blade 1. Over." The call crackled over the two-way radio.

"This is Blade 1, go ahead." I answered.

"How are you coming on those stockyard roads? Over."

"All clear. I'll be home in about twenty. What's for breakfast? Over."

"Hank couldn't make it in from town, so Joe's on the grill. You might want to pass on that breakfast. Over."

"Ten-four on that. I'll do a grilled cheese myself, I guess. Over."

"Cook one for me while you're at it Andy. Over."

"I don't want to hurt Joe's feelings. Order some biscuits for me, will you. I'll bring my chisel. Over."

"You're braver than I am. See you in twenty. Out"

The light conversation served to wake me up enough to drive again. The snow had stopped and I was looking forward to sleep after breakfast.

The bunkhouse dining room was full of cowboys and the smell of coffee and pancakes. The breakfast line was set up to handle a full crew this morning and I went through the line, avoiding Joe's coffee and opting for juice instead. Stony told me the juice was a good move as I sat down at his table.

"You look like hell Andy. If I didn't know better, I'd say you'd been out all night."

"Thanks Stony, I love you too!"

"Clearing those roads was a big deal for us today Andy. It means we can stay on schedule with the stock delivery. I want you to know we appreciate you staying with it until you finished it all. You put in an eighteen hour day. Get some sleep. We'll take it from here for a while."

There was an envelope taped to my locker door in the bunkhouse. Inside I found a $100 bill and a hand written note.

Consider this an unofficial bonus. Take that girl of yours out on the town the next chance you get.

Thanks again, Stony

I woke up about two-thirty in the afternoon, showered, dressed and went down to the dining room. Nobody was there except Joe. He made up a plate for me with the leftovers from lunch and went outside. I was alone in the place. I could see my car from here. Somebody had cleared the snow off of it for me. The other cars still had about eight or ten inches on the roofs. I finished eating, and then drove into town.

It looked like Charlie had cleared the sidewalks and parking lot for Martin. There was a stack of mail on the table. I turned up the thermostat and reached for the phone to call Terri. She didn't answer, so I called her at the restaurant. She was just leaving, so they called her to the phone.

"Hi Andy. Are you in town?"

"Yeah. It looks like I'll be here for a couple of days or so."

We made plans for dinner and I picked her up around 7:30. We talked about my long day clearing the roads and the $100 bonus, then had lobster for dinner and topped it off with bananas foster for dessert just to see the flames from the brandy.

After dinner the look in Terri's eyes progressed from

sparkling laughter to a cold, accusing stare as she told me that Charlie had called her a couple of days ago and he was staying at the motel. She asked me when I knew that, and I told her I had seen Charlie there a day or so after he arrived. I told her that Charlie wanted to be the one to call and tell her himself after he got back on his feet a little. The look in Terri's eyes when she talked about Charlie was disturbing. She didn't say anything on the way back to her apartment. I'd never seen this side of her. I dropped her off at the door. On the way home the sign at the bank showed 10:37 p.m. and 24° Fahrenheit. It seemed colder than that.

A letter from Johnny was on the bottom of the stack of mail on the table.

Dear Andy,

I saw Gloria the other day at the Center and she asked about you. I'll never forget the day in Cheyenne. Gloria was so scared about leaving home for Denver she could hardly talk until she saw you tempting Bronson with that sandwich. She got caught up in what was going on and forgot about why she was with us. She still laughs about it and asks about you two every time we see her. It's funny how the Lord works sometimes. Four broken lives were jammed together in an old Chevy Blazer to find comfort in each other for a few hours and begin relationships we'd cherish for years.

Your Aunt Margaret is doing well these days. She saw some old friends over the Christmas holidays for the first time in

*almost thirty years and has been to visit
them in Denver a couple of times. We had
to take Bronson to the vet a couple of weeks
ago because he lost his appetite, if you can
believe that. The vet said he had a fever and
gave him some liquid medicine to squirt in
his mouth twice a day, antibiotics I think.
After he tasted it for the first time, he refused
to open his mouth for me and went the other
way every time he thought I was about to
medicate him again. It was funny to watch
your Aunt Margaret try to hold him between
her knees with one hand on his collar while
he backed himself into a corner of the
kitchen trying to avoid me. He finally gave
up and let me do it. After a couple of days
he began to eat again and he made up for
lost time. As you know, he's never been shy
about eating.*

    *We've been watching the weather
reports to keep up with the snowfall in your
area. It looks like you've had a busy winter.
How do you like it?*

    *I hope you've found some peace about
Charlie and Martin. They are in our prayers
here, along with you and Terri. We're
hoping that, over time, you will all find that
your relationships have been enriched by
encountering each other.*

Johnny

Terri and Charlie's relationship didn't seem
"enriched" to me, but then what chance had she given

him? She hadn't seen his good natured compliance with Annie's ambush over dinner, or his genuine efforts at the Christmas dinner to make it a memorable family experience for everyone. She was focused only on the past while Charlie appeared to be struggling with the present and trying to build a sober future.

It hadn't been a pleasant goodbye at her door. For the first time in a long while we hadn't talked about when we might see each other again. I tossed and turned until after 2 a.m. then turned on the TV and started watching an old black and white movie with John Wayne that was so old he wasn't even the star. He looked to be about twenty.

I must have dozed off in the chair because the next thing I heard was Martin's truck heading out of the driveway. The clock read 7:30 a.m. and the sun was already up.

After my shower I walked the four blocks to the main highway and ate breakfast alone at the coffee shop of the new hotel they'd opened last summer. I couldn't get last night out of my mind.

Martin was still gone when I got back to the motel, so I left him a note and drove south on highway 82 past Carbondale and Basalt toward Aspen. The peaks Johnny and I had seen on that Fourth of July holiday drive took on a new character with snow covering the entire landscape. Outside Snowmass there were cross country skiers on the far side of a meadow, their tracks in the snow betrayed by the shadows from the mid-morning winter sun.

I stopped to watch as they continued their smooth, rhythmic march across the white expanse. Six of them evenly spaced in single file moved slowly over the gentle hill, rimlighted by the same sun that betrayed their single track across the snow in the meadow. As they moved toward the crest of the hill I watched, knowing they would likely disappear for a time.

After they were gone I continued to watch, my thoughts colored by those last few minutes at Terri's door. It was as if our lives had moved in opposite directions after Charlie arrived. I wondered if Terri had disappeared to the other side of the hill.

I continued on toward Aspen. The river cut a wide path through the snow beside the road. The fast running clear water was broken only by a few patches of white snow still covering the largest rocks on the shaded parts of the river.

It was noon when I arrived at the sidewalk cafe in Aspen. The prices on the lunch menu rivaled the lobster dinner last night with Terri, so I chose to order one of the least expensive items, a "Prime Bleu" hamburger made of a half pound of prime ground beef topped with crumbled blue cheese and chopped pimientos. It was about twice the price of the burgers on the lunch menu where Terri worked. I didn't stay long in Aspen.

It was a half hour before sundown when I arrived back at the motel. I stopped by the office to tell Martin I'd be going back to the ranch tomorrow morning and asked if he needed me to do anything around the place before I left. He told me everything was okay around the place right now, but he'd like to have dinner with me at his place about seven. I told him okay.

We talked about my job on the ranch and how Charlie was doing on his job at the new hotel on the main road through town. It was close enough for him to walk to work and he was making enough as a night clerk to pay Martin his rent. The manager of the place was one of the elders at the church.

"How is Terri doing these days, Andy?"

"We went out last night and talked about Charlie for the first time since I started working at the ranch. She isn't happy about Charlie living here in town, especially since it's here at the motel, and she's upset with me because I didn't tell her when he got here. She was angry that I honored Charlie's request to let him be the one who told her he was out of rehab and living here."

"How did you handle that?"

"I just told her the truth about Charlie asking me not to tell her. Not much was said after that, but I could feel the anger in her voice and see it in her eyes. I don't think we'll see each other again for a while."

"I'm sorry to hear that Andy. You know, you weren't wrong when you didn't tell her. You were just honoring your word to Charlie. Charlie needs people to support him now and that was a good thing to do. She's just not letting go of the past and until she does that, she'll have a hard time dealing with anything having to do with Charlie. Give her some time. Give Charlie time to try to build a relationship with her again. You know that what happened between them is not up to you to fix."

"I guess not. How are things around here? Has Charlie been able to keep up with the things you need help on?"

"He's pretty handy to have around and so far, he's kept himself sober."

"Do you think he can stay that way?"

"Nobody really knows that Andy, not even Charlie."

"Stony offered me a permanent job. I don't want to take it unless you're sure Charlie can handle things for you around here."

"Do you want to take it?"

"Not if it leaves you in a lurch when things get busy around here."

"Look Andy, I've lived in this town for a long time and I have lots of friends I can call in a pinch. You and Stony are two of them, and Annie could hire an army to come in here and help me if I needed it, so don't let this place hold you down if that's what you want to do. You'll be twenty-one this year and you need to spread your wings a little. I just thank God for putting us together when he did. I needed that window to be painted that day, and you needed a job. Who do you think brought you around here anyway?"

I didn't respond to his comment about God bringing me here.

"Okay, I'll call Stony and move my stuff out to the ranch in the morning. They have some open rooms in the bunkhouse. If I don't see Charlie tell him hello for me. I'll be around once in a while to check up on you two."

"You know you'll be in our thoughts and prayers Andy, and so will Terri."

"I'll call you when I'm in town Martin, and you call me if you need anything."

I packed my clothes and cleaned out the little kitchenette refrigerator and cabinets before gong to bed. When I left the next morning I waved at Charlie as he was walking back from his job along the other side of the road. He looked like it had been a long night for him.

I brought all my clothes and other belongings into my room at the bunkhouse and began unpacking. I didn't have quite as much room as I had in town, but the window had a spectacular view of the mountains to the south and west. I decided to wait until after supper to unpack.

That evening when I was loading the dresser I found the Gideon bible I had thrown in the back of the drawer when I first arrived at the motel. It must have been in the drawer when I dumped it out into the bag. A lot had changed since then.

For some reason I thought about Bronson when I looked out the window with the bible in my hand. I opened it to Exodus and read. That night I dreamed of a burning bush on a brilliant white, snow covered mountain slope … but there was no voice from the bush, no revelation, no command … only silence and a long, slow trip back down the mountain to the cold, shadowed valley.

Midnight Roundup

Friday June 11, 1982

My eyes are stinging from sweat, my arms ache from pulling wire, and fatigue permeates my very soul. Benny and I had repaired fence across the washed out canyon crossings in rocks, mud, and glaring sun for five days in a row from daybreak 'til dark. Early summer thunderstorms had taken their toll on the ranch with flash floods and scattered herds. This was the last of the fences and dark was settling in as we pushed hard to finish. We knew the cattle guards were next on the agenda, but that was tomorrow and we were living in the moment and the job at hand. Life on the ranch could be hard, but it made me feel more alive.

The bunkhouse never looked better than it does tonight. Hank had fixed barbecued ribs, potato salad and coleslaw for us. We each grabbed a rib on the way to the shower before supper. Later we topped off the meal with blackberry cobbler and vanilla ice cream.

After supper we checked the "Work Board" in the hall for tomorrow's assignment and found out that we were both scheduled for the same small cattle guard repair. We should be through by noon on Saturday.

Benny said we were going to paint the town Saturday night.

"We? You want me to go along?"

"Sure! You're up for it, ain't you?"

"I guess so, you just never invited me before."

"We earned it, Andy! Let's have some fun!"

Saturday morning Benny decided that we'd have more fun if we headed over to Grand Junction where he grew up. I reluctantly agreed to go with him, so we skipped lunch at the ranch and left right after we cleaned up and threw a couple of small bags in the back of his pickup. Lunch in Glenwood Springs was a roast beef sandwich "to go" from Blimpies, chips and a coke. Benny stopped on the way out of town to get some beer and ice for the cooler. He cracked open a beer to go with his sandwich as he drove past the Glenwood Springs city limit sign. I got a little nervous.

We found an inexpensive motel and rented separate single rooms, "just in case we get lucky" as Benny put it. He knocked on my door about a half hour after we checked in and told me he'd made some calls and we were gong to meet his brother and some friends at a restaurant and club called the "Midnight Roundup." He also said we might want to "catch some zee's" before we left for the club, so he went back to his room.

There wasn't much on television, so I decided to take Benny's advice and sleep for a while. After all it had been a killer of a week at the ranch.

We got there about 8:30, just as the country and western band was beginning to set up on the small stage beyond the dance floor. Benny waved to his brother at a table near the bar. He introduced me to his two friends Laura and Trish, and his brother Jack and his wife Marissa.

There was already a pitcher of beer on the table beside the fried cheese sticks and potato skins. The waitress brought two more glasses and menus. It didn't take long to figure out that Benny and Trish had some history and she'd brought Laura along to keep me occupied. We all ordered steak of one kind or another, mostly with fries and a vegetable side … along with more beer, of course.

The music started about the time we finished eating and it wasn't long before everybody but Laura and I were on the dance floor. We talked over the music for a few minutes, then she grabbed my hands and asked me to dance.

Laura was a tall shapely brunette about my age with a free spirit and an infectious laugh. I told her I wasn't much of a dancer, but she said it didn't matter how good I was, we could have fun. She led me out on the dance floor during a slow song and wrapped her arms around my neck and put her head on my shoulder. We stayed on the floor through three songs before we joined Benny and Trish back at the table. Jack and Marissa were wrapped up in each other in another slow dance ignoring everything but each other.

By 10:30 or 11 o'clock Benny had switched from just beer to ordering a boilermaker — a beer with a shot glass full of bourbon dropped into it. I was slowly sipping just my second glass, trying to stay sober for the drive back to the motel. Trish was hanging all over Benny and there wasn't much doubt about where she intended to spend the night.

Laura and I danced a few more times … she seemed to get a little closer with every slow dance and made a point to tell me that she had driven her own car if we wanted to get out of here. I told her I'd better wait and drive Benny back to the room because he was too drunk to drive, and so was Trish.

About 12:30 Laura asked me if we could get some air away from the table and grabbed my hand again while she walked away.

"I've got an idea Andy, let me talk to Trish and see if she wants you to drive her and Benny back to his room. I don't think it will take much convincing. After we get them off the streets we could get some breakfast somewhere."

Her lips were warm and willing and her eyes sparkled in the dim light. That infectious giggle and soft embrace made it impossible to tell her no. Besides, I was ready to get out of this smoke-filled room and stop sipping warm, flat beer.

On the way out Benny stumbled into a guy sitting at one of the tables. He was drunk too, and he stood up, ready to fight. Benny pushed him backwards into his chair and the guy's buddy stood up and knocked Benny to the floor. The security guard stepped between them and asked if he needed to call the cops. I wrapped my arms around Benny from behind him as he stood up. I told the guard we were taking him home now. He motioned us toward the door and put his hand on the chest of the other guy to keep him from following.

Benny had sobered up a little from all the commotion and struggled to get free of me. His brother calmed him down, took his truck keys out of his pocket and gave them to me to make sure I was driving.

Trish was worried about Benny because his mouth was bleeding a little, so we all decided to go to someplace for a cup of coffee to let Benny cool off and clean up. We left the coffee shop a little after one o'clock and I drove Benny and Trish back to the room. As soon as they closed the door to Benny's room Laura drove up beside me and I got in her car and we drove away.

"Leave it to Benny! The last time he came home he wound up hitting a tree in his own yard. That's why his truck has that grey primer fender. He's just lucky the tree was on his dad's place instead of in town somewhere. Keep an eye on him when you two are out together Andy, sometimes things get a little wild with him."

"I've only known him for a couple of months since he started working on the ranch. This is the first time I've been anywhere with him."

"He's a good guy as long as he's sober, but you might want to stay away from the bars when you're with him and you should probably do most of the driving."

"I'll keep that in mind."

"Do you still want breakfast?"

"Not really. I just wanted to get Benny off the road."

Laura stopped the car on a side street and turned toward me.

"Well, Andy we're finally alone. Need a ride back to your room?"

I nodded "yes."

Laura smiled and turned the car around.

The next morning we left a note on Benny's door:

Benny,

*Laura and I will meet you at the
restaurant across the street around one or
one-thirty tomorrow for lunch if you want.
Hope your lip is up to Mexican food. I'm
buying.*

Andy

Sunday morning we took Laura's car, bought some coffee and rolls and drove toward Grand Mesa. She showed me one of her favorite places on a high bluff above Grand Junction where there was a grassy meadow next to a grove of trees and a running stream. We talked about her growing up around here and how she had known Benny from the time they were freshmen in high school. She asked me about how I got to the ranch and I just told her about living in Glenwood Springs and a little about Platteville and Bronson's antics with the chocolate cream pie and whipped cream mustache at Thanksgiving and such. We walked and talked until time to meet Benny and Trish. It was a grand morning.

After a pretty bad Mexican lunch I drove Laura's car and the four of us spent Sunday afternoon in Colorado National Monument just west of town.

Benny and I got back to the ranch around midnight.

6 a.m. came early on Monday. Benny and I were assigned to maintenance duty in different parts of the ranch. I was assigned to fix a gate in the high end of the ranch between ranch property and BLM (Bureau of Land Management) leased property.

The road was rough and steep to the high ridge where the aspen trees stood on the far side with their light green leaves dancing in the breeze against a background of darker fir and spruce. There were thick posts on either side to support the heavy weight of the iron gate but rain, time and what appeared to be the marks of more than one errant vehicle turning the sharp corner with a loaded trailer had combined to make the post on the hinge side lean enough to jam the gate open against the rocks.

I hooked the trailer hitch on the four wheel drive pickup I was driving to a nearby tree with a heavy chain to anchor the truck from behind, then hooked up the cable from the front mounted winch to the leaning post. The winch was controlled by a switch on a remote cable so you could stand well clear of the direction of pull in case the cable broke, so I worked several feet to the side and eased the post back to its upright position with the pull of the winch. I braced the post against the weight of the gate from two directions with cables and long metal stakes driven into the ground with a heavy sledge hammer. As I finished up by packing the rocks around the base of the post, I mixed up a small batch of quick-set concrete in a large bucket and poured it around the post and over the rocks.

By then it was lunch time and I stopped to let the concrete firm up around the post before I unhooked the winch. I grabbed the cooler from the seat of my truck and found an inviting rock by the trees for a place to sit while I ate lunch.

From here I could just see the snow-capped peaks above Aspen in the distance to the southeast. I figured it must have been about forty miles or so, but the air was so clear it seemed closer. I was in the most isolated part of the main ranch, only accessible by the dirt and rock road about seven months of the year. I'd heard Stony talk about bringing snowmobiles up here in the winter to hunt elk with hunters from other places willing to pay high prices for guided trips in years back, but they'd stopped that several years ago.

After lunch I walked across the ridge toward that stand of aspen trees. The only sounds were the call of ravens and the sound of a deer escaping from my approach toward his midday hiding place. From here the red truck looked small against the steep mountainside beyond.

It was time to finish up so I walked back to the truck. I unhooked the truck from the post and checked and adjusted the hinges on the gate. I also put on the new latch and padlock Kelly had given me this morning so the keys would match up with the main master keys.

By the time I finished, the shadows of the aspen had grown long and, at this altitude, it was chilly on the shadowed side of the mountain. It had been a good day to drink in the magnificence and solitude of this part of Colorado.

On the way back I stopped to watch as a twin engine plane landed on the ranch airstrip below. That probably meant that Stony would be taking the big corporate bosses for a look around the ranch over the next couple of days to survey the repairs after the flash floods. Stony referred to it as "baby sittin' the big boys."

Over the winter I had plowed the snow off the airstrip a few times, mostly so they could fly in to go skiing or hunting. There was a 5,000 square foot lodge for them adjacent to the two-plane hangar.

By the time I got back to the bunkhouse supper was mostly over and there was a poker game already underway in the far corner of the dining room. I saw Benny throw his cards down on the table and stalk away for a minute before the next hand was dealt. It appeared he wasn't having a good night. About eleven o'clock Benny stormed out of the bunkhouse and drove away.

Laura had talked about his gambling habits along with his drinking. I was glad that the ranch rules didn't allow liquor in the bunkhouse. If you wanted to drink, you had to go into town. The next morning I noticed Benny's truck was still gone as I left the bunkhouse for the equipment barn. I was scheduled to use a tractor with a power auger to help a fencing crew set a new fence a couple of miles away.

Benny's truck was still gone when we came back for supper. The word around the crew was that he had disappeared before and came back after a four day binge. Stony almost fired him then. Benny came back later that night and Stony had him in his office for a talk the next morning. Benny said he was "in the doghouse" with

Stony, and he'd be working a lot of strange hours for a while.

July 1, 1982 — Rocker 7 Ranch

"Hey you!" I heard as soon as I stepped into the dining hall.

I looked over to see Stony having breakfast with Martin. We continued to banter as I walked across the room toward their table.

"I thought I recognized that voice. How are you doin', Martin?"

"I was just checking to see if you were still alive out here. We haven't heard from you in a while."

"Stony's a slave driver … he probably got that from you. It's good to see you!"

I tried to shake his hand and he pulled me into a brotherly hug and we continued to talk while standing.

"I was going to call you to see if you wanted to come into town for the Fourth. We're having a little gathering, as usual, and I thought you might want to come in and have some watermelon with us. What do you say?"

"Well, it sounds good, but I've already made plans for the weekend."

"What's her name, Andy"

"What makes you think my plans are with a girl?"

"What's her name?"

"Okay, you got me. Her name is Laura, and she lives in Grand Junction."

Stony stood up from the table, told us he had to "work for a living" and left. Martin's mood changed as we sat down and continued to talk.

"Charlie is staying sober and doing pretty well now, for the most part, but he tried to call Terri the other day and she wouldn't talk to him. So I called her later and she said she didn't want anything to do with her dad, and that he's my problem now. He's broken up about it and I'm concerned it might drive him over the edge."

"Terri's always insisted that she doesn't want to see him. She's convinced he'll hurt her again. She's pretty bitter about him. It will take more than a few months of sobriety to make up for what she and her mother went through to turn things around."

"Have you seen Terri or talked to her lately?"

"No. I called her and left a message back in March, but she never called me back. She's convinced I'm conspiring with Charlie."

"I'm sorry to hear that. I was hoping you could act as a go-between to get them together and talk. Charlie needs a lift right now."

"I'll try to call her again, Martin, but she probably won't talk to me either."

"I'd appreciate it Andy. By the way Charlie told me to let you know he'd like to see you sometime, just to talk. He values you as a friend and wants to let you know how much it meant to him to get him located at the motel after the hospital. It connected him with people who care. It would give him a lift if you could stop by and see him sometime when you're in town. He's still working the night desk at the new place on the highway. You can catch him there or at my place usually. He's taken over the maintenance for me like you did while you were there, although he doesn't have much use for painting. Remember him, Andy. Right now he's a troubled soul. Anything that supports his spirits would be a godsend."

"Tell Charlie I'll stop by sometime soon, maybe Monday on my way back from Laura's. He'll probably be at work by then."

"Good! I'll tell him."

"I'm glad you came out this morning, Martin. It's been a while. And how are you feeling lately? Are you behaving on your diet and exercise?"

"Yea, mostly. Annie's taken to calling Charlie for reports on me, so I don't get any slack, but yes, Andy I'm feeling good and starting to do a little more all the time as I can. I try not to get in too much trouble with Charlie or Annie."

"It's been good to see you, Martin, but I've got to go. It looks like the crew is loading up and they'll razz me all day if I don't help load. I'll try again to contact Terri before I see Charlie Monday night, but I can't make any promises she'll answer the phone."

When I returned to the bunkhouse that night I tried calling Terri, but just got the answering machine again. I left the number and told her what would be the best time to reach me over the next couple of days at the bunkhouse.

Benny was barely holding on to his job, and Stony had changed his work schedule to nights, holidays and weekends, so he wouldn't have much time to hit the bars when he was off or play poker in the bunkhouse at night. Stony had assigned Benny to work on the ranch over the Fourth of July weekend tending the stock, so I didn't have to tell him I didn't want to drive to Grand Junction with him.

Terri never called back, so I stopped by the restaurant on my way through Glenwood Springs Friday night to see f I could catch her at work for a minute. They told me she had quit about a month ago. I drove on to Grand Junction to see Laura.

Over the long weekend Laura and I stayed pretty busy with a couple of parties at some friends' houses. She told me she wanted to take some courses this fall at

Mesa State College there in town. She didn't know what she was going to study, but she knew that she had spent enough time since high school "going nowhere," as she put it, at her department store job and wanted to get a degree. She said she liked living on her own and would keep working to pay the bills and go to school as much as she could, so that might cut into our time together over the weekends. Most of the time, she thought she would probably be either studying or working.

"Okay, Laura, I understand. And you know that this winter when the snow starts on the ranch I'll have to be available to keep the roads clear, just like I did last year, so my hours will be unpredictable. We'll just see each other when we can."

"I'm hoping for a dry winter this year, Andy."

We watched fireworks in the city park on Sunday evening, the Fourth of July. Afterwards I heard all about her plans and dreams as well as her decision to move out on her own just after high school because she was fighting with her parents too much. She said she loved them and wanted to stay close, but they didn't recognize her need for independence. She'd moved out last December, just before Christmas. Trish had helped her find this little house on the edge of town and loaned her some furniture and a few things to get started. Trish was 23 years old and already divorced. The subject turned to my life after a while and I talked about Texas for the first time since I had told Martin.

Laura was a good listener. As we sat on a bench in the city park she snuggled her head on my shoulder and I told her about Mama and Daddy and the bus trip to Denver. She giggled when I told her about my first encounter with Martin and taking almost an hour to paint the trim on that little window.

I told her that I was mad at God for not answering my prayers when I was younger, and that lately, I wasn't sure if there even was a God. She turned to face me with a questioning look.

"Do you really mean that Andy?"

"I mean it when I say I'm not sure."

She put her head back on my shoulder without saying anything. After a few minutes she moved away from me a little, so she could look me straight in the eye. I could see the frustration in her face.

"I still pray, Andy … I prayed for someone I could really talk to, besides Trish … and here you are."

I didn't know how to answer that. We walked back to the car in silence, hand in hand.

Late Monday afternoon I headed back toward Glenwood Springs and found Charlie at the motel a couple of hours or so before he had to go to work, so I offered to buy him dinner at a little café near his job.

"I called Terri last week and left a message for her to call me back at the ranch. Unless I missed it or she called over the weekend, I haven't heard back from her. I'm sorry."

"Martin told me you hadn't talked to her for quite a while. I know I'm the reason you two aren't seeing each other any more, and I hate that. I didn't see it coming."

"Look Charlie, if Terri wanted to continue to see me, she could have, she didn't have to shut me out too … that was her decision. I'm glad to see that you're making progress, I just wish Terri would allow herself to see it too."

"Some days are hard, especially when I think about Terri and her mother. A few times I've started for the liquor store or the bars … and then I remember you and Martin showing up just when I needed help. You, with that naïve bargain we made for me to stay sober for a week, and Martin, praying with me all night after I drank that beer which broke the bargain. Those prayers that night literally brought me to my knees. I could see it all so much more clearly. I saw myself hitting Terri's mother, then remembered the broken promises, the lost marriage, and I felt the venom of Terri's resentment. My entire shattered life lay clearly before me and I wept, right there in Martin's kitchen. I sat on the floor and wept beside the stove where I'd made omelets for breakfast that morning.

Martin's prayers continue, you know. His church has welcomed me without reservation, and I've even made friends outside the bars, outside the transient drunken world I had constructed over the years. I also thank God for connecting you and Terri and ask that he'll touch Terri's heart, not only to forgive me, but you, whether you get back together as a couple or not. I'm learning that peace can only come as we forgive others, as well as forgiving ourselves. And I want that for her ... true peace, even if we can't be father and daughter we once were when she was little. I also want that peace for her with you through that forgiveness. Thank you, Andy. You were there exactly when I needed that connection, and it gave me assurance that, even with my failings, Terri had someone in her life who cared enough to make a deal with me, whatever your motives about me at the time. You were an answer to my prayers ... even before I prayed them."

It hit me like a hammer. This man was sincere about turning his life around. I was glad time was short before he had to go to work. I made a lame attempt to accept his gratitude and told him goodbye.

I ordered more coffee and a piece of apple pie and

lingered for a while. From here I could see Charlie at the desk of the inn where he worked. My conversation with Charlie haunted me. How could I be an answer to something I didn't even believe in anymore?

A couple came in to register and I could see them talking to him. After a few minutes I could see them laughing with him about who knows what. This isn't the same hopeless man I had seen in the moonlight at 2 a.m. that first night at the motel, shuffling around, shoulders slumped, head down, smoking cigarette after cigarette, struggling to find himself again. Something had happened in these months ... something extraordinary.

The following Saturday, 7 p.m. — Rocker 7

Dear Walt,

You've been on my mind all week and I wanted to write you, but the work around here has been dawn to dark and beyond with cattle sales, stock delivery and such.

Terri's dad, Charlie, is making some real progress putting his life back together. I met with him for supper on Monday and we had quite a talk. Well, he talked mostly. He's staying sober and has a steady job now. He's connected with Martin for a permanent place to stay in exchange for doing the maintenance around the motel, like I used to do. While we were talking and later, after he left, I remembered your letter about how to deal with his alcoholism and Terri's complete rejection of him.

I'll admit that when I read your words about giving me a place in Charlie's life I had no intention of participating in his life. My only concern was for Terri. But it seems I was too late. I had already been there for him. In our conversation over dinner, he made just that point that, by finding him a place to stay and connecting him with Martin, I had helped him turn his life around.

Terri and I haven't seen each other for a while because she found out that I had not told her when he arrived back at the motel after rehab. She accused me of conspiring with her father against her and making it easy for him to stay in the same town where she lived, even after I knew she didn't want him there. I don't know how to fix that since she won't return my calls.

It is ironic that I am now writing you about how to deal with Terri. We are no longer dating, but I am concerned about her bitterness and I'm afraid that if I do see her again I won't know what to say or do. I haven't seen Martin since I talked to Charlie, but I plan to take your advice about observing the reactions of those you trust and talk with him about Terri soon.

Again, I know these are tough questions to ask from such a distance, but I've always known I could depend on you to be candid about things and speak from the heart.

Tell the guys at church that I think of them every time I write you and I'd like to hear from them.

It looks like I'll be staying here at the ranch at least through the winter. I have agreed to keep the roads clear of the snow again for my boss, Stony. You'd like him. He never wastes a minute, but he always takes time to help if you need him. He's been a friend of Martin's for decades and they seem close.

As Always
Andy

I went down to the dining room and played poker long enough to lose $20, then decided that was enough and turned in for the night.

Sunday morning I called Laura. She had gotten a registration catalog from the college and she told me about what courses she might take. I told her I'd try to make it over there next weekend.

I decided to take a drive up the road from Carbondale along the Crystal River. The longer I'm in these mountains, the more I feel at home among the rivers and the constant view of snow on the high peaks. As the road climbed toward the town of Crystal, the canyon became more beautiful and intimate as it narrowed toward the headwaters. A large aspen grove beckoned from the left side of the road with its stark white trunks supporting a canopy of lighter green. After a short walk among the aspen I continued on for another few minutes then stopped by the old mill near the marble quarries. The sound of the late summer river flowing across the rocks accompanied me as I ate my two ham sandwiches scrounged from the bunkhouse kitchen. It was comfortable by the river, not like the lower parts of the ranch where the temperature was predicted to top 90 degrees today. Up here it was a little too cool in the shade with the breeze across the river, so I stayed in the sun.

I watched trout in the cold, clear water below the rock, mesmerized by their rhythms. They hovered, circled, darted out chasing food, and then retreated into the deeper water under the rock again. A fisherman wearing chest high waders prepared his fly rod for action, then carefully entered the water about fifty yards downstream from me on the opposite side of the river.

He began a cadence bringing the rod forward and back, paying out line as he stroked, slowing the pace as the line lengthened until with the last stroke his rod stayed forward and the fly settled in the water about forty feet away, just upstream from a large boulder. He took in the slack line as the fly came back toward him downstream past the rock, his eyes intent on the water. When the fly approached him he gently raised the tip of the rod to bring the fly out of the water and started the process all over again. Four times he brought the bait past the rock with no results. On the fifth repetition he let the fly settle for a few seconds then suddenly jerked the rod upward and set the hook, the graceful fly rod arching and trembling against the fight. After a few tense moments the rod action began to calm as he reeled the fish in the last few feet. Holding the rod tip up to keep tension on the line, he reached down with a landing net and carefully scooped up the fish, then walked to a nearby rock to sit lightly while he gently separated the fish from the net. After admiring his catch for a few seconds he looked in my direction and held the fish up in triumph. I applauded from my ringside rock. He grinned then bent down to carefully release his trophy back into the cold running water. His rhythm continued … the cadence of his rod, his concentration as the fly drifted by his targeted spot in the river. He continued slowly up river past me, breaking his patterns only to change a fly, release a fish, or walk around a tricky spot in the river.

I leaned back against the rock behind me and dozed for a few minutes. When I woke up I was alone except for the fish hovering in the cold water below, circling, darting, and returning to position, as if the fisherman was only a delusion.

Raindrops on the rocks interrupted the moment and after a few minutes I headed for the car in a hurry to escape an afternoon shower common to the mountains. I watched through the windshield as the rain peppered down on the river surface where the fisherman had released his first catch an hour ago. I wondered if he had found shelter or stayed on the river, confident in the knowledge that both he and the rain were at peace with it.

I turned off the radio as I drove back toward Glenwood Springs. This time I wanted to hear nothing but the sounds of the tires on the pavement and the wind past my open window. Occasionally I could hear the sound of rushing water as I passed near a section of white water rapids along the river. I thought about Terri and what I would say if she finally called me back or I saw her by chance on the streets.

Instead of turning off to go to the ranch, I decided to go into town to see Martin. I should be able to catch him before he leaves for the Sunday night service if I hurry.

Martin was just about to get into his truck to drive to church when I caught him.

"Hello, Andy! Did you decide to go to church with me tonight?"

"You know better than that, Martin, but I was hoping I'd catch you for a minute before you left."

"Okay, you got me. What's up?"

"After Charlie and I talked, I began to think about what I would say to Terri if I did hear from her. Telling her I talked to Charlie would be like waving a red flag in front of a bull."

"I can't tell you what to say, Andy. But I do know that you and Terri have a very real connection, and in the long run, I believe a very real mutual trust. Just be honest with her. Tell her about talking with Charlie and how you see his progress. It's up to her to see through her anger and draw on that trusting relationship you've built together. If she ever gives it a chance, that could be the key to their reconciliation. But things like this are God's business and whether you realize it or not both you and Terri are in our prayers every day. Receive that support and remember it if that conversation with Terri ever comes, and be okay with it if it doesn't. It's not up to you to solve this. Leave it in God's hands."

I said goodbye to Martin as he pulled out of the driveway for church. I left the radio off as I drove back to the ranch.

Sunday, August 1, 1982 — Grand Junction

"Do you think twelve semester hours is too much for me to handle while I'm still working full time at the store, Andy."

"Why are you asking me. I've never taken a college course either. If you think it's too much, you can drop one can't you."

"Yeah, I guess. I just don't want to start something I

can't finish and I probably won't know how much work it is for a while."

My own words hit me, "I've never taken a college course." Was I planning to work on the ranch forever? I hadn't thought about it before.

From the time I left Texas until now I had always reacted to circumstance. Mama's death and Aunt Margaret's cancer had both precipitated my running from an unbearable circumstance and each time I had been provided for, through no real effort of my own. Even the job at the ranch had led to room and board along with the job. Where was I headed for the next forty years? I didn't know how to plan beyond the next month.

On the way back to the ranch I thought about the future. I liked working for Stony. I liked being outside in the fresh Colorado air. But could I see myself there in five years, or even next year? If I decided to go to school, what would I study?

I arrived at the bunkhouse just before nine and grabbed a late supper from the bunkhouse fridge. Cold fried chicken and a glass of milk hit the spot pretty well.

Meanwhile in Brownsville, 9:47 p.m. Texas time

"I'm going to call it an early night, Walt. I'm a little tired tonight."

"Okay, honey. I need to answer this letter from Andy. I'll be up in a little while … goodnight!"

Walt was concerned about Shirley lately. She seemed tired a lot. He was glad she had a doctor's appointment tomorrow. It was just a regular physical, but she'd promised to mention her fatigue to the doctor.

He knew Andy was almost twenty-one now, but he still remembered him as a devastated fourteen year old boy dealing with the loss of both parents. The last time he saw him was about two weeks before he heard Andy had gone missing from Corpus. Walt remembered the sigh of relief when he heard from Andy's Aunt Flora that he had just taken a bus to Maggie's house. It was a wonderful answered prayer report for the congregation which had covered Andy with prayer while he was missing.

The connection with Andy had been tenuous over the years, but was still very much alive, nourished only by an occasional letter and Walt's continued prayers. Walt's letters answering Andy were always carefully considered and written only after seeking guidance from the Word and earnest prayer. Andy was like family, a brother in Christ he'd walked with through very difficult times, and who was now seeking counsel from his elder. Walt felt the weight of giving a valid reply in that counsel.

For several days he had been in prayer about this latest reply, yet he still was at a loss to find the words to guide Andy in dealing with what could be a volatile personal situation. And then he finally began to write.

Dear Andy,

   It's always good to hear from you and know that you are well.

   I hope you've had that talk with Martin about Terri by now. The Lord has connected you with Martin there as he connected us in those difficult times here in Brownsville. The Lord has a way of leading us to where we need to be, even when we try to go kicking and screaming in the opposite direction. Do you remember our Sunday school lessons about Jonah? You might want to read that

*sometime and remember the discussions we
had in that little room among your friends.*

*When you wrote about Terri's reaction
to her father living in Glenwood Springs,
it put me in mind of Jonah's attitude about
Nineveh. The Lord's methods for Jonah
were a little extreme, but eventually Jonah
followed God's instruction. Keep that in
mind as you see their lives unfold, and keep
an ear on the Word of God for guidance.
You may have been Terri's "ship" from
which she has been hurled for a life
changing encounter. But it is all in God's
hands, just be there for her with your honest
concern. I think the words will come to you
then.*

*I'm pleased to hear that Charlie is doing
well, and that he recognizes your part in his
story. Attentiveness to those who play a part
in one's recovery is vital to recovery from
addiction. It helps them realize that their
choices affect the lives of those around them.*

*Your life has profoundly affected mine
by requiring much prayer and thought in
answering your concerns from across the
years and miles. Thank you for staying
connected.*

*The guys send you a rousing greeting.
By the way we finally heard from Monte and
I sent him your address. Don't be surprised
if he contacts you. He got a kick out of
hearing you were working on a ranch. He
still remembers your refusing to get on that
pony when you were eight and how you two*

played cowboys and Indians around my
house.

Your brother in Christ,
Walt

He sealed the envelope, checked to make sure the
address was correct and added the stamp. His mind was
clear now. He put the letter in the mailbox on the porch
and raised the flag.

A walk around the neighborhood was just the ticket
for him now that his mind was settled for now about
Andy. The Texas August air was much cooler at eleven
p.m. than it had been when he arrived home from work
at 6:30. He walked for about a half hour under the
street lights in his upper middle class neighborhood and
wondered what Andy's life was like now on a ranch in
Colorado. Monte was right, it didn't seem like a place
where Andy would be comfortable. A lot must have
happened for Andy in the last six or seven years.

The following Friday — Rocker 7 Ranch

When I came in from work there was a letter in my
box from Walt. I was in a hurry, but I sat down to read it
before I hit the shower.

I had forgotten about studying Jonah in Sunday
school. We all tried to figure out how big the fish would
have to be to hold him. When Mr. Johnson asked us why
Jonah was on the ship in the first place nobody knew.
I dug in my dresser for the Gideon bible to refresh my
memory.

After quickly reading the book of Jonah, it all came
back to me. Jonah resented that God had appointed him
to preach to the people of Nineveh, a city he hated, so he

booked passage on a ship going the opposite direction to keep it from happening. He couldn't stand the thought that Nineveh might be saved by his preaching, just as Terri couldn't stand the thought that her drunkard father might recover after all the damage he had caused to her life. Terri had run the other way by refusing to talk to him or anyone "consorting with him," including me.

I understand Terri's doubts about Charlie, but since my conversation with him I can see real hope.

It's almost six o'clock. Gotta get in the shower and hit the road for Grand Junction.

I talked Hank out of a couple of his famous pork chops and some other stuff I could eat on the road along with a thermos of hot coffee. I had most of it eaten by the time I passed the Glenwood Springs city limit sign.

Westbound on the open highway I watch scattered clouds accumulate to form a small thunderhead above the northwestern horizon. Occasional lightning strikes along the diminishing profile of a small mountain range catch my eye as the sun sets in front of me in an impressive display of orange and yellow lighting the edges of the clouds. After sunset the lightning grew stronger and more frequent in the increasing darkness as the thunderstorm grew. I was glad the storm was traveling away from the highway.

I saw Trish driving away from Laura's driveway just as I arrived. I was glad she was leaving. I knew she was Laura's friend but I didn't want to have to deal with her crazy ideas and loony conversation tonight. Laura walked out from the porch to my car door just as I stopped. The window was open and she leaned down to give me a kiss before I could even open the door.

"Hi good lookin! Got any plans for tonight?"

"I was planning to cruise the bars for chicks. How 'bout you?"

"Do I qualify as a chick?"

"Well, I don't know. If you'll let me get out of the car we can research this profound question, if you like."

She opened the door from the outside while she replied.

"I like."

When we walked inside I could see that Laura had everything planned, a candlelight dinner with Cornish game hens and asparagus, soft music, white wine, and French silk pie for dessert.

"We're celebrating, Andy."

"I would never have guessed. And what are we celebrating?"

"I'm officially a student at Mesa State College, as of yesterday. I passed the exam last week, paid my tuition, and registered early for classes yesterday. I even got the schedule I wanted for classes, so I can get enough hours at work to pay my bills. I'm so excited!"

"Wow! You thought you wouldn't be able to register for another couple of weeks. That's great."

"Yeah, my exam grades got back early, so I made it for early registration."

We sat on the couch after supper while she explained her schedule and how it might work out for us to have some time together if she could do most of her studying during the week. I let her talk on, but I was too absorbed in her sparkling eyes to retain much about the details of her class schedule. There was so much anticipation, so much perceived potential for the future.

We spent most of Saturday exploring the campus. I felt out of place, but Laura was so excited I went along with her, all the while wondering what the future held for me. I had no answers.

Monday, September 20, 1982 — Rocker 7 Ranch

Bare ledges just below the peaks show a dusting of snow above the golden aspen groves and the chill in the morning belies the changing season. Kelly and I are scheduled to rig the dump truck for plowing snow again just in case we have an early storm. The livestock crews have been busy bringing cattle down from the high meadows in preparation for winter.

"Are you really expecting snow down here in the valley this early, Kelly?"

"You never know around here, Andy. One time we had to go up on McClure pass to help clear it because the state boys didn't have their act together October first. They got a surprise blizzard and we were the only ones around here rigged for it. You never really know about things after the middle of September."

"I guess it all pays the same."

We serviced the snowmobiles and ranch vehicles for the winter over the next few days. It was a welcome change to the hot, dirty work of maintaining fences on a ranch this size.

Thursday morning I went into Glenwood Springs to pick up some parts and supplies to finish the vehicle maintenance so I called Martin and offered to buy his lunch at a restaurant in town.

"Have you heard anything from Terri lately, Andy?"

"No. I haven't talked to her since February. I guess she's through with me. I just wish she would give Charlie a chance since you said he's still sober and working."

"Annie talked to Piper a couple of weeks ago. Piper said Terri moved to Vail and has a job in one of the ski resorts. I guess she didn't want to take a chance on seeing Charlie around town."

"It doesn't surprise me that she'd want to leave a place where she couldn't face the past."

"Are you still seeing that girl over in Grand Junction?"

"Laura? We see each other when I can get away from the ranch, but she's started school this fall and she's still working so I don't know how often we'll be able to get together for a while with my winter job and all."

"Is she working full time?"

"Thirty five to forty hours a week, maybe more at the store during the Christmas rush. She's taking twelve semester hours to start to see if she can handle both."

"That's a pretty ambitious workload. Is she a good student?"

"She said she had good grades in high school. I think she can probably handle it. If enthusiasm counts she'll do well. She's really excited about it."

"It's that enthusiasm that can keep her on track if she's serious about school."

On the way back to the ranch I thought about Martin's words. I realized that I hadn't shown as much enthusiasm toward anything as Laura does since I left Texas. Maybe that's what drew me to her, her zest for life … and of course those dark, sparkling eyes that could look into my soul and know whether I need a laugh or a listening ear … a caress, or space to think.

I hadn't been enthusiastic about anything since Mama died, except of course when I let go of the world to play Frisbee-catch-and-slobber with Bronson for a few minutes, or let myself be absorbed by the essence of these mountains … or caught up in a moment of silliness and joy with Laura. I hoped for a dry winter this year.

I got back to the ranch about six-thirty, just in time for supper and sat down beside Benny in the dining room.

We made small talk about the work on the ranch while we ate. After we'd both finished eating he looked at me and said, "I've got a problem Andy."

"What's going on Benny?"

"Can we go outside to talk about this? I'd rather not talk here."

"I lost my truck the other night."

"What do you mean 'lost'?"

"I got picked up for DUI the other night and they impounded my truck. I had to call Floyd for bail money and a ride back out here. Stony doesn't know about it, but I'll have to tell him when I get a court date. I know he's gonna fire me if he finds out about it."

"What are you asking me to do about it Benny?"

"You met my family in Grand Junction once. Just play along when I tell Stony I need to go back home because of a family emergency on the court date. He knows we're friends and he might ask you something about it."

"You want me to lie for you, is that it Benny?"

"Not lie exactly, just tell him you don't know what's going on with my family."

"It's a lie, Benny. He's going to find out sooner or later. You're better off just to tell him up front and get it over with. You've been working a lot of extra time the last couple of months, he can spare you a day or two for court."

"You don't understand. He'll probably fire me on the spot when I tell him about the DUI."

"Did you miss any work time yet?"

"No."

"I can see your truck in the parking lot. You must have gotten the money to get it out on your own."

"Floyd loaned me that too. It just about cleaned him out."

"Look, you've been working graveyard shifts, maybe you can get to court without taking off work at all. You might just lose a little sleep that day. Why don't you wait until the court date is set, and if you do need to talk to Stony about time off, I'll go in there with you ... but I'm not going to lie for you. Do you have a lawyer, or are you just going to pay the fine and get it over with?"

"There's no getting out of it. I tested almost twice the limit with the blood test. I'm just going to tell the judge I'm sorry and pay the fine. It's the first time I've been picked up."

"Okay Benny. I know you're in a tight spot, but you understand, don't you. If you lie to Stony, that would make it a cinch that he'd fire you, and maybe me too if I go along with it. Just take it one step at a time."

Later I sat down in my room and thought about the day. It was 9:13 p.m. I wondered what Laura was doing right now ... probably studying. I thought about her unbridled enthusiasm juxtaposed against the desperate tone of Benny's request.

I realized I had some choices to make.

Donald H. Borland

Thursday, January 20, 1983 — Rocker 7 Ranch

The snow is coming down sideways in the wind and it's almost impossible to see the road. Only the top half of the fence posts mark the way now and it's almost dark. I'm heading for the barn and a good meal. I'll need to wait until tomorrow to start the plowing again after the blizzard slacks off and I can see the road.

Benny's in the corner of the dining room playing poker again. He never misses a game, and the roads are too bad to get into town tonight. Supper smells good. Hank made up a batch of beef stew served with hot cornbread for tonight and it couldn't have been a more welcome meal in the middle of this blizzard. I went back twice for refills.

There's a letter from Laura in my box.

Dear Andy,

I couldn't stop thinking about our time together over semester break, so I thought I'd write before my classes get too busy this week. I was sorry you had to leave when you did. Mother and Daddy really liked you, but they weren't too happy when I told them after you left that you stayed at my house while you were here. We had another argument, but she asked me, and I couldn't lie to her. They'll get over it by the time you see them again. I went to church with them the next Sunday and it seemed to smooth things over, at least for now.

The extra three semester hours I signed up for this semester look pretty easy so far. The professor is a young guy and knows that we aren't majoring in art, we just need the elective so he's pretty cool about things. I think I can do most of the work in class.

I'm glad you said Benny is still around at the ranch. You seem to be a good friend for him. Yesterday Trish told me about how you helped him keep his job through that DUI thing last fall. He's a good guy when he can stay out of trouble.

I miss you tonight. I know you're busy with the weather now and I pray for your safety out there in the cold. Write when you can. I love getting your phone calls, but I can't read a phone call over and over again before I go to sleep, or keep it on the nightstand.

Love,
Laura

P.S. A picture would be nice too. Can somebody around there take a picture of you next to your snow plow?

I read her letter again before I put it in my locker and went to bed. At dawn the next morning the snow was still coming down, but the wind had slacked off and I figured I could get some work done. After a quick breakfast I fueled the truck and started out on the road toward town so we could get supplies in if we needed them.

When I got to the highway intersection I saw something that didn't look right on the side of the road toward Carbondale. There was a snow drift that seemed out of place about twenty yards off the pavement where the fence line should be and there was a dark spot on one side. I drove up next to it, careful to stay out of the ditch. I reached for the radio microphone.

"Blade 1 to Rocker 7 base. Over"

"Go ahead Blade 1."

"I'm stepping out of the truck for a minute to check out something. Over."

"Okay Andy. What's up?"

"I'm at the main highway turnaround and there's a snowdrift out of place over the ditch by our fence line. I want to see what's under it and get back to you. Over."

"Ten-four Andy. Watch your step out there. Get back to me in a minute so I'll know you're okay. Over."

"Ten-four base. Blade 1 out."

They must have started the county snow plows by dawn because the road had been cleared along here.

I left the truck window open so I could hear the radio if they called and stepped out of the truck across the deserted highway toward that drift. All I was carrying was a snow shovel. The snow in the ditch was over two feet deep and difficult to walk through. As I approached the dark spot on the drift I began to make out more detail. It looked like a car window.

I brushed the snow back from around the little bit of window I could see and confirmed that it was a vehicle. From its direction it appeared that they had veered off the highway for some reason, gone across the ditch and landed here. There still wasn't much light through the clouds and with the snow covering the rest of the vehicle glass I couldn't see inside. I made a guess about where the door should be and began to clear it with the shovel. The door was either locked or jammed too much for me to open it, but by now I could see that there appeared to be someone in the driver's seat.

I heard a radio call from the truck.

"Rocker 7 base to Blade 1. Over." … "Rocker 7 base to Blade 1. Over."

It took me a couple of minutes to get back to the truck to answer.

"This is Blade 1. I've got a vehicle buried in the snow here. It looks like there's someone inside. Send out a call for help. They aren't responding to calls through the glass. I'm going to break the glass and try to see what's going on. Over"

"Ten-four Blade 1. We'll call it in. Break in and call back when you can. Over."

"Okay. It takes me a couple of minutes to get to them from the truck, so I'll just monitor you unless I need something else. Right now send an ambulance and rescue. I'll try to get them free and keep them warm. I'm heading back to the vehicle with blankets and a kit. Over."

"Ten-four. Take care Andy. Out"

I had left the shovel at the scene and picked up a small sledge hammer, two emergency blankets and a first aid kit to take back with me. I broke out the passenger side window with the hammer, unlocked the door and struggled to open the door against the weight of the remaining snow. I tossed the hammer inside, just in case I needed to break back out of here again, then tossed in the blankets followed by the kit. There was no visible blood in the car, and only one person. The ignition was still on, shifter was still in park and the heater controls were turned on, but it was obvious that the engine hadn't been running for hours.

I tried wrapping him in one of the blankets, but his body didn't feel right. I tried to check his pulse, but couldn't find one either on his neck or wrist. He was cold to the touch and the color of his skin didn't look good. When I pulled his head back from the steering wheel I could see his open eyes. There was no life in them, only a blank, dead stare. I knew I was too late. I could hear the sirens in the distance.

The highway had been recently cleared but it was probably before there was enough light to see where the vehicle had landed and it was too far away from the pavement for the headlights to pick it up in the dark. The county snow plows had no doubt passed him early this morning and had no way to know where he was in the dark.

The paramedics said he appeared to have died from carbon monoxide poisoning as he ran the heater to stay warm and the snow trapped the exhaust inside the car. The engine had more than likely died because the snow choked the exhaust and the air intake for the carburetor was blocked. They'd seen it before. They said he would have frozen to death in those temperatures anyway without the heater. That was no comfort. I walked back across the road to the truck with the blankets, hammer, useless first aid kit and the shovel all gathered up in my arms. As I was loading it back in the truck a highway patrolman came over, clip board in hand to get a brief statement from me.

I told him about how I found him and he wrote it down on his clip board. He spoke in a low, emotionless voice.

"Thank you for your cooperation. We'll take it from here. You can go back to work now.

I thought to myself: 'What a useless gesture this is after he's already dead. It was just like the prayers for Mama after she was already sick. What's the point?'

When he left I sat on the running board of the truck with my head between my hands, staring at the pavement, the flashing red lights still reflecting off the ice along the edge of the pavement under the dark snow clouds. My feet felt numb inside my snow boots so I got back in the cab of the truck, then turned it around to head back toward ranch headquarters plowing the other side of the road as I went. It took a few minutes for the heater to warm back up and then I noticed that the snow had stopped and it was getting brighter under the clouds. I called in on the radio and told them I was back on the job. They told me that they'd gotten the word on the driver from the ambulance crew and wanted me to head back in to the barn.

I couldn't forget those eyes. They looked like the ones I imagined on that dead Viet Cong soldier Johnny told me about. I remembered the sorrow in Johnny's voice when he told me about it. I drove without really seeing the road anymore, lost in cold gray memories, wondering who the first person was who saw Daddy when he died. I wondered if Daddy's eyes were open. I couldn't remember what he looked like any more.

I turned off the road into the main ranch compound and Stony flagged me down from the parking lot in front of his office. Kelly was with him. I rolled down the window to talk.

"Kill it and come on in my office for a minute Andy."

We walked up the stairs to Stony's office.

"Kelly's going to finish your shift for you Andy. Sit down for a minute, while I free up some time and we'll go over to the bunkhouse for a bite to eat."

"It's okay, Stony. I can finish the shift."

" I know you can, but sometimes it pays to talk things out a little after something like that. Besides, Kelly needs a refresher on how to run that thing. You've let him get too soft."

Just like the day he hired me, Stony got on the phone and initiated some things so the crews could get started while he took a break from the office. He never seemed to lose control over what was happening anywhere on the ranch, but he let his men do the jobs they were hired to do without interference. He only stepped in to direct their work when he needed to and he had a reputation for keeping loyal employees for years longer than most ranch foremen.

"Okay Andy, let's go see if Hank has anything interesting over there in the kitchen."

He put his hand on my shoulder as he opened the door and we walked outside in the cold air and he began to talk, "It's a tough thing to find somebody like that. It grabs your soul and won't let go for a while. But life goes on, you know. Even for his family, life will go on and they'll come to remember him as they knew him. You never knew him when he was alive, so all you can see is his death. But you need to remember that for every death there was a life before it. And that life is what the person is all about, not what you saw in that car. His life, good or bad, is what folks who knew him will remember. And you know Martin will tell you that if he had faith, he's in a better place now."

I heard the words and knew what he was saying to me was true, but they also rang a little hollow because

I also knew that the death of a loved one can destroy everything familiar and reassuring in life.

We went in the back door to the kitchen and Stony went straight to the refrigerator to see what kind of pie was left over from last night. He picked out two pieces of pecan pie and asked me to get us a couple of cups of coffee. He told me a little about the days when he worked for Martin. He told me to knock off for the rest of the day, take the weekend off and go into town or something. Kelly could finish up, or tell Floyd to do it. They needed to get out on the road again anyway and the weather looked like it was clearing up for a while.

I took a shower and drove toward town. As I turned at the highway I could see the tracks in the snow where they had dragged the car out of the ditch. I pulled off the road to look at the tracks. It looked like such a simple thing. He'd probably just misjudged the edge of the road in the blizzard and missed the slight curve to the right. Once he was across the ditch and hung up on the fence he had no way out. The snow was coming down so fast he couldn't try walking and his only protection was the car itself. Life is so tenuous. A matter of a few feet one way or the other can be the difference between life and death.

I wanted to escape from things for a couple of hours so I drove on into town and took in an afternoon matinee. The sun was getting low on the horizon when I came out of the theater. I drove to Martin's place and knocked on the door.

"Hey Andy. Stony called and told me what happened out there. I was hoping you'd come by for a while."

"Do you have a room for a wayward soul tonight?"

"Sure! Take the key to number fourteen. Are you not working tomorrow?"

"No. I'm not due back 'til Monday."

It was good to make small talk with a friend. He didn't ask me about this morning, we just talked about nothing in particular over a home cooked dinner. He told me some funny stories about Stony when he first worked for him over thirty years ago. He said Stony was pretty naïve when he first started and the guys in the crew played a lot of jokes on him at first. But he said it wasn't long until Stony caught on to them.

"They sent him out to 'outflank' a rogue bear and drive him into the net they'd be holding to herd him into a trailer. After he got out of sight they sat down and had a good laugh and a cup of coffee.

What they didn't know is that Stony was watching them from behind a tree while they were having their laugh. He quietly got in the crew truck and let it coast downhill until he was out of earshot, then he drove it back to the office and he and I had our own laughs.

They weren't laughing by the time they came into the office about three hours later after they walked the four and a half miles over rough mountain roads back to the office. When they got there Stony and I told them he had caught the bear by himself, chained him in the back of the truck and drove him up to the ridge and let him go. We told them he was so tired from wrestling that bear that he forgot all about them and just drove back to the office. They didn't give him any more trouble after that. Once in a while we still laugh about that phantom bear."

"It sounds like you two have some history."

"Over thirty years of it. But I'm getting tired, and you ought to get some sleep too. Breakfast here around eight thirty?"

"Sure."

I brought my clothes in from the car and turned on the T.V. After a few minutes I turned off the television and took out Laura's letter again. Sleep came hard. I woke up again and again from dreams of him slumped over the steering wheel with the engine running.

Charlie called Martin to tell him he wouldn't be there for breakfast because his replacement was running late at the inn. I was a little relieved that he wouldn't be having breakfast with us, it was just simpler this way.

After breakfast I picked up the morning paper from the kitchen table and saw the headline on page two: "Local Man Dies in Blizzard."

The story gave his name as Donald H. Borland, age thirty seven, a local restaurant manager survived by his wife and two sons ages twelve and fourteen. Funeral services were still pending. He'd left work around seven p.m. from Glenwood Springs driving toward his home in Carbondale. The estimated time of death was around two thirty a.m. Friday.

Now that I knew he had a family and a little bit about who he might have been the images changed ... Stony's words about how he might be remembered by those he left behind came rushing in. I wondered what his sons called him. I knew I had to be at the funeral to find out about Donald H. Borland, the man, not the dead man in the car behind those cold, dead eyes.

I stayed in town Saturday, mostly just walking the streets downtown. I walked by the old hotels in the downtown area, past restaurants and shops, and watched while the train unloaded passengers coming in from Denver. I waited until I knew Laura would be home from work and called her ... I needed to hear her voice.

I could hear the sparkle in her eyes in that infectious laugh, so full of life and energy. For a few minutes she erased the pictures in my thoughts while we talked about her classes and her job. She told me things were a lot easier at work since the Christmas rush was over. The conversation eventually turned to my work and the blizzard that had come through Thursday night.

"I had to shut down the plowing Thursday night at about seven. It was blowing hard and the driving snow made it almost impossible to see the road. I couldn't get out again until dawn. They closed the main highway south out of Glenwood Springs around eight o'clock that night and didn't reopen it until almost dawn."

"We heard about the road closures. Yesterday the news said a man was killed in the blizzard. I'm glad you were able to stop working until it was over. I worry about you sometimes out in the bad weather."

"Laura ... I was the one who found him."

There was silence for a few seconds.

"You found the man I heard about on the radio?"

"Yes. His car was stuck in the ditch close to where the ranch road hits the highway. I was plowing the ranch road Friday morning when I saw a snowdrift by our fence that didn't look right and stopped to check it out. When I called it in on the radio I didn't know that he was already dead ... His name was Donald Borland and he had two sons. The highway patrolman on the scene wrote on a clipboard what I told him about discovering the car, had me sign the form, and told me that was all he needed ... I could go. It was as if he dismissed his whole life after he had his paperwork finished. I couldn't bring myself to leave until the ambulance left a few minutes later. I watched them drive slowly away with no siren, just flashing red lights on an icy highway. I didn't even find out his name until I read it in the paper this morning."

"You don't sound good. Are you okay?"

"… I'm going to the funeral service Laura. I need to know who he was. I need to get those gray pictures out of my mind."

"Do you know when the funeral is?"

"Not yet. I'll keep an eye on the newspaper for the obituary. It will probably be early next week."

"I'm going to the funeral with you."

"You don't need to do that. You'll lose a whole day of class or work. I'll be fine. I was going to ask Martin to go with me."

"Good! Then I'll get to meet Martin too."

"But …"

"… Don't try to talk me out of it. We can get the Glenwood Springs paper at the bookstore on campus too. I'll probably know about the funeral as soon as you do, and it's not even a two-hour drive."

"Are you sure? I don't want you to come if the roads are bad."

"I'll be there. They always clear the Interstate first. Just tell me where and when to meet you."

"Okay! I give up. It should be in the paper by tomorrow, I'll call you then. I'll let you get back to your books now. Good night Laura."

"Good night Andy."

I didn't know why I had told Laura about finding him. I just blurted it all out.

I wasn't sleepy, so I turned on the T.V. for a while. The weatherman said it was going to be clear and dry for the next four or five days, but the temperatures overnight would be down around zero. I thought about the funeral and how cold it would be for the family around the grave and then I realized I didn't have a suit or overcoat that would be right for the service.

Tuesday, January 25, 1983 — Glenwood Springs

Charlie loaned me a suit and an overcoat for the funeral and I'm meeting Laura here at my room at the motel around ten this morning … "How does this tie go anyway! I'll never get it right!"

A knock at the door interrupts my frustration. It's Laura.

"Good morning, Andy!"

She reaches up and gives me a light kiss before I can reply.

"Hi Laura. I'm glad you came. Come on in while I try to wrangle this tie into shape."

"I used to tie my little brother's tie before Sunday school when he was little, do you want me to help?" She said as she took off her coat and threw it on the bed. I had turned around facing the mirror again to re-tie it for the third time.

"I guess so. I'm not doing any good with it."

I turned back around just as she was coming toward me again and I was stunned. I had never seen her dressed up for anything like this before. We had always been casual together and mostly she wore jeans when we went out. She was stunning in her navy blue dress, pearl necklace and heels. She looked puzzled at my reaction to her.

"Are you okay Andy?"

"Now that you're here I am."

She came close enough to reach my tie and deftly tied a near perfect Windsor knot in about thirty seconds and stepped back to look at me.

I couldn't take my eyes off of her... and I guess it showed because I saw my normally take-charge Laura blush for the first time since I had met her. She quickly moved on, trying to dismiss her discomfort at my reaction.

"You told me you didn't have a suit. This one looks pretty good on you. Where'd you get it?"

"Charlie loaned it to me. He's about my size. I did buy a pair of shoes, though ... You're gorgeous today Laura!"

"Why thank you."

She blushed again as I reached out and took her in my arms. She put her head on my shoulder as if we were about to dance.

"Thanks for coming Laura. I guess I needed you today more than I thought I did. I've been thinking about my dad and wondering about the first person to see him after the accident, who he was and where he is now. I guess I'll never know about that. I just need to know more about Donald Borland before it's too late."

Laura looked up at me with the beginnings of tears in her eyes and said, "I'm here Andy. We'll find out together."

The funeral was in a small rock church building outside of Carbondale. There was a traditional steeple above the white double doors at the entrance and stained glass windows down each side with pointed arches at the top of each one. When we arrived there were about twenty five cars in the parking lot along with the hearse and two other funeral service cars. Laura and I signed the registry book near the entrance and we sat down near the back. Memories of Daddy's funeral and Mama's funeral came rushing forth with the flowers and casket on display at the front. There were more flowers along both sides and the first two pews were reserved for family. I tried, with no success, to push back memories of being ushered to the front pew at both their funerals and watched uncomfortably as the family was seated about ten minutes after we arrived. Laura squeezed my hand a little tighter as she sensed my growing discomfort.

The next half hour was filled with music, prayers, and short accounts about Don's life as related by his closest friends. From that we learned that he was a devoted family man with a dry sense of humor that could assault you when you least expected it. We heard from his closest college friend that he sometimes struggled in his studies, but persevered through it all with hard work and determination, earning his bachelor's degree in business administration.

During the pastor's message he spoke about how he had known Don all his life and recalled his free-spirited antics in Sunday school class, early signs of the dry sense of humor others had spoken about. He then turned to Don's profession of faith when he was fourteen, his marriage to Lillian when they were twenty-one and his willingness to stay involved with the church ever since, first volunteering to help maintain the church grounds, and later working with the children as their own children began to be involved in church activities. But most of all he spoke of him as a man of humility and faith, always ready to help someone in need. Always ready to go to the Lord with them in prayer.

He then spoke of the hope of eternal life all believers have, and that, even in the pain, Lillian knew that he was now with the Lord and that she'd see him in that glorious eternity. She had spoken of it only this morning … even through the tears of loss and heartache … even as she and the children were learning to live without his earthly presence … even as she prayed for strength to raise her children alone. All of this was a testimony to Don's life

... the pedestrian walk of his faith and the strength that faith had imparted to others by his living testimony.

The casket was then opened and the invitation given to pass by him for one final time. Laura and I stood quietly when the ushers directed our pew to move toward the casket if we wanted.

I let Laura go first and put my hand on her shoulder as we moved toward the front.

I wouldn't have recognized him from the cold blank stare I remembered on that awful morning. He looked warm and peaceful now, eyes closed in repose, dressed in his Sunday suit with those he had loved nearby, waiting to say goodbye. I paused for a few seconds, hoping to replace the nightmare images with new ones, coupled with new knowledge of who Don was.

Then I moved on, Laura at my side.

Laura and Me

A year and a half later
July 1985 - McClure Pass, Colorado

The backdrop is an incredible canopy of aspen leaves and white bark as we stand, newly married, before the small gathering of family and friends. Johnny and Martin share the duties of best man and Trish stands crying next to Laura as her maid of honor. There were about twenty people there for the simple ceremony.

"I now give you Mr. and Mrs. Andrew King."

Laura was even more gorgeous than ever as we walked back down the rock path toward the car. Annie grabbed us both at the same time with a big hug and kissed us each on the cheek as we neared the end of the path. Stony opened the door to the limousine parked at the bottom of the path where Benny was busily tying cans on the back bumper. Laura's little brother was taking the wedding pictures and stuck the camera through the door for one final picture before we left. Laura's dad passed me an envelope full of cash through the window, then stood arm in arm with her mother as we pulled away.

I really missed Aunt Margaret. She wasn't able to come because of her health, but we'd had a long phone conversation with her yesterday before the wedding. She and Laura had developed quite a close relationship in recent months, even though they had met only once. Laura had called her a few times after that and told me Aunt Margaret shared some very interesting things about my time in Platteville with her and Johnny. She never would tell me everything they talked about.

Annie insisted on paying for the honeymoon —

five days in a five-star hotel in San Francisco with a chauffeured limousine from the airport and on call the whole time. Charlie had lined all of it up for Annie, since the hotel was affiliated with the one where he worked.

It was a glorious five days, but we knew we had to get back home to Grand Junction so Laura could begin her summer classes and I could start my new job Stony lined up for me. I'd be making local deliveries for a ranch equipment company there. The work schedule would allow me to take part-time classes at the college starting in the fall.

The last night in the hotel after dinner I took out a piece of hotel stationery from the desk drawer.

> *Dear Walt,*
> *A lot has changed since I wrote you last. Are you sitting down?*
> *I've been married for almost a week now. Her name is Laura and she's the best thing that's ever happened to me. We're on our honeymoon in San Francisco and I'm writing to you while Laura is in the shower. No, we're not rich. Annie, a friend of ours is though, and she paid for the whole trip. Annie is a lifelong friend of Martin's who keeps an eye on him since his heart problems. You'd like Annie, she's full of life and has a great, giving spirit.*
> *I'm enclosing a Polaroid of the two of us with the Golden Gate Bridge in the background. I'll be moving to Grand Junction with Laura right after the honeymoon. My boss at the ranch, Stony,*

*lined up a job for me there that will allow
me to go to school at the state college.
Laura's going to school there too.*

*It's funny how things work out
sometimes. Mama and Daddy's deaths have
stayed with me for a long time and there
have been times when I couldn't get past it.
But Laura has helped me change all that.
For the first time I can let go of it and get on
with life.*

*I know newlyweds are always excited
about each other for a while, but I know this
is deeper than that first-blush enthusiasm.
Laura is special. She knows my soul already
and I'll move heaven and earth for her. It's
time for me to get on with life and I wanted
you to know that I think we have what I saw
in you and Shirley in the time I stayed with
you. You and Shirley shared your strength
together even when you lost that baby. I
could see it in you. That is what I already
feel with Laura.*

*Aunt Margaret isn't doing well right
now. The radiation they're giving her is
making her pretty weak. She wasn't able
to come to the wedding. Laura and I are
planning to go to Platteville when we can
manage the time. Aunt Margaret asks me if
I've heard from you every time we talk.*

*Tell the guys at church I got "hitched."
Use the return address on the envelope to
write when you can. And thanks for being
there when I've needed your advice over the*

years.
    Andy

When I looked up from the letter Laura was standing behind me waiting for me to finish. I handed the letter to her to read before I put it in the envelope. She sat down beside me at the desk and wrote on a new sheet of stationery:

> *Dear Walt,*
>   *I'm writing this after Andy let me read what he wrote to you. I know how important your letters have been to him over the years. Andy has a special place for you in his heart. Don't be surprised if you hear from me once in a while too, as a part of Andy's life.*
>   *He tells me you are a man of faith. Keep us in your prayers as you have kept Andy all these years.*
>
> *Your new partner in prayer,*
> *Laura*

The next morning we dropped the letter in the hotel mailbox as we headed for the airport.

The rest of the summer we were busy getting me settled into my new job and Laura was getting a jump on the next school year with two summer courses. Between the end of her summer courses and the beginning of the semester we took a long weekend to go to Platteville to see Aunt Margaret and Johnny.

It looks different now, somehow smaller. There's a new grocery store on the highway so you can't see the mountains anymore from the boulder Bronson and I used to call our own. Everything is green now, but I still remember the mud from that first spring thaw after the record winter snow. We passed the church on the way to the house.

Johnny met us at the door.

Bronson got up from in front of the couch to meet us. He was moving slower now. Arthritis had set in and he was gray around his mouth, but he still picked up his Frisbee and brought it to me. We went out in the back yard and I tossed him a couple of easy throws before he sat down for a break. He must be twelve or thirteen by now.

When Bronson and I came back in the house Johnny was in the kitchen putting lunch together for us and Laura was helping. I sat down in the living room and Bronson took up residence against my foot.

We waited for Aunt Margaret to come back from her bible study before we ate lunch.

She looked more tired than I'd ever seen her when she got there, but she made the effort to give me that big hug and even messed up my hair just to make me feel at home. I was almost expecting a grape soda next.

Laura stood in the kitchen door smiling at us and waited until the formalities were over before she said hello to Aunt Margaret.

"I know you sent me a picture from the wedding and the hotel in San Francisco, but I need you two to stand over there by the window and let me take one of you right now."

"Okay. Laura let's get this over with."

She took a couple of pictures of us then Johnny had Aunt Margaret stand with us for another one. Bronson sat on my foot for that one.

We ate lunch and talked around the kitchen table for an hour or so before Aunt Margaret decided to take a nap in her bedroom.

After she closed the door Johnny invited us to the front porch away from Aunt Margaret's bedroom.

"Mother's cancer didn't respond to the radiation this time. The doctors have only given her a few more months. She didn't want me to tell you, but I didn't want it to be a surprise for you if we need to call you soon. She didn't want it to spoil your time together as newlyweds."

I knew she looked tired, but I didn't realize that things had progressed that far. I gulped, looked down and then replied.

"Thank you for telling us, we needed to know. We won't let her know you told us."

When I looked at Laura she turned her eyes away from me, stood up and walked to the edge of the porch.

I asked Johnny if it was alright for Aunt Margaret to still go to her bible study right now. Before he could answer, Laura spoke up.

"It's the best thing she can do right now ... it keeps her focused on her faith instead of her cancer."

We were quiet for a while. Johnny went back inside.

On Saturday morning Laura was up early fixing breakfast for everyone. The smell of fresh coffee was enough to wake Johnny up first and he and Laura had been sitting at the table talking for a while before Aunt Margaret and I got there.

After breakfast Laura ran us all out of the kitchen and cleaned up. Johnny went to the post office to pick up a package and I sat down in the living room with Aunt Margaret.

"Johnny told me about his time in Viet Nam and his recovery afterwards. I had no idea what you were going through when you left Texas to come back here. I didn't know I was going to be such a burden coming into the middle of that."

"No, Andy! Don't think that! We were just glad you knew you could come here. It wasn't a burden to us. It was good for Johnny to be concerned about helping you through that time. He almost thinks of you as a brother now, and he really loves Laura."

"At first I just wanted to get away from Texas. I didn't know what I was asking of you, but the last few years it's become clearer to me what you both did in my years here."

We continued talking until Johnny came home about the same time Laura finished up in the kitchen. Over the rest of Saturday we drove around the area so Laura could see it and we bought dinner at a local restaurant. We thought about going into Denver, but decided Aunt Margaret wasn't up to the trip. Bronson got the rib bones left over from dinner when we got home. Johnny put most of them in the refrigerator for later because he said Bronson's teeth weren't up to devouring them like he could when he was younger.

Laura suggested that we could go to church with them the next morning before we left for Grand Junction. Aunt Margaret looked in my direction to see if that was okay with me. I grudgingly nodded yes and said, "We'll come later after Sunday school."

During the opening prayer they prayed for Aunt Margaret along with a few other people. The pastor shook hands and greeted me by name as we were leaving. I guess Aunt Margaret had told him we were coming. We offered to buy Sunday dinner and Johnny suggested a restaurant over near the Interstate. He asked the blessing before the meal and included Laura and me for continued blessing in our life together and Aunt Margaret for healing and peace.

Laura squeezed my hand as he prayed.

Martin's Request

Three months later
9:17 a.m. October 15, 1985

Laura answers the phone on her way out the door to class.

"Hello. Charlie?"

"Is Andy there?"

"No, he left for work a couple of hours ago. What's wrong, you don't sound good."

"It's Martin. He's in the hospital with another heart attack. He's asking for Andy."

"I'll get in touch with him at work as soon as I can, but it may be a while if he's out on the road."

"Yeah, tell him to come as soon as he can. I've already called Annie. She's flying in from Laramie in about an hour. He was asking for her too."

Laura called the office and caught me just before I got out on the road with a delivery. I picked her up and we were on the road within an hour. We arrived at the hospital before noon. Annie was in the waiting room outside the cardiac care unit along with Charlie and Pastor Bernard. Stony was in the room with Martin. They only allowed one or two visitors at a time for no more than five minutes. When Stony came out he motioned to me that it was our turn. Laura and I walked quietly into the room.

He had oxygen tubes, heart monitors and all kinds of wires hooked up to him along with an IV drip. It was a lot more than the last time when I saw him after a heart "episode." This looked more serious. He was pale and his eyes were closed at first, so I didn't say anything. Laura stood by the door. He opened his eyes after a few seconds and smiled. His voice came in a hoarse whisper.

"Hi Andy, is that Laura with you?"

"Yes. I guess you'll go to any lengths to get me to bring Laura to see you, huh."

"She does brighten up a room."

"Yes she does.

"Hello Laura, you two come on over here closer"

"The doctors won't say it, but I'm not sure I'm going to get out of here this time and I need to ask if you'll do something for me."

"Of course Martin. Just name it."

I was afraid he could see that I was holding back the tears when Laura took his hand in hers.

"Would you pray with me Andy? I've never heard you pray and I know it's in your heart. It would mean a lot to me if I could just hear you pray."

Laura looked up at me and took my hand as well. We knelt by his bed, Laura still holding his hand. I paused for a few seconds and the words came along with the tears.

"Father, it's been a long time since I talked to you. You know that Martin is very dear to me. He's been the father I needed and I thank you for that. I now come to you asking that you'd bring him through this. He needs you to heal his heart. You are the only one who can do that, and you know how faithful he has been to you. Do this for him. We ask it in Jesus' name."

Then Martin began to pray.

"Thank you Jesus. Thank you for being faithful to Andy all these years, even when he didn't know it. The prayers of many have been lifted for him over the years and I have been blessed to hear him acknowledge your presence here today. We ask that you continue to bless him and Laura as they live this glorious journey together … Thank you Jesus …"

His voice tapered off even as he said those last words, but we continued to hear the heart monitors with their rhythmic sounds. He must have just dozed off from fatigue.

I heard Laura whisper "Thank you, Jesus."

It was my first earnest prayer since Mama died.

He died that night in his sleep. He was eighty one.

The following Saturday …

Laura and I drove back to Grand Junction after the graveside service. We didn't talk for the first few miles.

"What good did it do, Laura?"

"What do you mean?"

"What good did it do to pray for Martin? He died anyway."

"You have no idea, do you?"

"I guess not. Why don't you clue me in about how God answers prayer. He didn't answer mine. Martin's dead."

"Were you listening to Martin in that room? He didn't ask you to pray for him to get better. He simply asked you to pray WITH him. His final wish was to just hear you acknowledge God through prayer. His own gain was not the issue. He was concerned about YOUR welfare. On his death bed he was concerned about YOU! His prayer was answered. Can't you see that! His was the same prayer I've had since that conversation we had in the park three years ago. I love you Andy, but does everything have to be about YOUR priorities?"

I was speechless. It was our first real argument, and I knew she was right. For the second time I could remember, I felt like a selfish ass.

For the first time since the wedding Laura didn't even ask me if I wanted to go to church with her the next morning, she just dressed and left the house without saying more than ten words to me. I showered, dressed, fixed a little breakfast and turned on the T.V.

She didn't get back to the house until after two that afternoon. I asked if she wanted to go out for Sunday dinner and she gave me a cold stare.

"I've already eaten, thank you. But you're welcome to go out if you like. Whatever's best for YOU!"

Her words bit to the bone. I grabbed my jacket and a couple of my class textbooks and left the house. I had intended to apologize for last night over Sunday dinner and tell her she was right. I guess she didn't want to hear it.

I had a burger for lunch and went to the campus library to get ahead on my studies for the week. After about half an hour I realized I didn't remember what I was reading. My mind was on Laura's words, "Whatever's best for YOU!"

I went for a long walk around the campus. Laura was gone to church for the Sunday evening prayer meeting when I got home. She came home a little after eight-thirty and walked straight across the room to me to kiss me hello.

"I'm sorry I blew up at you, Andy. I know it was hard on you to see Martin like that, I should have been more understanding."

"You were right Laura. I didn't hear what he wanted, I just said what I wanted to happen. I didn't want him to die. I didn't want to go back to the motel and not find him there. I didn't want to have no one there to listen to my problems. That prayer was about me. I didn't take into account the fact that he might be too tired to go on …

that he might want to go on to, as he put it one time, 'see Jesus face to face' and have all his physical problems behind him."

We sat and talked until almost midnight.

October 23, 1985 - Brownsville, Texas

The letter on his desk was from Laura King, Grand Junction, Colorado.

Dear Walt,

Andy is at work right now and I only have a few minutes to write you. His friend Martin passed away last week. Andy and I were able to be with him for a few minutes in the hospital at the last. Martin said that he had never heard Andy pray, and then asked Andy to pray with him, just so he could hear it. Andy prayed for Martin's recovery.

A few hours after that Martin died and Andy went back into his shell about unanswered prayer. I got mad and told him that he was selfish because he had expected God to do what Andy wanted, instead of just praying with Martin because he asked him to pray with him. I told him that the prayer should have been to comfort Martin instead of answering Andy's need for Martin to recover.

It was our first serious argument, and I'm afraid I hurt him deeply. I've known about Andy's doubts about prayer almost since we met, so I should have been more

understanding. I should have been there for
him instead of blowing up like that.

He's depended on you over the years
more than you know. He has kept all your
letters and has shared them with me. Since
the prayer meeting at my church last Sunday
you have been on my mind. I'm hoping you
can give me some direction, some insight
about where we should go from here.

Please send any reply to my parents'
house. The return address is theirs. I'll
share your responses with Andy if you think
I should, or when the time is right. And
keep Andy and me in your prayers as you
consider this.

You're partner in prayer,
Laura

Walt takes out the photo of Andy and Laura on their
honeymoon to see if he can get a better idea about who
Laura really is. He'd asked the Lord to work his will in
Andy's life for most of Andy's life. Maybe, in God's
timing Laura had been placed there to share in that work.
For a young lady in her twenties she seemed to have a
good understanding that prayers are our response to what
God is already doing in our lives, and that answers to
prayer are sometimes not what we expect.

Andy had been hurt by his unrealistic expectations
for miracle cures, and he wondered how he could have
counseled Andy differently when his mother died.

Walt took out his bible and began to read, hoping for
biblical guidance for Laura and Andy.

... two days later — Grand Junction Colorado

The trailer is loaded and I double check the tie-down chains to make sure my load will stay put. It wouldn't be good for a 12,000 pound tractor to come loose on the highway to Montrose.

It's a typical clear day on the road. I should be back by mid afternoon if things go right. The drive to Montrose was uneventful.

"Sorry Andy, Fred is the only one who is authorized to sign the transfer papers and he left the office a few minutes ago with a customer. He said he'd be back in about an hour."

"Okay Jack. I think I'll take a walk down to the coffee shop back toward town."

I can't get the argument with Laura out of my mind. I know I should probably forget about it, but I can't. Laura and I are okay with each other now, but her words still echo in my head, "Does everything have to be about YOU?"

About a block toward town I notice a small Catholic church with the door open. I can see someone through the door kneeling in prayer and stop to observe. The young woman kneeling reminds me of Laura. I can't ignore her humble pose, the same pose Laura had struck at Martin's bedside. I watch unobtrusively for a few moments until she rises and walks quickly out the door. I turn around so she won't realize I've been watching.

She's gone now, but I continue to watch the candles burning. I step slowly toward the door and finally go inside. The sanctuary is empty.

Stained glass windows take me back to my church in Brownsville. The Sunday after I was baptized I prayed for Mama there ... I had knelt at the bottom of the steps to the pulpit in the same way.

"Are you here for confession?" a gentle male voice asks from behind me. I turn to see the voice … he's a priest.

"I'm not Catholic."

"That's okay, but that wasn't what I asked, was it?"

I pause, not quite sure what to say.

"Can we talk for a minute, Father."

"Of course. What's on your mind?"

We sat on the front pew and I told him about Martin, the bedside prayer, and Laura's reaction to my comment about unanswered prayer on the way home.

"Was your prayer earnest?"

"Of course … I desperately wanted Martin to recover."

"I understand that, but what I am asking is whether you, in your own heart, truly believe that God has the power to have healed Martin; or is your attitude one of demanding that God do your bidding, no matter what God's plan in Martin's life?"

"I truly don't know Father."

"Perhaps we should pray about that."

I sit quietly for a moment, unsure how to answer.

"Thank you Father, but I have to go now. I'm expected back."

"Are you sure."

"I have to go now. Thank you Father."

I turn and walk quickly back to see if Frank is back yet. He comes in a couple of minutes later, signs the equipment transfer and we unload the tractor … I'm on the road back to Grand Junction surrounded by silence and self doubt. Echoes of his words ring in my head about demanding that God do my bidding. Annoyed and alarmed by his stinging perception, I force my thoughts to other, more pressing matters to block out the words.

Thankfully the traffic in Grand Junction is distracting enough to occupy consciousness as I arrive back in town.

Saturday is a busy day at work with several local deliveries and there's no room for self reflection. That evening Laura and I had a quiet meal and each of us worked on our studies until almost midnight. Sunday morning we had breakfast together before she left for Sunday school.

I hadn't spoken of my encounter with the priest to Laura, but his words weighed heavily on my mind again in the quiet morning. I walked back to our bedroom and found the Gideon bible hidden in the back of a dresser drawer.

But where would I start?

I closed my eyes and opened it to a page somewhere near the middle and blindly pointed my finger, Proverbs 19:20-21:

> *"Hear counsel, and receive instruction,*
> *that thou mayest be wise in thy latter end.*
> *There are many devices in a man's*
> *heart; nevertheless the counsel of the LORD,*
> *that shall stand."*

I read the passage several times, astounded at the wisdom it brought to bear on my lingering questions. Had both Laura and the priest served as counsel? Was the 'device' in my heart a selfish petition for my own desires?

I shoved the bible back in the drawer and opened my business class textbook where there would be no dilemmas, no judgment of my motives, only facts, figures and business principles to memorize.

November 1, Grand Junction, Colorado

Laura picked up the letter delivered to her parents' house on her way home from work and stopped at a fast-food place for a cup of coffee while she read the letter from Walt.

Dear Laura,

I'm heartened that Andy has you in his life. As you know, Andy has been forced to deal with more than his share of the death of loved ones in his young life. Death is hard for any of us to face, even when we are strong in our faith. Martin was a wonderful sounding board for Andy and he will miss him almost like he would a parent. The Lord placed Martin in his life the same way he did his Aunt Margaret, Maggie as I knew her in high school.

I was closely involved in Andy's life both after his father died, and when his mother was in the hospital during her final months. It was a difficult time for Andy, but his decision to run away to Maggie turned out well. She has a wonderful heart for those who are hurting and she took him in as her own. Get to know her if you have the chance, she is a genuine blessing to anyone who connects with her.

Maggie told me a few years ago that Andy had withdrawn from earnest prayer, so it's no surprise that Martin's death brought about this reaction, after all, as far as I know, the last time he prayed for anyone's healing, his mother died that very night.

*As for you Laura, I can only remind you
that the Lord is in charge of Andy's life,
and the Lord's time does not necessarily
correspond to our perception of WHEN
things should happen. Who but the Lord
knows when Andy will be ready to come
home to the faith he knew and professed
at a very young age? My observation over
the years and miles has been that the Lord
has had his hand on Andy and we are best
served by trusting Him for Andy's well
being. After all, Andy married you with the
Lord's blessing didn't he? Stay close and be
ready to respond when Andy is ready to deal
with God. And keep praying along with me
and more people than you or Andy know.*

*Your partner in prayer,
Walt*

Laura sat for a few minutes sipping her coffee and silently praying for Andy. She carefully folded the letter and put it away before she drove home. She got home about seven.

We were looking forward to the Thanksgiving break so we could go to Platteville again and visit with Aunt Margaret and Johnny.

Bronson was not there over Thanksgiving. They put him to rest a couple of days before in the field near the boulder where he and I used to look toward the mountains. Our Platteville Thanksgiving just wasn't the same that year.

I spent some time alone sitting on that boulder while

we were there, then walked down to the intersection so I could see the mountains. They looked somber under the heavy clouds until the sun broke through just before sunset and rim-lighted the early season snow along the high peaks. Bronson would have liked that.

December 23, 1985, 6 p.m. — Glenwood Springs

Annie's holding her annual pre-Christmas dinner for volunteers at the church for the Christmas Day bash. The crowd has grown to twelve people, but there's no mystery anymore about why they're here. Annie affectionately calls the group of volunteers "Martin's Mob." Charlie, Piper and Stony are sitting at Annie's table with two more chairs reserved for Laura and me.

We were late coming in from Grand Junction, but Annie was keeping the party alive with stories about when she and Martin were growing up on the ranch. In typical Annie style, she had everyone's meal put on her check, as long as they agreed to have one scoop of sherbet for dessert in honor of Martin. Laura was a little overwhelmed by Annie sometimes, and this was no exception.

Laura and I went to our room at the motel after dinner.

Christmas Eve morning Annie grabbed Laura after breakfast and took her shopping. I stayed at the motel with Charlie. Martin had asked Annie to let Charlie stay on as manager there. Annie actually owns it.

Charlie and I automatically sat down at the kitchen table to talk, as if Martin were still in the room, only this time Charlie made the "real" coffee.

"Piper told me something last night Andy. She said she heard from Terri a few days ago and she asked about you."

"Terri? Did she say how she was doing?"

"She said she sounded rattled, like something was wrong, but she wouldn't tell her anything."

"Does she know how to contact her?"

"No. She said she'd call Piper back in a few days, but she thought you might be in town for the Christmas Day dinner at the church."

"Did she tell her that I'm married now?"

"She said they didn't talk long enough to tell her anything like that this time. I guess Piper and Terri have talked a few times since Terri moved to Vail. That's about all she knows."

Charlie and I talked for a while about Terri's refusal to be around him, or me for that matter. Laura and Annie got back around two that afternoon.

I still did not know what to say to Terri if I saw her, except to follow Martin's advice and be honest with her about how I viewed Charlie's progress, and of course let her know I married Laura. I needed to talk to Martin. My conversation with Charlie about Terri had served only to build more anxiety for me.

I needed to tell Laura about Terri's call, but I wanted to wait until after Christmas Day.

The church had eleven families for dinner this year. Laura took over one of the chairs by the window to read stories to the younger children while they sat on the floor around her. It wasn't long before almost everybody had gathered around to listen. Laura had no idea how many people were listening until she finished the story and everyone applauded. She blushed when she looked up to find me leading the applause.

Charlie, Stony and I took over passing out the pile of presents under the tree and I realized once again the sense of brotherhood in the room, each family having their own dignity regardless of the circumstance of their lives outside of this room. It was warmth of spirit, it was true unselfish fellowship.

Before we finished with the cleanup Laura was already planning next year's dinner with Annie. They talked and laughed about the day's events while they scraped dishes and loaded the dishwasher. Charlie and I took out the last of the trash again.

On the way back to Grand Junction we talked about the party, Annie, Charlie and Stony. I knew I had to say something to her about Terri, but I still needed to gather my thoughts, so I let the opportunity pass again for the time being.

January 1, 1986, Grand Junction

Laura woke up to the smell of fresh coffee and bacon around nine-thirty New Year's morning. She put on her robe, and slipped quietly into the hallway and stopped at the kitchen door where she could see Andy at the stove. This was only the second time Andy had cooked for her since they were married. She leaned quietly against the door frame and watched as he continued to cook. When he turned to go the refrigerator he saw her smiling at him from the doorway.

"You spoiled it. I was going to bring you breakfast in bed."

"Good morning to you too! You should have cooked something with a quieter smell."

"I'll keep that in mind the next time I cook breakfast for a woman who's sleeping in my bed."

"I'd better be the 'next time' woman or my family will be visiting me in prison after I kill you."

"I'll keep that in mind."

After a leisurely breakfast we decided to take a drive

through Colorado National Monument just west of town. It was magical with two inches of fresh snow clinging to the rocks and cliffs. We stopped at one of the turnouts along the top edge of the canyon to look back across toward Grand Junction.

"Charlie and I had a long conversation when we were there. He told me that Terri has been in contact with Piper over the last couple of years."

"Wow, it's been a long time since you've said anything about Terri. Has she decided to get in touch with Charlie again."

"I don't think so. Piper told him she was asking about me."

"You? Does she know we're married?"

"I'm sure Piper has told her."

"Did she say what she wanted?"

"I guess not, anyway Charlie didn't tell me anything except that she was asking about me. I just wanted you to know so you won't get the wrong idea if her name comes up sometime."

"I trust you Andy. Thank you for telling me about it."

"If she wants to see me about Charlie's recovery I'll need to talk to her, probably alone, but I'll tell you before it happens."

"I understand. You've told me enough about what happened for me to know that if you can help them mend their rift I want you to try. Charlie deserves it, and from what you've told me about Terri's attitude she needs it."

We snuggled quietly in the car from the overlook until almost dark then drove back into town. I couldn't stop wondering about what Terri wanted to talk about.

Terri's Return

Two days later
Friday, January 3, 1986, Glenwood Springs

Through the window Piper can see a woman pacing back and forth nervously on the apartment landing … it's Terri! What's she doing here?

"Terri? I saw you through the window. Are you okay?"

"Oh, sorry Piper I didn't mean to worry you. I was just about to knock. Can I come in?"

"Sure. I'm about to have some lunch … want a sandwich?"

"Yeah, sounds good."

Piper wondered what was going on. Terri seemed rattled. She'd never seen her like this before.

"How are things in Vail?"

"Not so good Terri. I'm leaving there."

"What happened?"

"Jack's in the hospital."

"Who's Jack?"

"I've been staying at his place for a while. He overdosed on coke, Piper. That's why he's in the hospital. I can't go back there. I'm afraid I'll wind up like him … or Daddy."

"Are you doing drugs too?"

"Just a few times, … at home with Jack. But then, when I found him like that last night, all I could do was call the ambulance … and pray he'd be alright."

Piper put her arms around Terri for a few seconds then they both sat at the table.

"How can I help you?"

"Can I stay here for a few days? I can sleep on the couch."

"Sure. Let's go down and get your things out of the car."

"Can we just sit here awhile. I'm tired. I came straight from the hospital. I didn't pack anything anyway."

"I'll fix those sandwiches, you just take it easy."

Their conversation went on most of the afternoon until Piper had to go to work at the restaurant. She was the assistant manager now.

When Piper came home around eleven she found Terri asleep on the couch. She was careful not to wake her.

Saturday morning Terri made the trip to Vail to pick up her things and visit Jack in the hospital. She told him she wouldn't be there when he got home. As she left the room she could hear him telling her he didn't need her anymore anyway — He had lots of friends. She remembered his 'friends' had brought him the package that had almost killed him. She drove back to Glenwood Springs in silence, her car packed to the roof with all her possessions.

She stopped by the restaurant about six-fifteen that evening to get the key to the apartment from Piper. As she walked toward the office she heard a familiar voice from a table by the window.

"Terri! ... Terri!"

It was Annie ... Charlie was with her.

Annie got up from the table and headed over to meet Terri. She grabbed her and gave her a big hug and greeting, then grabbed her by the hand and headed toward the table. Charlie stood up. He looked uncomfortable, but anxious to see her. He gave Terri a hug for the first time since he had seen her in the hospital the day she and Andy picked him up over four years ago.

"Hello, honey. How have you been?"

Terri didn't answer him in words or the warmth of his embrace.

"Your Dad and I were just about to have dinner, why don't you join us?"

"I just came to see Piper for a second, I really have to go."

"She'll be back here in a minute. She had to go take a delivery or something in the office. I didn't know you were in town or I would have invited you to have dinner with us in the first place. Sit down, honey. You can't run off now!"

Annie pulled out the chair between her and Charlie and borrowed an extra chair from an empty table for Piper.

"Really Annie, I can't stay. I just need to see Piper and go."

Instead of sitting down, Terri headed for the office again, found Piper, got the key and slipped out the back door, relieved to be away from there. When she got back to the apartment, she unloaded enough clothes for the next few days, all the while fuming about her encounter with Charlie. She was still awake when Piper came home.

"Why did you run away from Charlie like that tonight? He's your dad!"

"He's the guy who hit my mother in a drunken rage. I don't consider him my 'dad' anymore."

Piper sat silently, trying to understand how she could still feel this way after Charlie's turnaround after rehab a few years ago. She also knew what a loyal friend he had become to Martin in those years ... but Terri had not allowed herself to admit that.

"I never knew my father at all. He left my mother

before I was born. Believe me, it's better to have Charlie than to have no dad at all."

Terri glared at Piper and left the apartment having no idea where she was headed. She drove toward the south part of town to the local bar where Charlie had been found the night he was taken to the hospital. She sat, considering the divergent roads she and Charlie had taken since then. There were looming questions punctuated by her own failings and regrets.

Was Charlie the drunk she remembered in the kitchen knocking her mother down, or was he the likeable guy who gave her that warm hug in the restaurant tonight? Is he trustworthy now? Is there any way she could forgive him for all those ugly years?

She went in the bar. It was almost midnight.

The next morning, Sunday, January 5, 1986

Terri rolls over on the couch, groaning and wincing at the bright light streaming through the window. Her mouth tastes nasty and she's nursing a giant headache … she tries to deny the blurry vision of Piper fixing coffee in the kitchen as she hears an excruciatingly cheerful "Good Morning" from somewhere in the room. She growls again and covers her head with the couch pillow … then sleeps until almost one-thirty. She awakes to an empty, sunlit apartment.

There's a note on the counter by the coffee pot.

*I had to go to work for the Sunday dinner
rush. You looked pretty bad this morning. It
must have been a rough night. I'll be back
around five this afternoon.*

Hope you're feeling better,
Piper

She pours a cup of coffee and places it in the microwave. There are cinnamon rolls on the counter.

The shower is long and hot ... and welcome, but the headache remains. Where's the aspirin?

Terri didn't remember how she got home last night, so she looked out the window to see if her car was there, finally spotting it on the other side of the parking lot straddling the line. She vaguely remembers walking from the car to the apartment, trying to remember the number, unsure of which stairway to use. Piper had left the light on and the door unlocked. She decided to go out for a late fast-food Sunday dinner alone.

She found her car unlocked ... not surprising, since she couldn't remember driving home. The sun was so bright on the snow she could hardly see ... no sunglasses to be found in the glove box ... there they are on the floor in front of the driver's seat, partly crushed by an errant step, lenses scratched beyond use. Squinting in the bright sun, she finally pulls out of the parking lot a little before three.

The feeling of isolation grows stronger as she eats alone at the table by the window and watches families swim in the hot springs pool a block away, the hot mineral water steam rising quietly above them as if in a silent movie. What is she doing here only three days after she made that call to save Jack's life. So many changes, so many questions and doubts manifest themselves now, here at this simple table with only the counter staff as company thirty feet away laughing and, thankfully, ignoring her presence.

She sits for a while distracted by the ever-changing scene on the other side of the window. Her thoughts wandering back to her childhood in Grand Junction, remembering a day of bright sunshine and snow when her mother and daddy took her up in the foothills for a day of sledding. She remembered how her father caught her in his arms at the bottom of the hill and suddenly stood up holding her high above his head as they laughed. He continued to hold her up against the brilliant blue sky as she put her arms out as if flying while he made airplane sounds, laughing again with her … it seemed a lifetime ago. Yet it seems so near to this brilliant day of snow and sunshine outside the window. She looks away as the tears come, her daydream shattered by the reality she knows now. She stays at the table in quiet solitude until after four, and then leaves, hoping Piper will be home soon to break the seclusion with someone she can trust, someone who can understand who she is right now and what she has lost. After all, Piper is her only reliable connection between her past and her present … except possibly Andy. He'd been there in the transition between her controlled, self-confident life here in Glenwood Springs and the failure that was life in Vail and she had pushed him away.

Terri waited on the apartment landing until about five-fifteen when Piper came home.

"Hi Terri. Are you feeling better now?"

"Yeah. I went out and got some lunch at a burger place over on the highway."

Piper opened the door with a single key she took out of a sack from a hardware store.

"It works! That's why I was late. I stopped by the store to get you a key on the way home."

She handed the key to Terri as they walked in the door.

They sat and talked for a while and Terri apologized for walking out last night. After a while the subject came back to the incident in the restaurant with Charlie. Terri seemed to get more distant then, but at least they kept talking.

The next morning Piper left early for the breakfast shift at the restaurant and Terri slept in until about nine. She fixed some breakfast and looked around for the morning paper to see if she could find a job and maybe get an idea of how much apartment rent was around here. As she picked up the newspaper she knocked something off the counter and reached to pick it up. It was Piper's address book. She tossed it back on the counter and started looking through the paper. After a few minutes she looked back at the address book, walked across the room and opened it.

"Andy and Laura King" were the first listing under "K."

Who's Laura!

She must be his wife.

Shaken, she leaned on the counter with the address book in her hand, staring out the window at the falling snow. She wrote the number and address down on a slip of paper, folded it and put it in her purse, not sure what to do next.

She turned on the T.V. and watched the weather report, ignored a couple of soap opera episodes, then decided to go for a drive. She headed toward the Springs

Motor Lodge, unsure of what she would do when she got there. She remembered throwing the Frisbee for Bronson and hearing Andy's cousin, Johnny, sitting with Martin, talking about their military service. And then there was Annie ... bigger than life Annie. It was Annie who'd called about Piper that night when she and Andy had picked up Piper from the sheriff's office in the early morning hours. She realized how much Annie and she had trusted Andy then. Annie's trust in Andy was reassuring when Charlie showed up in the hospital. In fact, if it hadn't been for Andy, she might have left Glenwood Springs then, instead of getting Charlie out of the hospital the next day. She knew that it was Andy she'd trusted from the time she met him ... until he'd taken Charlie's side after rehab.

She drives slowly past the motel. There's no one outside. It looks like there are only a few people staying there. She wonders if the car parked near the office belongs to Charlie. A left turn at the next intersection takes her off the main road and into the neighborhood. She circles the block and parks under a tree about half a block away from the motel office. There's the big blue spruce that Martin loved, and the picnic tables where they'd eaten hot dogs and hamburgers. She sits for almost an hour before observing Charlie get into his car and leave. Martin was gone now, and Charlie was living in his place.

She thought about her Saturday night escapade at the bar. Her world had turned upside down since that first summer with Andy, and she couldn't admit that she was the bad guy now. It's three in the afternoon when she arrives at the bar. One drink won't hurt ...

9:30 p.m.

Piper hears a key in the door lock. It must be Terri. It takes more than a minute for her to succeed in unlocking the door. Piper reaches for the knob just as Terri coaxes it open. Terri's breath makes Piper take a step back.

Terri crashes on the couch in her clothes. Piper doesn't sleep.

10:15 a.m.

Terri has gone down to do her laundry in the apartment laundry room. Piper dials the phone.

"Hello, Grandma?"

"Good morning, Piper! How are you this morning."

"I'm not sure, Grandma. Terri's staying with me for a while, but she's not doing so well. She came home drunk last night. That's the second time since she got here last week. And sometimes we argue."

"Why is she staying there? I thought she lived in Vail."

"It's a long story, Grandma. She moved out of where she was staying in Vail."

"Is there something I can do for you ... or Terri."

"I don't know. I just needed to talk to you."

"I'm glad you called, Honey."

They talked for over an hour, about Terri and how to help a friend in trouble. They hung up a few minutes before Terri came back with her laundry. Piper and Terri had lunch, but didn't talk about last night before Piper had to go to work.

Terri was alone again in the apartment. She turned on the T.V.

Wednesday evening, January 8, 1986

At seven o'clock Charlie walks in the front door of the church, just in time for the Wednesday night prayer meeting. The scripture reading for tonight is Psalm 32, the same scripture Martin had read the night Charlie came back from rehab — and the scripture he prayed Terri would come to know on her own.

Psalm 32 begins: "Blessed is he whose transgression is forgiven, whose sin is covered ..."

After the reading, the elder in charge of the meeting begins to take prayer requests. For a few minutes they hear about various illnesses and other concerns familiar to the congregation ... then Charlie stands quietly in the back of the room waiting for his turn to speak to his church family.

"Most of you are familiar with my continuing prayer for my daughter Terri, that we might be reconciled again as father and daughter, and that she might come to know the Lord through that. I received a call yesterday from my very dear friend Annie, who told me that Terri is back in Glenwood Springs, at least for now, but that her situation is of grave concern. She is staying with Piper, Annie's granddaughter. You remember, she helps out at the Christmas dinner ... she's told us that Terri has started drinking heavily sometimes. I can only imagine that our relationship, because of my own drinking, plays a major role in this since she refuses to talk to me. I ask for your prayers that she will find it in her heart to forgive my transgressions against her and her mother, and that the Lord will keep her safe as she deals with this. And I pray for guidance through all of this for Terri, for me, and for all those the Lord may put in her path, that the Lord's will be done in her life, and that His grace will be evident. Thank you."

Prayers at the church continued until about eight o'clock. Afterwards, several of the congregation spoke privately with Charlie offering assurances of their support and any practical help that he might need in this.

Charlie drove home, pausing briefly as he parked to look at the dark windows of the now vacant room he had occupied on that first night out of the hospital ... he wished Martin were here. Later in his bedroom he wept while kneeling to pray once again about Terri's future. He began by asking the Lord to let her know the joy revealed in Psalm 32.

Sunday, January 19, 1986 — Grand Junction

Around three p.m. Terri stops at the curb to review the city map. Andy's house is on Mesa View Court. It should be another couple of blocks ahead. As she turns the corner she can see the house number on the left. The driveway is empty. She sits at the curb for a few minutes, nervous about seeing Andy and wondering what Laura is like.

She drives away for now and heads for her old neighborhood. She hadn't been back there since she moved away after high school and her mom had remarried and moved to Denver. It was strange to see their house with a different color trim, a new garage and a landscaped yard her dad would never have maintained. The trees seemed larger and the street narrower now. There was no snow on the ground in Grand Junction right now, so she explored the park across from her old junior high school. They had changed the swings and slide, but the benches were the same old heavy timbers she remembered sitting on when Frankie stole a kiss from her in the seventh grade. It seemed like yesterday ... it seemed like a lifetime ago.

This was also the park where she'd been before she went home to find Mom yelling at Daddy in the kitchen about his drinking losing him another job ... then he said a bad word and hit her while Terri watched through the back screen door. Daddy didn't come home again after the police came and talked to Mom. It wasn't the first time they had yelled at each other. Mom had taken Terri with her the next day when she went to see the lawyer.

It's dark now. Terri glances at her watch under the street light... it's almost six-thirty. She decides to try Andy's house again.

There are two cars in the driveway. Laura must be there too. Terri hesitates for a minute, and then Laura walks outside carrying what looks like a bible, then leaves in her car. Terri waits for a few minutes before approaching the door.

Andy is in the kitchen when the door bell rings. He puts down his economics text book on the stack of papers to answer it, only to stand speechless for a moment ... he stammered, "Terri? ... What ... when ... what are you doing here?

Of all the times he'd thought about seeing Terri again, he never thought it would be Sunday night after dark on his doorstep. He stood speechless in the open door.

"Aren't you going to say hello?"

"... Hello Terri ... Wow! It's been a long time ... about four years, I think. Did you know I got married this year?"

"I heard about it ... her name's Laura, isn't it?"

"Yeah, that's right. She's gone to church right now. You'll have to wait until she gets back in about an hour and a half to meet her."

"I'm sorry to just show up like this, Andy, but I need

to talk to you … can I come in? It's getting cold out here."

Andy realizes how startled he must look, steps aside and invites her into the small living room, offering her the chair beside the fireplace. He sits on the couch. They make small talk for a few minutes catching up on things from the last four years, both Terri and Andy avoiding saying anything about Charlie. Andy knows there's something wrong. She looks drained. When Andy comes back from the kitchen with the coffee he finds Terri standing by the fireplace, staring into it. He stops, just to observe for a few seconds, and then rattles the cups a little so she'll know he's there. Terri looks up from the fireplace.

"Thanks, Andy."

"You said you needed to talk about something."

"I moved back to Glenwood Springs … I'm staying at Piper's place for a while. I was afraid to stay in Vail … I had to call an ambulance for a friend of mine because he overdosed on cocaine. I could see myself on that gurney someday if I stayed there with him. I was alone … there was no one left there for me, except his doper friends. I had to get out. Piper's letting me stay with her until I can get the money together for an apartment. She's a good friend."

"Were you doing drugs too?"

She hesitated …

"Terri?"

She turned away from Andy's eyes, and looked down into the fireplace.

"A couple of times, but I haven't since I left Vail. I don't even know where, or how they got it."

Andy grabbed her shoulders and turned her toward him again so he could see her eyes. He could see the tears beginning to come. It reminded him of Aunt Margaret's eyes the night she told him she had to leave Brownsville to go back to Denver and take care of Johnny. This wasn't how he had pictured his conversation with Terri. He had thought he'd be trying to convince her to forgive Charlie, but this time it was Terri who needed the help … for herself.

"Why did you go to Vail in the fist place, Terri?"

"I just didn't want to live in the same town as Charlie."

"You mean, it wasn't because you were mad at me?"

Terri wiped away a single tear.

"No, Andy. I couldn't see past my anger at Charlie. You just got between us."

"Have you seen Charlie since you've been back in Glenwood Springs?"

"Yeah. I stumbled into him and Annie having dinner at the restaurant where Piper works, but we didn't talk."

"Why not?"

Terri didn't reply.

As Laura turns the corner she can see a strange car parked at the curb in front of the house and wonders who might be visiting on a Sunday night.

Andy sees the curtains next to the driveway light up with the headlights of Laura's car … She's back a little early … he's a little apprehensive about this.

Laura opens the back door and comes in through the kitchen.

"Hello?!"

Andy rises nervously to meet her at the kitchen door and gives her a quick kiss on the cheek.

"Laura … you've heard me talk about Terri."

"Terri?"

"Hello Laura ... I ... I hope I'm not intruding. I'm just in town for a little while."

Terri told Laura that she had come back to town to visit some old friends and just stopped by for a minute to say hello. Laura wasn't buying it. I knew she could see Terri's red eyes, but she graciously accepted her explanation and we talked while Terri and I finished our coffee. Nothing more was said about Vail or Charlie. Terri left about nine-thirty.

Laura and Andy talked about Terri's visit and he filled her in about it, asking her to keep everything confidential. She nodded and kissed Andy before she picked up the dirty coffee cups and put them in the sink. It was clear to her that Terri was still connected to Andy and that he was nervous about it. All she could do was let Andy know she didn't doubt him, or the strength of their marriage.

Andy's speculations about the real reason for Terri's visit make for a fitful night's sleep.

Journey in Faith

The following Wednesday, January 22, 1986

Johnny walks down the hospital corridor toward the cafeteria where he saw the pay phones earlier, wondering how to tell Andy the bad news. It's 11:42 p.m.

"Hello, Andy? It's Johnny"

"Hi Johnny. Is everything okay?"

"We brought Mother to the hospital again tonight. You know she had that bad spell over Christmas. She doubled over in the kitchen after supper tonight, so I brought her back to the hospital in Denver."

"What do the doctors say?"

"They've advised us to call the family in. Can you make it?"

"Of course. We'll be over as soon as we can pack."

"Good, Mother asked me to call you."

The next morning Laura and I told our professors and our bosses that we'd be gone for a few days and got what class assignments we could before we left. We pulled into Denver Thursday night and drove straight to the hospital. It was seven-thirty.

Johnny had given us her room number and some brief instructions on how to find it. Memories of the hospital where Mama died flashed through my mind … the walls seemed to close in around us as we walked down the final long hallway to her room. We saw a large, crowded waiting room about fifty feet past the door to her room. I could see Johnny there talking with someone. The door to her room was closed, so we decided to see Johnny first. He introduced us to a couple of people in the waiting room from the Center for Hope and another from their church in Platteville … more flash backs to Mama's last day.

We knocked gently on the door to her room. The lady visiting patted Aunt Margaret's hand, told her she'd be back tomorrow and smiled at us as she left. There were all kinds of tubes and wires connected from her to the machines in the room.

Aunt Margaret weakly held both hands out toward us, inviting a hug. She asked if we'd seen Johnny yet and told us she was glad we came to see her. I saw her bible on the nightstand beside the bed, the same one she'd carried to church that first Sunday morning after my arrival in Platteville. The old, worn bookmark was placed somewhere near the middle and her name was engraved on the zippered leather cover.

After we had visited for a few minutes, she asked Laura to read one of her favorite Psalms. She was asleep before Laura finished, peaceful and breathing well … the electronic beat of her heart steady for the moment.

Johnny was staying in Denver with some friends so he could be closer to the hospital, and Laura and I were staying in Platteville at Aunt Margaret's house. Watching the falling snow in the beams of the headlights reminded me of that night in the front seat of the bus when I came to Denver for the first time. It was very dark and cold when we got to the house. I struggled with the lock while holding the screen door open with my elbow. I flipped the switch by the door and looked back at Laura through the doorway and was struck by how vulnerable and attractive she appeared, struggling with both hands to lift our one heavy suitcase. I played the white knight and took the suitcase from her, struggling to hold it up with one hand myself … we both laughed about it while we shivered.

We lit the gas stoves in the living room and bedroom, and spread the down comforter on Aunt Margaret's bed. I wiped frost from the window and looked out over the snow covered flatland toward the mountains.

"What are you looking at, Andy."

"I was just remembering the first night I came here. I was fourteen … It was cold that night too. I haven't seen Texas in ten years."

"I love you, Andy."

It was a long night for both of us.

The next morning we fought a cold wind blasting across the Colorado snow as we loaded the car for the trip back into Denver. I finished scraping the snow and ice from the windshield as the car warmed up. Breakfast consisted of bacon biscuits and hash browns-to-go from a McDonalds in the edge of Denver.

At seven-thirty we found Johnny outside Aunt Margaret's room talking to the doctors. The door opened and we heard the heart monitor's continuing beat. Aunt Margaret appeared to be asleep. When Johnny is finally able to talk with us he tells us that she has gone into a coma and probably won't wake up.

Their pastor from Platteville is in the waiting room along with Esther, her best friend, and the director of the Center for Hope in Denver. Johnny joins the group in the waiting room and we follow along. He tells us what the doctor said and the pastor invites us to join them in prayer. We all move the chairs into a tight circle and join hands. The pastor leads:

"Father we come before you today recognizing the work that you have done in Margaret's life over the years, and celebrate her passion for the welfare of others so evident over her entire life. Many young mothers have sought her guidance … and made the decision to spare the life of their unborn child because of her biblical counsel. All of us in this room have been richly blessed through knowing and being loved by her as well, and we thank you for that. Give her peace now, and give her loved ones peace about her final journey ... that you know her, Father. And if it is your will to take her soon, we have your assurance that she will be with you in glory. Thank you Lord. We ask it in Jesus' name ..."

Then Johnny began to pray:

"Lord, you know us all better than we know ourselves. She was your tool to bring me back to you from a defiant, destructive life. I will never forget finding Mother asleep in that chair with your Word open on the table beside her. It was evident that she had been seeking your voice in my deliverance, even after my transgression against her. And I heard her request for prayer that same day, and now know that you answered those very prayers — in your own way and time. What a gentle, loving spirit you have allowed me to know all my life. I join in my brother's prayer that she may know your peace now and remain free from the pain she has come to know these last few months ... and come into your presence as she has openly anticipated in the midst of this family of believers represented here. Give us the same hope she enjoys, that we will see her again in your presence. Your will be done, Lord ... Amen."

We all continued to sit silently for a few minutes. Laura squeezed my hand when I looked out the window at the snow continuing to fall. I could see Johnny's red eyes revealing the pain he must now feel, the grief of final loss already coming. The pastor took his bible into her room. Johnny followed him into the room a minute or two later. They left the door slightly open. We could hear them, each of them alternately reading scripture to her for half an hour or so. The pastor came out and left Johnny sitting beside her bed, his hand holding hers, the heart monitor still audible.

In this setting, I imagined what it must have been like in the hospital room the day Mama died in Brownsville. I had seen her the morning of that awful day and she had whispered to me she loved me. Later at Mr. Johnson's house when we said the blessing over lunch, I prayed for her to get well … Mama died that afternoon. That was the last time I prayed until that day in Martin's room at his request.

We stayed in the hospital the rest of the day, eating lunch and supper in the cafeteria and the waiting room. They told us it could be a matter of hours or days, so we left for Platteville again around nine-thirty. The weather had cleared, but under the clear skies it had only gotten colder. The stars were brilliant and the snow covering shone silver under a three-quarter moon … another cold restless night softened only by the warmth of each other under the down comforter. The call came at four-fifteen Friday morning. Johnny came home to Platteville that afternoon and told us the funeral would be Tuesday at two.

Saturday morning Johnny went through Aunt Margaret's desk looking for the long-forgotten life insurance policy and other papers he needed. In the process he found a picture from her high school prom. It was signed "Love, Wally." More pictures in the box included one of Aunt Margaret and me in the park when she came to Brownsville and one of Bronson looking through the screen door from the old porch which had served as my bedroom.

Johnny also told us something I had been too self-absorbed to realize while I lived here. She was single and seventeen when he was born ... twelve hundred miles from home in Brownsville. In 1945 she came to Denver to live with her grandmother and start a new life with a new baby. Again, in 1970 she had sacrificed her life's calling at the center to move here to Platteville and nurse him back to health in the years following his injuries in Viet Nam. She had stayed involved with the center as much as she could, and even during her chemotherapy was involved in helping to place young misplaced mothers-to-be temporarily in loving homes when they needed it. Gloria was just one of many, and the only one I had briefly known.

Although I lived in her house for over four years, I had never asked her to tell me the story of her life or much about what the Center was all about. She seldom asked for anything more than simple prayer and the chance to reach out to others who were hurting. I had experienced that myself when I showed up unannounced from Brownsville — she never thought about the extra responsibilities, she just invited me into her home, loved me as her own, and prayed for me. What more precious gift can anyone receive.

2 p.m. Tuesday, Denver

The funeral was overwhelming. The little church in Platteville was not big enough for the expected crowd, so they held the service at First Presbyterian in Denver. She had been a member there from 1945 until she moved to the old family place in Platteville in 1970 when Johnny came home from Viet Nam. For over twenty years her full time occupation had been to counsel young mothers-to-be in the nearby church sponsored "Center for Hope." She was instrumental in creating the Center and had stayed intimately connected with it until her death. Then the pastor related to us what Margaret had said to him when she left Denver for Platteville to be with Johnny full time. She said, "I don't know why all this has happened, but I know that Jesus is calling me there for a reason … Johnny needs me now. Pray for both of us … pray that we won't lose sight of Jesus when things get tough … and that we'll be who Jesus made us to be in the lives of those troubled souls who need His touch so much."

Her words quoted from that pulpit cut to my soul. I knew that I was one of those troubled souls she'd been called there for. I knew her prayer in those words to her pastor had been answered. And I could still remember Johnny's words in that prayer three days ago in the hospital about her faithfulness to him at his lowest ebb.

During the eulogy they recognized those who had been born to mothers who were counseled at the center she helped to form in partnership with First Presbyterian. When asked to stand, more than one hundred people responded, their ages spanning over thirty years. One of those who raised his hand was a young boy standing next to an attractive lady about my age who looked hauntingly familiar.

I couldn't get her face out of my mind, and after the service was over, I found Johnny and asked him about her. He said "Why Andy, that's Gloria and her son Jeremy. You met her in Cheyenne the day we got Bronson. She's been a volunteer at the center ever since she got her life back together after Jeremy was born.

I located her after the service was over and asked her if she had picked up any big skinny dogs lately. She turned with a puzzled look on her face and asked me what I said.

"I said, 'have you picked up any big skinny dogs at the animal shelter lately?'"

She thought for a minute, then smiled and said "Andy, is that you?"

"It's me. We've grown up a little since then haven't we? And who is that you're with?"

Gloria gave me a sisterly hug and stood back to look at me.

"This is my son, Jeremy ... Jeremy this is Andy."

"Hello sir."

I could see his eyes were still red and he continued to look down at the floor with his hands in his pockets.

"Hi Jeremy, it's nice to meet you."

"Jeremy is in the third grade now. He's a pretty good speller ... I can't believe Margaret's gone. She made such a difference for Jeremy and me ... and so many others. Margaret was his favorite spelling buddy whenever she could manage some time to visit. They were very close."

As we were talking Laura stood beside me and silently looked on. I knelt down to Jeremy's level and gently lifted his chin so he could see my eyes.

"She was my Aunt and I loved her very much too. I know how you feel. When I was about your age she came to Texas and helped me through a tough time. We used to go to the park and sit on a bench and read about Moses from the bible. She knew all about Moses in the desert and God talking to him through the burning bush. The way she read to me made me feel better. Was she fun to learn spelling with too?"

He smiled a little and raised his head to look at me on his own and nodded his head.

"Remember her the way she was when you were together learning to spell those words. Remember her smile. Remember her voice when she was happy about your good spelling. And remember her laugh. I know she probably laughed with you sometimes. She used to mess up my hair when she played with me sometimes. That's the way I remember her ... laughing and messing up my hair. It almost makes me laugh ... even now."

Jeremy put his arms around my neck and held on for a minute, then let go and pulled back a little, then said, "She messed up my hair too when she laughed ... I miss her."

"I know you do Jeremy, but it'll get a little easier after a while. Just take care of your Mom. I know she misses her too."

He nodded his head, took Gloria's hand and asked "Are you okay Mommy?"

"Yes, honey. I'm okay. We'll remember her together, alright?"

Gloria looked at me with eyes beginning to tear and said "Thank you," silently mouthing the words so Jeremy couldn't hear.

I introduced Gloria to Laura just before Johnny signaled for Laura and me to get into the funeral limo for the ride to the cemetery. It was quiet inside until we heard the blip of a siren as the police car stopped traffic for the funeral procession to commence. As we rode through the freeway interchange we could see the line of cars behind us as they entered the cloverleaf entrance we had just driven through. Another blip on a siren signaled the other drivers on the freeway to yield to the procession. As we pulled into the cemetery we could see the temporary cover over the open grave from a distance. Johnny shifted nervously in the seat of the limo as we approached ... the strain of the day was wearing on his nerves.

Around the opening an all-weather carpet was spread on top of the snow-covered ground and there were padded folding chairs for the family just in front of the support frame for the casket. The sun was out and the air was still ... a perfect winter day to remember ... and say goodbye.

They transferred the coffin to the waiting support frame carefully, respectfully making sure that every detail was in order, and then signaled for the family to exit the car. Laura got out first and I followed. Johnny took some extra time to gather himself before he stepped out. I could see he was still nervous, and I realized that he had misplaced his cane. It was probably still at the church by the driveway where we had gotten in. He was nervous about slipping on the snow at his mother's funeral. I whispered to Laura that he didn't have his cane and stepped back beside him to steady his walk. Laura came beside him on the other side and we walked, slowly, carefully across the fifty feet of hard-packed snow to the chairs. We sat down and waited while the rest gathered around.

I glanced back toward the limo and saw a familiar car parking on the other side of the cemetery driveway. It was a new, white Lincoln ... it was Annie. Charlie was with her. They came forward just long enough to express their condolences and then stood on the outside of the group. Other people I did not recognize sat around us in the reserved seating section under the canvas roof. Johnny said most of them were close friends from the Center. I saw Gloria and Jeremy sit down on the end of the row behind us. The graveside service was brief in the cold weather.

Laura and I steadied Johnny's steps to the limo as we walked back. We asked the driver to take us back by the church to get Johnny's cane before he took us back to the house in Platteville. We arrived back at the house around five-thirty.

There were three ladies from the church in Platteville in the kitchen doing final preparations of food for our dinner along with sandwiches and other finger food for any guests who might visit during the evening. Johnny was exhausted and sat silently in the living room recliner. A few people from the local church came by and spoke with Johnny. I only knew two of them. The ladies from the church left after Laura and I had a light meal and they washed the dishes and put away the leftover food. Johnny didn't eat that night. As Laura and I prepared for bed Johnny passed by the door to say goodnight before he went to bed and we could see the pain in his eyes as he knew his mother would never sleep in that room again. Laura closed her eyes in a silent prayer before kissing me goodnight. It seemed a longer prayer than usual. I looked out the window at the snow under the moonlight and wondered if Aunt Margaret had found Mama and Daddy in heaven yet. Behind the closed door, Johnny's room light was still burning after midnight.

Wednesday morning I woke up to the smell of coffee, bacon and hash browns. In the kitchen I found Laura and Johnny talking quietly, the bacon and hash browns on a platter. His face was drawn and he kept his eyes on the floor as they spoke. Laura smiled at me as I came in the room and said "good morning." Johnny attempted a smile and poured me a cup of coffee before I asked. His attempt at good humor is a transparent facade. I know his pain. I know the isolation of grief and hurt of this loss. I wondered what Johnny's future held. Was there an Exodus from home in store for him as there had been for me?

"Laura fixed us some breakfast, Andy. Do you want some eggs to go with the bacon?"

"Sure Johnny. I see them on the stove. I'll get them."

We made small talk while we finished breakfast. Not much was said about yesterday. Laura and I packed the car and were ready to leave by around ten-thirty Wednesday morning.

"I'll go through Mother's things and see if there's anything she'd want you to have and give it to you next time you're here. I guess that may be a while with your school and all. Call me when you get a chance, Andy. I really want to stay in touch, and I know Mother would want that."

I gave him a brotherly hug that lasted longer than usual and I heard Laura tell Johnny that he is still in her prayers and that we'll stay in touch. I watched him in the mirror as we drove away. He looked tired as he walked slowly with his cane back toward the empty house.

The weather was warming a little as we drove through Denver on our way west toward the mountains and there were a few clouds shrouding one of the higher peaks.

"I heard what you said to Jeremy about remembering Aunt Margaret's laugh, Andy."

"It's a good thing to hold on to ... those good memories and mind pictures of how she looked when she was happy."

"What color was your mother's hair, Andy?"

"She had brown hair ... and hazel eyes. She laughed at the ducks in the park when they fought over the bread we threw to them ... until Daddy died. Then she didn't want to see the ducks anymore."

"What's your favorite memory of her when you were little?"

"We used to go to the movies on Saturday afternoon, just Mama and me. We always got buttered popcorn to share. She said I was her 'date' while Daddy was on the road, and then she'd smile at me and tell me I looked just like him. It was always fun even when the movie was bad. We'd get a hamburger afterward and make jokes about how bad the movie was."

Laura talked about the times her family had gone camping and how much fun it was to look over the valley from "Land's End" on the western edge of Grand Mesa. She said the wind blew straight up as it hit the top of the cliff along the edge of the mesa.

"That's my favorite memory of my grandfather, Andy ... the day he tried to fly a kite off the edge of Lands End. He always loved kites and every time we went to the park in town with him he brought a kite — even if there was no wind — so he was prepared, just in case a breeze came up."

"You said he 'tried' to fly a kite up there?"

"He had it all planned with a special heavy duty kite he built just for the occasion. When we got up there he made sure we were all watching when he made his way to the edge. He had my dad hold the kite away from the edge while he threw some grass over the rim of the cliff to get an idea of where the updraft was. Of course the grass blew straight up about two feet in front of him and he was delighted, so he motioned to my dad to bring him the kite. He gave the string to my dad and eased as close as he could get to the edge. He tossed the kite up and out to make sure it got into the updraft. Well, as soon as the wind hit the kite it nearly pulled my dad off his feet, then Grandpa's 'heavy duty' kite folded in half like a sheet of paper and stayed attached to the string. The wind kept it up anyway for just a moment and Grandpa yelled 'It's flying!' and all of us laughed. A few seconds later the kite came loose from the string and blew somewhere out over the edge. Grandpa and Dad sat down on a rock by the edge and laughed until they cried."

"Your Grandpa sounds like quite a character."

"Oh yes! But I'll never forget the smile on his face on the trip back down the mountain. That's how I remember him."

"How long has he been gone."

"He died of a sudden heart attack when I was fourteen. He always said he wanted to go quickly … the Lord answered his prayer."

We arrived back in Grand Junction Wednesday night, glad to be home. Thursday morning brought a return to the realities of work and school for both of us.

Saturday, February 1, 1986

I arrive home from work to an empty house. Laura won't be home until after the store closes around five so I decide to take advantage of the quiet to write Walt.

> *Dear Walt,*
>
> *You probably know by now that Aunt Margaret lost her battle with cancer a few days ago.*
>
> *Even though I lived in her house for four years I didn't know how many lives Aunt Margaret had touched over the years. At the funeral there were hundreds of people who knew her and wanted to tell her goodbye. Johnny is having a hard time with her death. I hope he can find some peace about this soon.*
>
> *Terri surprised me a couple of weeks ago by showing up at our house here in*

*Grand Junction one Sunday evening. She
told me some troubling things about her life
in Vail. She said she tried drugs a couple
of times there, but has now moved back to
Glenwood Springs to stay with a friend for a
while. She never really told me why she was
there, but I could tell she had something on
her mind, probably about her dad Charlie.
We talked until Laura came home from
church, but she never really finished what
she intended to say.*

*Laura was very gracious about finding
Terri here in our house talking with me that
night and has told me she understands my
part in Terri and Charlie's relationship. But
I'm not sure whether I should try to contact
Terri or wait for her to contact me again.
I don't want her to get the idea that I'm
interested in seeing her again, or that there
is any problem between me and Laura, but I
still feel connected to her somehow.*

*I know you don't have enough
information on this to give specific advice,
but you always seem to point me in the right
direction somehow. Laura and I speak of
you often when we are unsure about our
decisions in life. You are loved and trusted
from afar.*

Andy

I mailed the letter at the campus post office on my way
to the library. Class makeup work filled the afternoon. I
was determined to get it out of the way so we could have

a quiet evening without studying. We both needed the "down" time and were looking forward to an evening alone.

I picked Laura up from work around five fifteen and we stopped at our favorite Italian restaurant for a dinner alone together. We splurged on a good bottle of wine and talked about Aunt Margaret and Johnny, Gloria and Jeremy. We finally realized we had been there over two hours before we asked for the check.

At home, pillows on the couch, candle light, our favorite soft music on the stereo along with quiet conversation restored our souls ... renewed our devotion ... rekindled the flame. The warm flickering light sparkled in her eyes and drew me in. We reminisced about the first night we met, and danced ... and found each other in the night.

Glenwood Springs the same Saturday night, 6:20 p.m.

Piper drives out of the apartment parking lot to her job at the restaurant as Terri, watching from the window above, stands hopeless and alone. The money she brought from Vail is long since gone and Piper has loaned her all she can afford, for this week anyway ... one lonesome twenty dollar bill.

Even the HBO movies are re-runs. Two hours of this is all she can stand.

The gas gauge reads about a quarter tank and the sign on the bank a block away flashes 8:22 p.m. / 22° F. The streets are clear and dry now, but the snow is still deep most places and the weatherman says there'll be heavy snow again beginning around ten.

Just one drink before the blizzard hits ... the bar is only a couple of miles away.

They never cleared the snow from the parking lot at the "Hideaway Lounge" after the last storm, so she picks a spot close to the door where it's melted away … mostly. Her tires crunch to a stop on the now re-frozen slush. Through the windshield an old neon sign in the window sputters the news that Budweiser is the king of beers. She sits for a minute, trying to remember the first time she went to a bar alone, then steps out into the still, cold night … each breath slowly rising as a vanishing mist. Only the sound of the sputtering sign breaks the stillness as she stands, shivering and alone in the cold night.

The brass handle on the heavy front door coaxes her into the dark, smoky, anonymous world inside. An old George Jones "cheatin' song" greets her on the other side and a tall cowboy punches A9 on the jukebox and buys some cigarettes from the machine. He strikes a match with his thumb, and the flare reveals his eyes following her tight fitting jeans to the bar.

She stares into the first drink — hesitating … forestalling the inevitable … then downs it all at once, the ice rattling in the glass as it lands back on the bar, empty. The bartender slides another round in front of her before she asks for it.

"It's on me," she hears from the barstool beside her.

She smiles and tips the newly filled glass in his direction as he slides onto the barstool beside her.

"It's a cold night to be out all alone."

"This will warm it up okay. Thanks … ?" Terri asks him his name with a furtive look.

"I'm Joe … and you would be … ?

"Terri … spelled with an "i."

She glances at his left hand to make sure there's no wedding band. After another drink the conversation gets "playful" and they move from the bar to a booth in the far corner. With every round of drinks Terri's misery slips farther away, lost in the eyes of this tall cowboy named Joe.

The streets are already covered with snow again as Joe turns out of the parking lot just after eleven in his four wheel drive pickup. Terri fumbles at tuning the radio to her favorite station as they head for his place a few miles out of town.

When Piper returned home after work Sunday night Terri's things were gone and there was a note on the refrigerator door:

> *I'm sorry you weren't here when I came to pick up my stuff today. I'll never be able to repay you for being here when I needed a place to stay and a listening ear. Thank you for that.*
>
> *But I have overstayed my welcome and I need to move on. I met someone and we're leaving town today. His name is Joe. I'll call you when I get settled.*
>
> *I left my key to your front door and the $53 cash I owe you beside the microwave.*

Terri

Denver, March 10, 1986

Gloria left the center and headed for Jeremy's school to pick him up, bought some gas then drove in the direction of the house. She was running a little late, so she made her stop at the grocery store quick …a dozen pork chops, two packages of brown 'n serve rolls, salad, a gallon of milk and a frozen apple pie. Jeremy pushed the cart all the way through the checkout line. Johnny would be at the house around 5:30 and it was already after 5.

They were housing three young mothers or mothers-to-be, ages fifteen to nineteen, in the old mansion. It was a temporary stop in life for them, hopefully a turning point in their difficult young lives full of all sorts of circumstances. Rich unforgiving parents, abusive relationships, and poverty had brought these three tender young lives together through a common unshakable fact ... they were becoming mothers and had no idea of how to handle it. They had all found their way to this old house with a house-mother only marginally older than they. They had all considered terminating their unplanned, unwanted pregnancy, but had somehow been connected with Gloria and her effervescent little red headed son Jeremy. Watching Gloria and Jeremy interact as mother and son had rekindled their hope ... they had all turned from the despair of the moment and a possible abortion, to the hope of imagining who their child could become.

Somehow this young house-mother had survived the same sort of despair and become their mentor, and her son Jeremy had brought a living, breathing hope for them and their children-to-be. He always seemed to show up in their darkest moments with a skinned knee, a question they couldn't refuse to answer, or some other childhood mini-drama, thereby embodying the life they had chosen to preserve ... and reminding them of why they had come here. Gloria and Jeremy were a godsend.

Earlier in the day Johnny had called Gloria at her office in the Center for Hope to tell her he needed to see her tonight. He hadn't told her what it was all about, but he'd sounded excited. The news must be good.

Gloria delivered the groceries to the kitchen where

Debra, one of the residents, already had dinner partly underway. Debra told her Johnny was in the study waiting for her. Jeremy went outside to play with the new puppy they had rescued from the pound a few days before.

"Hi, Johnny."

Johnny stood up and gave her a hug before they sat down to talk.

"Gloria, we have some wonderful news. We have a new benefactor for the Center. It means we have enough money to pay off the mortgage on the residence and even remodel the main Center building. The bank called me this morning and told me we received a very large anonymous contribution. The money had already been deposited with the stipulation that it was an anonymous gift, no strings attached!"

Tears began welling in her eyes as the news penetrated that there was enough for them to proceed with Margaret's long-postponed plans. The news Johnny brought contradicted years of struggle for Margaret just to keep the Center alive, often barely meeting only the most urgent needs, financial disaster always lurking in the background.

"But, who … ?" Gloria questioned.

"The bank told me that it was someone who came to Mother's funeral. They couldn't tell me any more. You were there, so you know there were hundreds of people who came. We may never know who it was. But the Lord knows, and that's all that matters."

Gloria sat motionless, tears of joy streaming down her face … while Johnny prayed a prayer of thanks and praise, then Gloria continued on in prayer, mentioning each of the current residents by name and, suddenly remembering the comfort Andy had brought to Jeremy in those few minutes after the funeral, she prayed in thanks for her connection to him and that his life would be blessed. Johnny then concluded their prayers with his mother's words, "that we won't lose sight of Jesus when things get tough … and that we'll be who Jesus made us to be in the lives of those troubled souls who need His touch so much; in Jesus' name, Amen."

After supper Johnny and Gloria talked about how to present the good news to the advisory board and what plans should be made for the clinic to move forward with the new funding.

Jeremy interrupted their conversation when he crawled up on the couch beside Gloria in his pajamas looking a little sleepy. She realized it was a half-hour past his bed time and took him to his bedroom after he gave Johnny a goodnight hug.

The trip back to Platteville seemed shorter that night than it had been for Johnny in a long time, but the house seemed just as empty and quiet … and cold.

He picked up his Mother's old bible he still kept on the table by the lamp and remembered her long-standing prayers for provision at the Center. Many of those prayers had been answered today.

The excitement of the day had distracted him from the task he'd started yesterday after church. It had been the first time he'd been able to look through Mother's things since Andy and Laura left. Before yesterday the house had been so overrun with emptiness he couldn't bear to invite any more of her memories inside.

Her past was in these old boxes … and the drawer of her writing desk that she had always kept locked. He reached for the small door on the left side where he'd seen her carefully place the key one day when she thought he wasn't watching. At the back of the compartment he found a blue velvet covered box … inside was an boy's high school senior ring and the key to the drawer. He switched on the small light above the writing pad and turned the ring slowly in the light, trying to make sense of it ... of who might have given it to her, and why she'd never said anything about them. It was too much to absorb.

After a few minutes he tenderly replaced the ring in the box and snapped it shut without touching the key ... and placed it carefully back in the compartment.

Andrea's Journey Home

Grand Junction, 5:30 a.m. June 2, 1986

Laura usually sleeps in on days when she doesn't have an early class or an early shift at work, but today we share a good breakfast before my overnight delivery trip. Our kiss goodbye at the door lingers a little … I look back as she stands in the door in her robe, watching as I drive away.

By seven the truck is loaded with the two tractors bound for Farmington, New Mexico. I open the cab of the truck and toss my small bag, a sandwich cooler and thermos of hot coffee inside on the seat. I make the final walk-around to check the load and tires and sign the transfer receipt for the tractors. Since the spring semester is over I can finally take a higher paying overnight load. It's only the second night I'll spend away from Laura since our wedding.

I make my first stop at Montrose, Colorado, to pick up some smaller additions to the load. It takes about thirty minutes to load up and head out of the dealership.

Less than a half mile on the right is the chapel where I heard those calm, soul-piercing words … "Are you here for confession?"

The door is closed today, but I stop before driving by, recalling the mute witness of the young woman kneeling silently, humbly in prayer.

At the next red light I sip my coffee, trying to stop the priest's words echoing in my head … a tap on the horn from the car behind startles me into motion after I realize the light is now green. I turn south on U.S. 550 toward Ridgway, settle into the rhythms of the road, turn up the volume on the radio and hope the loud country music on the radio will drown those nagging words.

After I drop the load in Farmington, the dealer lets me leave the truck secured on his property for the night, and take a company pickup to the motel. I check into a room and shower, then head into town for supper at a local seafood place I had seen advertised on a billboard along the highway. There's a movie theater next to the restaurant and I decide to kill some time and take in a double feature. It's a little after eleven when I get back to the room.

From the second floor outside walkway I can hear the moaning brakes of eighteen wheelers coming to a stop at the nearest intersection. As I put the key in the lock I hear the scream of an ambulance and turn to watch as it heads west into town … then relative quiet invades for a minute or two. A car door closes below and I watch from above as a small family of three unloads their luggage into their ground floor room, the young father carefully lifting his child from the back seat of the car, trying not to wake him. I continue to watch quietly until they finally close the door to the room behind them.

Entering my room, I leave the overhead light off, close the drapes and sit on the edge of the bed. The dark emptiness surrounds me … I turn on the bedside lamp. It's strange to be alone at night now, no quiet conversation, no kiss goodnight. The sheets are stiff and cold, the pillow too thick, and the blanket too thin for the temperature set on the a/c thermostat. I turn it a little warmer and go back to bed. The clock radio reads 1:12 a.m. … at 2:03 I get a drink of water and go back to bed again … then the burning bush flares about twenty feet ahead and I hear another siren in the background mixed with a voice coming from behind. I turn to see the voice, but see only the young woman kneeling silently at the altar, the voice still booming everywhere and nowhere ... "ARE YOU HERE FOR CONFESSION?" ... it's Martin's voice ... it's nobody's voice ... I wake up in a sweat tossing the cover to the floor, and turn on the lamp, blinking wildly, staggered by the light. Out of sheer reflex I stumble across the room trying to make sense out of confusion. It's 3:42 ... I need more water. I sit in the light, trembling inside, searching for calm in the room ... not finding it.

What was that all about? ... No peace until daybreak ... waffles and coffee alone at Denny's ... I pick up the truck from the dealer again, and face the long drive ahead.

8:17 a.m.

After stopping for fuel I head out on the road. As I drive away I'm immediately captured by the vacant look of an exhausted young woman sitting on a boulder beside the highway. Her large suitcase bears a cardboard sign reading MONTROSE COLORADO. Something about her draws me. She looks to be in her late teens ... distraught and weary.

I pull the rig onto the shoulder just beyond her and watch in the mirror as she struggles with the heavy bag. Coming to a full stop, I set the brake and step down to the pavement.

"Let me help you with that!" I yell as I move toward her, take her bag and heave it up to my shoulder. She doesn't look well.

"Thanks. I can hardly lift this thing anymore."

I put the bag into the floor of the cab, leave the door open and help her up into the cab. Dirty, disheveled red hair frames her pale gaunt face, and penetrating eyes peer through dark circles as she tries to decide whether she can trust me. Nervous hands cling to the door handle as she resolutely looks straight ahead and avoids eye contact.

"How long were you sitting on that rock?"

"A while … not many people want to pick up hitchhikers anymore."

We drove in silence for a several miles.

"My name's Andy … I've got some cheese, crackers and a couple of soft drinks in that cooler over there if you want some."

She shakes her head "no" but looks down at the cooler.

"It's okay, really. I just had breakfast and I brought that for a snack later down the road. You look like you could use a bite."

I open the cooler with my right hand and give her the package of sliced cheese. After a couple of minutes she opens a package of crackers and a coke, and eats in silence, still clinging to the door to keep as much distance between us as she can. After a while I hear a nervous giggle and look over to see her smiling.

"They call me Andy sometimes too" she says as she looks away through the passenger window. "My name is Andrea, but some people call me Andy."

We laugh together about it and some of the tension clears.

"I think I'll call you Andrea, if you don't mind."

The conversation begins slowly at first, but over the next fifty miles or so I tell her about Laura and why I had been in Farmington last night. She didn't volunteer much about herself, except that she hadn't been in Montrose for the last few years. After a while she dozed off for what looked to be some much needed sleep and didn't rouse again until I stopped on the south edge of Montrose.

"Where are we?"

"Montrose. You had quite a nap … I need a break and some lunch … let's get a burger or something … my treat!"

"No, you've done enough already. Thanks for the ride. I'll just call somebody to come get me from here."

"Okay, but I'm going to wait here until I know someone's on the way to get you."

Andrea walks over to the pay phone at the corner store and dials two different phone numbers with no success. She tries to look up something in the phone book and drops it back on the shelf in disgust. Then she looks at me across the parking lot and shrugs her shoulders before walking back to the truck.

"Why don't you at least let me take you where you need to go? I've got all afternoon to get back to Grand Junction."

"Okay, keep going for a few blocks up here, then you'll make a right."

As I pull away from the store I tell her the only rule is to keep me away from dead end streets, so I won't have to back out with this thirty foot trailer. She laughs and says she can't make any guarantees.

About ten minutes later we park in front of an old run-down house with two kids playing in the driveway. Andrea looks confused, gets out and knocks on the door. She talks with the woman who answers for a minute or two and then goes next door to talk with someone there. The woman there invites her inside while I wait and watch from the truck. After about ten minutes Andrea comes back outside looking shaken and returns to the truck. Her eyes are red and she trembles as she gets back in the truck.

"What's wrong, Andrea?"

"She's dead. The neighbor lady said Mama died two years ago ... she had pneumonia and nobody found her until it was too late."

"I'm sorry. Is there someone else in town you can call? Do you have any other family here?"

"No. Daddy left a year before I did and there's nobody else ... anywhere."

We sat there for a few minutes, Andrea biting her lip, trying not to cry in front of me without much success. I started the engine and drove back toward town, unsure of what to do next. I knew she didn't need to be alone now ... memories of the awful feeling in the pit of my stomach the day Walt told me Mama was dead floated past and I shared Andrea's emptiness and loss.

I stopped in the parking lot of a large restaurant along the main highway through town and suggested we go in and have some lunch while we considered things. I know she must be hungry, but she mostly just picks at her plate in silence so I don't push conversation, knowing food can never fill the void. After a while I decide to tell her about leaving Brownsville:

"Daddy died when I was eight, then Mama died when I was fourteen."

She looked up, shocked at my words coming so cleanly out of the heavy silence, but didn't reply ... I continued.

"Two weeks after Mama died I took a bus from Brownsville, Texas, to Denver without telling anybody I was leaving. It was the loneliest two days of my life."

Her eyes narrowed as she questioned me sincerely, "Why Denver?"

"My great aunt lived there, and I knew she'd understand ... I just knew it in my heart because she'd already been there for Mama and me when Daddy died. I lived with her and her son for the next four and a half years."

"I don't have a great aunt … I don't have bus fare … and I'm two months pregnant."

Those last three words stopped the conversation again. She looked down at her plate, tears welling up, not saying anything else. After a couple of minutes she turned away and stared out the window trying to avoid looking at me again.

"Where's the father?" I asked.

"He didn't take the news about being a dad very well." She pulled back her long red hair away from her right ear to show me the cut and bruise, probably from a large ring on his fist. The marks from three stitches were still plainly visible. "I filed charges on him and he skipped out. I don't ever want to see him again."

She sat looking out the window watching a young mother pushing a carriage on the sidewalk across the street. "I can't have this baby … I can't even take care of myself, much less a baby."

I didn't know what to say after that so I drank another cup of coffee and we sat for a while longer. In the silence of the moment I realized why I had been so drawn to her as she sat on that rock by the road. She reminded me of Gloria with that long red hair and the same apprehensive look I remembered that day in Cheyenne … and she reminded me of myself twelve years ago, alone and on the road, away from a place where she could no longer live.

And then it came to me … "I have an idea … are you through with lunch?"

We leave the restaurant, drive back toward the highway and park the truck at the curb on a side street next to the Catholic Church. The front doors are still closed, so I leave Andrea in the truck and knock on the side door of the church. No one answers. I walk around back and find the caretaker pruning some shrubs.

"Hello!"

He stops working and turns toward me. "Si?"

"Is the Father here?"

"Padre?" He motions for me to follow him to the other side of the building and points toward the church office.

"Thanks."

I see a priest sitting beside the open window... "Father?"

He looks up at me with a puzzled look, smiles and opens the door to his study.

"We meet again" he says and reaches forward to shake my hand.

"You remember me?"

"Of course! It's not every day I have someone declare so clearly they're not Catholic while standing in the middle of the sanctuary ten feet away from the confessional ... what brings you here today? ... are you ready to pray now? ... sorry, I have a habit of anticipating conversations ... I'm Father James."

"It's good to see you again, Father. My name's Andy. I'm afraid I was rude the first time we met, but it was a difficult time for me and I wasn't thinking straight."

"An appropriate time to pray I'd think ... but what brings you here today?"

I explained how I had come to know Andrea and a little about her situation before we walked out to the truck to get her. We all went back to his office, closed the door and talked for a few minutes before Father James called someone and arranged temporary local accommodations. For tonight she'd be staying with a family who lived nearby. He dialed the number of the family where she'd be staying, talked with someone for a minute, and handed her the phone before motioning to me to step outside for a minute to talk.

"You've been God's blessing to that girl today. Thank you for that."

"I don't usually pick up hitchhikers, but she looked so vulnerable sitting on that dusty rock by the road ... I've been there ... I couldn't leave her sitting there."

"You have a good heart, son. I'll be praying for you as well ... I prayed for you before ... that you'd come back so that we could finish our talk. Can you stay a while? I promise not to ask you again to pray with me."

"I need to get this truck back to Grand Junction today. I'm already running late.

"Of course, Andy."

"What will happen with Andrea now, Father?"

"Well, since she told me she just turned eighteen, it will be up to her of course, but if she wants assistance we'll be here to help her get back on her feet."

I went to the truck to get her suitcase and when I returned to the office I could see Father James and Andrea through the window ... they were in prayer, so I waited before I went in. Her eyes looked a little less hollow as she squeezed my hand in a shy thank you gesture and gave me a quick surprise hug before going back inside. I can't shake the sense of both relief and loss as I drive away ... and remember last night's disturbing dream (or possibly nightmare) about the burning bush. Was the girl kneeling at the altar Andrea? If the dream had not come, would Andrea and I have crossed paths? How did I know to take her to that church? ... I hadn't voluntarily been in a church in years, except for funerals ... and that one strange day when I encountered Father James here. The dream and the events of the day hang stubbornly in my consciousness like an advertising jingle I can't get out of my head.

As I drive back toward Grand Junction I stop the truck on the shoulder to watch a hawk circling above the fence a few yards from the pavement. It's not a lazy purposeless glide, but a calculated hovering, full of tiny precise adjustments, at times almost stationary, as he faces the prevailing wind directly, intently. Like a falling missile he drops from the sky, talons open, poised for action, disappearing behind a small bush. After a few seconds the purpose of the drama reveals itself in his claws as he climbs back into the sky with his prize, a small rodent of some sort, struggling weakly in the bird's killing grip. I can see the small dust cloud briefly rising from behind the bush, and evaporating in the next gust of wind over the summer prairie. I sit for a few more moments remembering today ... Andrea sitting on the rock ... the news about her mother's death ... and now witnessing this natural violence in the continuum of life. This day has been a revelation of sorts that in creation, life and death are two sides of this same coin of existence. Without the death of the rodent the hawk and his offspring will die, and even though Andrea's mother died, life continues in Andrea's womb toward a future generation.

I see a dust-devil across the road, birthed by the heat of the day, destined to a sure demise with the first stiff gust of wind or encounter with a large tree, and am reminded of the fleeting nature of that voice from the burning bush ... it was silenced as soon as consciousness returned, but the enigma remains.

... it's getting late, I need to go home. I need Laura.

Resurrection

July 7, 1987, Glenwood Springs, Colorado

Charlie looks out the window from the breakfast table. There's that old beat-up car again, parked halfway down the block with someone sitting inside. It's the third time this week he's seen someone sitting there in that same car. He grabs the leash and hooks up Bruno on the way out of the house, heading down the block for a closer look. As he crosses the street and turns toward the car it pulls out from the curb and u-turns before he can see the driver, but he runs to get close enough to get the license number.

There's not much doubt that the driver didn't want to be seen by him, so he heads back to the motel to call the police and report it. He asks for Sergeant Burns, a friend from church.

"Hello, Larry?"

"Hey, Charlie how are you doin' this morning?"

"Everything's okay here, I guess, but there's something I was hoping you could check on for me."

Charlie told Larry about the car and gave him the license number. Larry said he'd check it out later in the day and get back to him on it.

"What do you think, Bruno?" Charlie asks, remembering that he hasn't fed him this morning. Charlie answers himself, "you think it's time for your breakfast don't you?" as he reaches for the pantry door to get the dog food.

Bruno is the half-grown mutt Charlie's keeping for some friends while they are on vacation. He's kind of ugly mixed brindle color with short hair and a long, unceasing tail. He eats with abandon, but his eyes bless you with an unmistakable "thanks" as soon as he empties the bowl and comes over to drool on your shoes. Bruno makes life chuckle around here, and Charlie will be a little sad to take him home in a couple of days.

About four that afternoon the phone rings. It's Larry.

"I checked on that plate number for you. There aren't any warrants for it, but I did find out something for you … Charlie, the car is registered to Terri."

"Terri!?"

"I double checked it. It's hers."

Charlie stood there collecting himself, unsure of whether this was good news or bad. Was she in trouble? Did she want to talk? Why did she run away when he approached her?

"Uh … thank you Larry."

"Do you want me to check her out to see if anything's wrong, or make sure she's okay?"

"No, I'd rather you wouldn't. I know she was here. I know she's not ready to talk right now. I don't want her to think I'm sending the police out for her. But if you hear anything more let me know."

"Sure Charlie. Peg and I will see you Sunday. Call us if you need anything."

Charlie sat down behind the office counter and stared out the window toward where she had been parked … and remembered a day in the sun before things turned bad between them … a day when he picked her up from the snow and held his four-year-old daughter above his head and made airplane noises … and listened to her laugh. The world was perfect then.

Wednesday night's prayer meeting came and passed three times, each with renewed hope for Charlie, each with renewed disappointment as the following days passed with no more sightings of the battered old car that was Terri's. Then the phone rang on a Thursday night just before ten. It was Larry.

"I thought you ought to know that the state boys came across Terri's car out west of town on the interstate. There's no sign of foul play, though. It looks like she had car trouble and hitched a ride. They towed it into town and gave it a good going over before I called you. It looks like the transmission gave out on it and she put up the hood and walked away, but that's all we know … For now we're just treating it as an abandoned car. The registration address of record is in Pueblo, Colorado."

Charlie stood by the bed holding the phone in his hand after Larry hung up, then slowly reached over and put the receiver on the hook, bowed his head and began to pray … the same prayer he'd prayed every night since that day he'd last seen her in that restaurant. But this time his prayer was filled with renewed anguish and hope … uncertainty and repentance.

One month later Glenwood Springs, Colorado

Rocky signals the waiter for another round of drinks. Terri sips the last of the "Old-Fashioned" drink in front of her, chewing on the last sliver of ice before biting the cherry in half. It was almost midnight when he put the $20 on the drink tray for the next two drinks and told the waiter to "keep it." About 12:30 they leave the club, both of them laughing and staggering a little as they head for the door. Rocky's new black truck is parked around the side fence and he drops the keys on the pavement as he goes past the front bumper. When he picks them up he's startled by the sound of the starter and the engine coming to life.

"What the h…" he says as he stands up to see someone sitting up in the driver's seat, surprised to see Rocky and Terri in front of him. The thief knows he's caught in the act and instinctively hits the accelerator slamming both of them into the fence, then jams it in reverse and smokes the tires leaving the parking lot, almost hitting a car as he enters the street.

Bewildered … Terri sees the cloud-shrouded moon evaporating into oblivion as consciousness slips away … blackness swims among ambiguous visions of her mother invading the night, painful visions, chaotic visions … then Daddy in the snow … sirens in the distance … then nothing … nothing …

In the waiting room Charlie sits with his head in his hands, silently praying, his friend Larry watching from the chair facing him, unable to comfort him in his pain. It had been one of the hardest things Larry had ever been called on to do. After years of praying with Charlie about Terri, he'd had to tell him this morning that she had been critically injured in the parking lot of a local night club.

Six hours later the surgeon enters the room and asks Charlie to come onto one of the smaller conference rooms nearby. Charlie searches the doctor's expression trying to glean any hint of the prognosis from his eyes.

"She's not out of the woods yet. Her pelvis and hip are broken and she has severe internal injuries. We stopped the internal bleeding, but her head injury is what concerns us the most. She struck her temple hard on the curb when she fell. We're not sure how much damage was done because of the bleeding and swelling. We'll just have to wait until she's conscious again and we don't know how long that may take. The longer she's in the coma, the less chance she'll recover completely. I'm sorry, that's about all I know right now. She'll be in the critical care unit when she comes out of recovery. You'll be able to see her, but she won't be conscious for some time."

The doctor's words laid Charlie's conscience bare ... convicting him that his old sins had festered into Terri's tenuous grip on life. He knew she wouldn't be here now, barely clinging to life were it not for years of revulsion to her own father and the resulting destructive patterns hard-woven into her adult life. The last time he'd even hugged her was when she and Andy picked him up that day in the hospital ... Andy ... he needed to call Andy.

Glenwood Springs, 6:30 p.m. the following Tuesday

Charlie leaves the hospital for only the second time since that awful Sunday morning. She's still not conscious, and he's so tired he can hardly see the road. While stopped at the traffic light, he begins to weep as he sees the club where it happened along the highway. He turns left into the parking lot and searches with his eyes along the fence ... THERE! That must be where it happened! He studies the scene from his car, agonizing over the bent steel post and the lingering stain on the curb and pavement where they must have cleaned up the blood.

Why had she been here? He answered that question to himself and pounded the steering wheel in agony, realizing that his own self-destructive life had led her to this. For the first time in years he needed a drink.

"Are you okay, mister?" a slow voice asked. The words came from behind through his open car window from an older, rough looking man who had just parked a few feet away.

"No ... and neither is my daughter."

"You look like you need a drink. Come on in with me and tell me about it ... I'll buy the first round."

Those words, seeming to come from years past, seem familiarly inviting ... a round of drinks and a non-judgmental ear to absorb some of the pain ... a respite in the storm. Involuntarily Charlie killed the engine and opened the car door, allowing himself to be duped by the false prophesy of comfort through a drunken stupor.

The stranger put his arm across Charlie's slumping shoulders ... Charlie can smell his drunkenness and half-supports him as they move toward the door of the club and go inside.

Sad steel guitar music steeped in dark and murky, smoke-filled air feels both familiar and ominous as they sit down. Neon signs punctuate the blackness above the bar as 'his new best friend' orders a pitcher of beer from a flirty, aging waitress. There's no way to avoid a view of her cleavage as she leans down to deliver the pitcher and pour the first frosty mug just full enough to make the head on the beer slide slowly down the side. She lingers over the table long enough to elicit a fat tip from Charlie's new acquaintance as he pays for the "first round."

The sound of the pouring beer and the memories of long nights watching foam slide down the sides of countless beer mugs seem so familiar, so simple to ease into. As Charlie reaches for the mug he hears the metallic sound of coins falling into the cigarette machine behind him and remembers the cigarettes he bought the night he collapsed in that parking lot years ago ... his last binge before rehab. Those cigarettes had cost him his last dollar in the world, just before his world had gone black ... he remembers the blood stain on the curb outside, probably from Terri's blood ... he lets go of the mug and says, "I can't do this, friend."

"Whadda ya mean? We just got here. Just let me buy you one drink and we'll talk about you and your daughter."

"Terri almost died in that parking lot outside because of my drinking. I can't do that to her again … hell, I can't do that to myself again!"

A fresh breeze blew through the barroom door as it opened before him on the way out. That breeze caught Charlie by surprise, but it was his confirmation that he didn't have to be here any more … he knew he was walking away from life's dungeon for good. There was no doubt that this was his last encounter with the dark familiar world of his past. Outside the bar he felt the easy yoke of Jesus, just as he had that glorious day as he left the rehab center. And he was finally able to actually smile for a moment, realizing that Jesus was in charge of her life as well, even if she didn't acknowledge it. He knows without question that there was the same hope for Terri as long as she continued to draw breath.

The motel was about ten minutes away. He knew he couldn't sleep anyway tonight, but he had to try. Annie's white Lincoln was parked in its usual place and he could see Piper through the window at the front desk. He quietly entered the back door, going straight to his bedroom and closing the door behind him. About fifteen minutes later he saw Andy's car through his bedroom window pulling in the driveway. It was the third night in a row that he and Laura would spend here. They were commuting from Grand Junction eighty miles away on the chance that Andy might be able to see Terri when (if) she wakes up.

Charlie knew the longer she stayed in the coma, the less chance there was she'd ever wake up, but he slept for the first time since Saturday night Everyone knew he

was home, but no one interrupted his privacy that night
... even so, he was back at the hospital by 4:45 a.m. Andy
and Laura joined him at six for a half-hour visit before
heading back to Grand Junction for the day.

Terri's hospital room, Thursday evening

Terri knows the voices are familiar, but can't attach
names to them in this heavy void ... confusion ... images
of silverware and napkins float by ... more familiar
sounds ... "What dressing would you like on your
salad?" ... nothing makes sense ... sleep ... beeping
noises ... light ... pain ... more pain ... can't tell where
it's coming from ... sleep ... blurry light ... muffled
voices again ... more pain ... the cherry's in the glass
all alone ... ♫ Jesus Loves Me ♪ ... blurry light moving
from one eye to the other ... a man in white is shining
light in her eyes, she squints, blinks. He's clearer now
... "Terri, Terri, don't be alarmed, I'm Dr. Gerard and
you're in the hospital. Can you hear me?

She feels the tube in her nose and something's
attached to her arm, but she can't raise her head to see
what it is.

"Can you hear me Terri?"

She musters the strength to nod her head "yes" and
realizes the beeps are coming from the machine next to
the bed.

"Welcome back! You've been asleep for quite a while
now, but we're taking care of you. Do you remember
what happened to you?"

She shakes her head "no" and after a few seconds
nods off again ... more voices ... what are they saying?
... I know them ... who are they?! ... Andy! She mumbles
as she drifts off again, no dreams this time, just sounds,

strange sounds, beeps and voices … and the pain, oh the deep, ever-present pain, dizziness and fatigue.

Hours pass as Terri remains in a deep, troubled sleep. About two a.m. Friday Dr. Gerard is called back to the hospital. Terri's vital signs have begun to go awry. A blood clot is suspected … at 3:15 they wheel her into surgery again. Terri briefly opens her eyes as she deals with new pain. The walls are in motion in the hallway, and the sound of swinging doors is followed by bright lights as human figures in light green surround her. More lights, more pain. One of the figures speaks softly to her as the bright lights go strangely dark: "Take it easy honey, I'm going to put you to sleep again so we can take care of that pain for you. Go to sleep for me one more time."

The world is afloat again, coming at her in all directions … there's Daddy telling Terri and her mother goodbye as they leave for church on Sunday morning … there it is again … the music from Sunday school, ♫ Jesus Loves Me ♪ … fading now … then louder again ♫ Amazing Grace ♪ this time … then through the screen door, mother in the kitchen yelling at Daddy … tears in his eyes, anger in his voice too … BAM! She sees Mother hit the floor and get back to her feet as Daddy leaves through the back door … crying, it's Mother … Daddy's car is gone.

Then nothing …more pain … unfamiliar voices, familiar voices, Daddy's voice praying in the dark room beside her … nothing …

9 a.m. the same day

I return to the waiting room to find Laura and Charlie talking quietly in the corner and decide not to interrupt. Laura has a tender way of listening in times of pain. Charlie needs that now.

A short, solitary walk outside clears my mind a little and along the way I remember the early days with Terri working at the restaurant and the July 4th gathering at the motel where Terri fell in love with Bronson. The painful, uncertain times following Charlie's return to town had altered the course of our lives. But we could never have imagined her bitterness would eventually lead to this. I return to the waiting room to find Laura and Charlie still talking. Charlie seems more at ease now. When Laura sees me from across the room she gives Charlie a long, reassuring hug before joining me.

So far Charlie had only observed Terri from a distance except for when he prayed fervently at her bedside earlier this morning following emergency surgery.

The nurse came into the waiting room to let us know that Terri was awake. Charlie looked relieved and apprehensive. Only one or two at a time could go in, for only a couple of minutes. She looked at Charlie as the assumed first visitor. He looked at me, pleading through his eyes for me to take the first turn. Laura stood back, allowing me to decide whether to go in alone or with Charlie.

Charlie shook his head "no" and lingered at the door again as I approached Terri's side. Her eyes were closed.

"Terri? Can you hear me? It's Andy."

Her eyes blinked open a couple of times and there was a hint of recognition.

"Andy." She whispered, barely audibly.

"You gave us a scare. Do you know how you got here?"

A tear formed in the corner of her eye and she nodded yes and whispered something unintelligible. I leaned closer and she said, "I heard them say Rocky's dead."

I nodded and whispered yes. She turned her eyes toward the window. A lone, lingering tear rolled slowly onto her cheek.

"I heard Daddy's voice yesterday."

I nodded toward the door where Charlie was standing. Her eyes followed mine and found him there, but did not invite him to come closer. Instead, she turned her eyes toward the window as more tears followed. After a few minutes she drifted into a restless sleep again. As I left the room Charlie stepped inside just far enough to watch her sleep, sat quietly in the metal chair beside the door, bowing his head again. Years of separation and Terri's mistrust weighed heavily on his shoulders. It was the same burden I had witnessed on him the first night he came to the motel before the rehab.

If he truly knows God, why is he suffering again? Why has God abandoned him in his time of need after we'd all witnessed his faithful return to sobriety? I know the pain of his unanswered prayers, his prayers for reconciliation must be as painful as mine were for Mama's healing. At least Terri is still alive and expected to make a long, slow recovery.

Turning from the door, I find Laura standing at the window. With the warm morning light streaming across her face, I wonder how we found each other, two people born 1,500 miles apart with no common thread to bring our worlds together ... only the chance of time and place in that club in Grand Junction, Colorado ... or was it chance that brought us together? Without my life-changing decision to take that bus from Corpus Christi to Denver I would never have met her ... and if Mama were still alive I'd probably still be in Texas.

More hours in the waiting room slip by. I nod off in the chair and in my dreams recall my "chance" encounter with Andrea after that nightmare of the burning bush the night before meeting her. Still in a sleepy daze, I marvel at that extraordinary day when everything came together for a lonely, pregnant girl sitting on a rock beside the highway. Even with the realization about her mother's death and the agony of an unwanted pregnancy, she found hope that day ... hope for the future in the prospect of burgeoning life in her womb through the words and reassurance of Father James. I try to imagine what her life might be today, a new mother in the town where she'd grown up, but no longer considered her home. That timid, anxious look in her eyes had been hauntingly familiar when we talked in the truck that day, but only days later had I fully realized that it was the same look I had seen in Gloria as she came down the steps that day in Cheyenne ... the frightened look of an uninvited life-change and overwhelming apprehension about this thing called motherhood. Jeremy had been the agent of change for Gloria into a vital young mother following the same difficult, yet rewarding road Aunt Margaret had traveled over forty years before, beginning with her own unplanned bus trip from Texas. I wondered what road Andrea was taking now.

Laura gently touched me on the shoulder to wake me and tell me that Annie had invited Charlie and us to have dinner with her in town. The hospital would notify us at the restaurant if Terri woke up again. They also told us they expected her to sleep through the night. Charlie said he wasn't hungry. As we left, I looked back to see him in a familiar pose, standing by the waiting room window, hands in his pockets, staring into the sunset. But, somehow today the weight of the world on his shoulders didn't seem quite as heavy as it had been.

The following Sunday 2:27 a.m.

Laura's slow, regular breathing tells me she's finally asleep after our long drive back home from Glenwood Springs. We'd arrived a little after midnight. We'd talked for a while after retiring, but I couldn't sleep. I wander quietly into the front room and turn on the lamp. Walt's letter lay unopened on the coffee table where Laura had dropped the mail on her way out the door to pick me up as we left town last week.

> *Dear Andy,*
>
> *I'm sure you remember my mother from the time you stayed with us that summer. I think you were twelve then and she was staying with us for a few months as well. She loved the way you and Monte used to listen to her tell stories about Africa while drinking your Cokes and eating your chips at our kitchen table on those summer afternoons. She always loved to recall the missionary days of her youth.*
>
> *She went to be with the Lord last month. The last couple of years her memory failed her mostly, but she asked about you and Monte only a few days before she died. I think she still pictured you two as boys. It seemed to please her greatly to describe you two sitting across the table from her, listening to every word she said. I think she probably stretched the truth a little when she told you about her adventures with the wild animals, but it was innocent enough.*
>
> *Only the Lord could have planned for those lazy afternoon story sessions over*

*chips and a Coke at our dining room table
to be such a rare blessing to her in her final
days. Thank you, Andy.*

*Have you heard from Terri again?
Charlie has been in my prayers lately since
your last letter, as has she. Be sure to let me
know if things change with them.*

*Give my love to Laura. Someday I hope
she and I will meet since the Lord has
connected us through you. Maybe Laura
and I can sit around my dining table and
tell "Andy" stories on a summer afternoon.
I'm sure I'd cherish those times as much as
Mother cherished her times with you and
Monte. I'd like to meet Terri as well, since
the Lord has seen fit to keep her in your life,
as precarious a relationship as it has been.
Keep in mind that, as much as we'd like to
be in charge of our destiny, the Lord can
change it in a moment. And, at times, those
changes can seem brutal or even tragic from
our human perspective. Through those tough
times our only real comfort is that God is in
control and all things are possible through
him. From what you've told me about
Charlie's life I think he must know that. I
pray that Terri will also come to know that
in time.*

*Always remember, you and Laura are in our
prayers.
Walt*

The letter must have come just before we went to Glenwood Springs after Terri's emergency surgery. Walt had no idea how prophetic his words about tragedy in Terri's life were. I answered his letter with a brief description of the latest unsettling events in Terri's life. I finally went back to bed a little after 3:30.

Three months later,
November 12, 1987 Glenwood Springs ...

Charlie looks across the parking lot of the motel toward the room in the corner with the new wheelchair ramp. Annie had a contractor build it last week. He's both hopeful and apprehensive about today ... the day Annie brings Terri home to the motel from the hospital, at Annie's insistence of course. Terri has no place to go, except here now, and is facing months of recovery followed by more months or even years of rehabilitation. In typical Annie style she'd insisted on paying for everything, including fixing up the room here to accommodate the recovery process. Charlie was uneasy about the arrangement. So far, he and Terri had only exchanged a half-dozen awkward words across the room or in hospital hallways, always with other people around. He hadn't been able to talk to her alone ... he knew his faltering words could never make up for the years of pain he'd caused, and the difficult years they may have yet to face.

A new white van pulled in the driveway and backed into the drive next to the ramp. Piper parked next to the van and helped as Annie brought Terri out of the van and into the room using a wheelchair, with Terri's leg propped up in front and her yet-unused crutches stowed beside her in the chair.

Terri sat in the easy chair next to the front window. There was a good view of the big blue spruce and the picnic tables on the lawn. While Annie and Piper fussed with the details of getting her settled, Terri remembered throwing the Frisbee for Bronson that summer and Annie sneaking him chicken under the table by her chair. They were good memories. It seemed strange that Charlie was here now instead of Andy and Martin. What is there about this place that continues to draw her? As modest as it is, there's a comfort about it, a silent unexplained hope.

"Terri? Are you Okay?" Piper's voice coaxed her out of her wandering thoughts.

"Sure. I'm just a little tired from all the fuss. Why don't you get settled in next door. I'll just sit here and rest for a while. Help me prop my leg on the stool and I'll be okay."

Annie and Piper unloaded Piper's car into the adjoining room. She'd be staying here for a few days while Terri needed help getting around. Terri sat alone and wondered how she'd wound up in this place only a few yards from Charlie's door, helpless.

Tonight would be the first night Terri would be completely alone without nurses checking her vital signs every few hours, or well-meaning visitors trying to keep her spirits up. She was a little apprehensive, but thankful to know that Piper was staying just next door where only a tap on the single wall between them would signal her for help, Annie had made sure of that. Overbearing as she is sometimes, Terri had come to love Annie like a favorite aunt, and Piper like a sister.

Piper came in around nine to make sure Terri was set up for the night with her medications within easy reach along with the telephone, a glass of water, TV remote and an extra blanket and pillow. Annie had made sure that there were enough hand rails installed in all the right places along the wall for her to use if she needed the bathroom during the night. By nine-thirty, Piper was satisfied with the arrangements so she took Terri's blood pressure one last time, wrote down the results on the clipboard and said goodnight.

As the door closed behind Piper, Terri felt truly alone for the first time in months. This sudden isolation, as temporary as it is, begets a new apprehension, new doubts. Who had she become in all of this? Charlie still had not directly approached her. His presence in her life is still only tangential, if remarkably persistent.

She turned out the lamp and opened the blinds a little. After all her efforts to avoid Charlie over the years, here she was, sleeping just across the parking lot from him, close enough to see that his light was still on. Just beyond his door the neon sign by the street proclaimed "VACANCY," inviting all who need rest to enter.

She needed rest now, but avoided drifting off for a while ... sleep was not always her friend. She'd never quite gotten past those strange, chaotic dreams which began in the days before she fully awoke in the hospital ... the days when her very survival was in doubt. When those dreams visit, there is little rest in the sleep, and headaches always follow the day after.

At eleven the vacancy sign goes out, but Charlie's light still burns ... no rest for him either ... Rocky's face floats by and his eyes are closed ... music in the background, Merle Haggard, I think ... silence ... pain ... I hear Daddy's voice ... is it Daddy or Charlie? ... can't decide ... can't figure it out ... praying ... Sunday school ... pink light ... Rocky's dead ...my fault ... shouldn't have been there! ... No! ... I know I'm sweating but I can't wake up ... silence ... nothing ...

Morning streams through the blinds painting the

kitchen in pink stripes. Terri blinks at the brilliance, suddenly awake and hungry at the same time. She can smell coffee. Is she allowed to have coffee? She can't remember yet, her mind still a jumble. Piper is asleep in the chair by the TV. When did she get here?

Terri moves carefully along the wall toward the bathroom using the rails for only the second time. She tries not to wake Piper, but the commode flush is pretty loud and Piper greets her as she opens the bathroom door.

"Good morning Piper. I didn't hear you come in. When did you get here?"

"I came over about three this morning. You banged on the wall a few times, but you were still asleep, so I didn't wake you. Did you rest?"

Their conversation about rest repeated itself almost every morning for the next two weeks as the nightmarish dreams remained her companions, but eventually Terri began to rest quietly most nights. The recovery began in earnest the day the doctor removed the last small cast. When Annie was satisfied that Terri could manage without help, Piper moved back into her apartment across town.

Charlie's morning chores became familiar as Terri observed his rhythms through the blinds, but seldom heard the sound of his voice. He would not approach her alone, always taking refuge in Annie or Piper's presence. Gone was the boisterous con man salesman, always looking for an angle — replaced by this unpretentious servant, always observant of others' needs. When she watched him clearing snow from the walks she remembered those days in Grand Junction when she begged him to let her help. He'd finally give in and help Terri's six-year-old arms pitch the snow to the side once or twice before losing interest and deciding to build a snow man. After a few minutes, he'd always stop shoveling until the snow man was just the way she wanted it. She couldn't remember the last time she wanted to build a snow man.

She wanted those days again. She needed those days again. She needed her "Daddy" again, but she knew she'd hurt him too deeply for that. She knew they would never build a snow man together again.

Sunday - January 10, 1988, Glenwood Springs

As Charlie stands near the front of the congregation with the other ushers waiting to help with communion his eyes wander to the back row of the sanctuary ... it's Terri! He tries not to stare at her during communion and is thankful that she does not come forward to participate.

He hardly hears the sermon, unsure of how to approach her here, or whether to approach her at all. The sermon drones on as his mind fills with possibilities, doubts and prayers for reconciliation, self-consciously fidgeting like a ten-year-old, anxious for the sermon to be over. As they stand for the final prayer, he briefly turns again toward the back and finds her leaving quietly using her walker with Piper at her side. Should he go after her? What would he say to her if he did? Instead, he decides to wait and seek out one of the elders after the service for prayer.

Terri didn't return to her room that afternoon and Charlie was still confused about her visit when he left for the Sunday evening services. When he returned he could see the light from her lamp through the cold, frosty window. At least he knew she was safely home. He missed her feisty spirit and was saddened by the slow progress of her recovery. Would she ever feel strong enough to stand defiantly before him again? For the next few weeks he didn't see her again, except through his window as he watched her come and go a few times, moving awkwardly on her crutches.

February 21, 1988, Grand Junction

I can hear Laura talking on the phone in the kitchen as I watch a basketball game in the living room. It's 3:30 on a Sunday afternoon and I'm avoiding studying for my classes until the game is over. I can see a snow-covered Grand Mesa through the living room window and wrestle with the possibility of clearing the driveway of new snow sometime before dark. The handle of my new snow shovel propped up against the porch rail mocks me through the window ... no more excuses! Shovel, then study, that's the plan. The game will be over in a few minutes anyway, and my team is behind. Click! The TV goes off as I step toward the coat rack by the front door. Laura ignores my attempt to tell her I'm going outside and continues with her phone conversation.

As I step out into the cold air I remember the days when a driveway like this would be cleared in a couple of minutes with the snow plow on the ranch. Oh, well! I pick up the snow shovel and talk directly to it, "Today it's just you and me, kid!" I look over the driveway and decide to start work by the street curb and move toward the garage, tossing five or six inches of snow from the driveway surface into the yard on either side. I'd been working for about 45 minutes when Laura showed up outside with a cup of hot coffee and coaxed me inside for a breather.

"That was Terri on the phone earlier."

I set the coffee cup down on the table and looked into Laura's eyes trying to get a sense of what was going on. I hesitated for a few seconds before replying.

"Terri called YOU?"

"Yes."

"What's going on?"

"She wants us to come to Glenwood Springs next week … next Saturday night. She wanted me to ask you to come. We talked for a long time. I'm asking you, too Andy."

"What's this all about? Why didn't you call me to the phone?"

"She asked me not to. She wants to talk to both of us together. I think she needs to make sure that you know she's not coming on to you. She just wants to talk without anything lingering in the shadows."

"Should I call her back now?"

"No. I'll call her tomorrow. We agreed on a time when she could be by the phone. She still has a hard time answering the phone in her room if she's not by her bed. Getting to her feet with the walker is still a struggle. I think she needs to do this in her own way. She asked me not to say any more and I want to honor that, okay?"

I looked at Laura again, struggling to find some betrayal of the purpose of all this in her eyes before replying.

"Okay … if that's what you want too, Laura."

She leaned over the table and kissed me on the cheek, then whispered in my ear, "It's what I want."

I couldn't stop wondering what all this was about as we finished our coffee and I went outside to finish the driveway. The uncertainty plagued my studies that evening after supper as I tried to write intelligent sounding answers to seemingly inane questions from my American history professor.

It was still dark Monday morning as I backed out of the driveway and headed for work. I had a snow plow to re-rig after some repairs. I'd be through in plenty of time for afternoon class.

Later in the week Laura and I made plans to go to Glenwood Springs during the day on Saturday for some skiing at Sunlight Ski Resort. It would be only my third time to ski since coming to Colorado. We called Charlie and reserved a room at the motel for Saturday night and told him we wouldn't likely be in until late. We didn't mention Terri's call to him.

Saturday Night, Glenwood Springs

After skiing most of the day, Laura and I drove into town and made the final turn toward the motel. Laura once again successfully deflected all of my efforts to find out what Terri wanted to talk about. When we arrived we saw Annie's Lincoln parked in her usual place next to her room. A few minutes later, Annie knocked on our door and invited us to Charlie's kitchen for dinner at six sharp. That wasn't like Annie. She usually wanted to take everyone out to dinner in grand style.

As we headed out from our room at 5:58, Laura took my arm and steered me down the sidewalk in the wrong direction. I stopped and reminded her that Annie had wanted us there at six sharp and we didn't have time for a detour.

"Relax, Andy it'll be okay, just keep walking."

She kept leading me toward the far corner of the motel and stopped a few feet from Terri's room.

"Go ahead, Andy … knock on her door."

I knocked gently on Terri's door and waited a few seconds, unsure of what was really going on here. The door opened and Terri greeted me using only a cane to help her stand. The last time we saw her she was still leaning heavily on her walker to stand.

"Aren't you going to say hello?" she said smiling a lot like the old Terri I had known. I stood motionless, stunned by the change in her in the past two months.

"Wow!" was all I could say.

"I could use a little help to get from here to dinner. Can I lean on your arm?"

I looked back at Laura and found her beaming at me, her eyes moist with tears of joy. She nodded "Yes" to answer my question about their premeditated plot. I gave Terri my arm and closed her door behind us as we walked carefully down the well-shoveled sidewalk toward Charlie's place. Laura fell in behind us as we walked.

"Daddy doesn't know I'm coming to dinner tonight, Andy. He hasn't seen me walk like this yet. We haven't talked really about anything yet since the hospital. It's as if we live in different worlds within sight of each other. He's been so faithful about providing everything I need, but we haven't spoken a dozen words to each other in all this time. On my own I can't break the silence … I need you here tonight. You are the only one who's kept us connected to each other. I need you to be here when I tell him I was wrong about everything."

We stopped for a minute and I hugged her in approval while Laura looked on.

"I've practiced what to say a thousand times, but I'm not sure I can say it the way I need to say it. I need you and Laura and Annie there to give me the strength to do it."

"We're here for you Terri … are you ready?"

"Without all of you here I wouldn't be … you'll help me if I choke up won't you?"

I silently nodded yes and took her arm more firmly than before. Terri took a few steps, and we walked toward Charlie's door. Terri stood at the door on her own as I stepped back. She knocked on the door as we heard Annie and Charlie talking inside. Charlie opened the door.

"Hello Daddy." ... her voice cracked as she said the word "Daddy" to him for the first time in twelve years, despite all her rehearsal for this moment.

Charlie's voice was almost a whisper as, bewildered, he fought for words not uttered in over a decade ..."Terri! ... " he could hardly breathe as he fought back the tears in surprised realization about what was happening. Were the years of rejection finally melting away?

He continued to stand — stunned, motionless — as Terri stepped forward into the doorway, raised her free hand, palm up and said through streaming tears and broken words, "Can you give your daughter a hug?" Time stood still for Charlie as they found each other in a long postponed father-daughter embrace, erasing years of bitter rejection in a single all-encompassing moment.

He suddenly realized that she might have trouble standing that long, and helped her inside to a chair. Then he knelt beside her, looked directly into her eyes and said, "I'm sorry for all those lost years, Honey. I watched you grow up from a distance far enough away to keep from embarrassing you any more than I did that night at your graduation. I stayed away because I didn't want to hurt you any more ... I missed you more than you can imagine."

She grabbed both his hands and replied, "I missed you too, Daddy. I'm sorry I was so hard on you for so long. It wasn't right. I wasn't there for you when you finally tried to make things right. I forgive you for everything Daddy ... can you forgive me too?"

"There's nothing to forgive you for, Honey. I was the one who traded my family away for the booze. I was the one who hit your mother that time. It was all my fault."

"I didn't believe you when you said you were going to stay sober ... I ran away from here so I couldn't see you again and I almost died because of it ... and Rocky died because of what I was doing to you."

Charlie leaned over toward Terri and held her again as they sat at the table.

"You can't blame yourself for what a criminal did to you and Rocky, Honey."

This was not the meeting he had envisioned. He'd never considered that Terri felt guilty too, and blamed herself for not making amends before that fateful night of violence in a dark parking lot ... and Rocky's death. He ached for her. He had no idea of how to comfort her in this.

Annie, Laura and I moved quietly into the next room as they continued to talk. It was clear that they needed to be alone tonight, that they needed to re-discover a lost relationship and begin the long road of lasting reconciliation.

After a while I stepped back into the kitchen. They were still deep in a conversation only they could fully comprehend and share. I asked them if they wanted to join us for dinner in town and Charlie replied that if it was okay with Terri, he'd rather stay here and fix dinner for just the two of them. Terri agreed, but asked everyone to come into the kitchen for a minute before we left for town.

"I'll never forget what you all did for me tonight, I'm not sure I could have ever mustered up the courage to be here by myself. All these months I've been here have given me a chance to take stock of who I'd become and where I was probably going. You've all been her for me and Daddy, but I've never been able to say thank you before … and thanks especially for being here tonight."

As we left, Charlie pulled me aside to tell me something, but as he hugged me all he could say was "Thank you Andy" before he went back to be with Terri.

Annie tossed the keys to her Lincoln to me and said, "I still like your style! You're driving. Let's go to dinner and leave 'em alone for a while."

Over dinner Laura and Annie told me about their long phone conversations with Terri the past couple of months and how much Terri had been motivated to get back on her feet for just this moment. Piper joined us at the table when she had a chance to get away from the office in the restaurant where she was now the manager. As she sat down I remembered that first meal with Annie here years ago and how Piper had been so embarrassed when Annie had pressed money into her hand. Tonight she was a confident manager, fully in control and thrilled that Annie and Laura had pulled off their plan to surprise me and let me in on Terri's moment of reconciliation with Charlie. We lingered long after dinner and dessert and Laura got to know Piper and Annie a little better. We got back to the motel around ten and found a note on our door.

> *Dear Andy & Laura,*
> *Daddy and I have begun a new*
> *relationship tonight and we both realize how*
> *important you have been in bringing us back*
> *together after all these years. Tomorrow we*

plan to worship together for the first time in
almost fifteen years. We invite you to join us.

Daddy's prodigal daughter,
Terri

Sunday Morning, 10:45 a.m.

As we enter the front door, Laura is surprised when we're greeted by several people who know us by name, and so am I ... it's been several years since we helped with the annual Christmas dinner. We join Charlie, Terri and Annie near the front of the sanctuary.

The first bible reading from the pulpit is Psalm 32 and starts with the words, *"Blessed is he whose transgression is forgiven, whose sin is covered ..."*

As we listened I thought about the first day I met Charlie and the venom I'd heard in Terri's voice as she recounted their history. That was the turning point in our relationship and revealed a simmering resentment that eventually brought her to a reckoning of her own, not unlike Charlie's near-death experience.

This was the first sermon I'd really heard since leaving Texas, the first sermon I hadn't rejected out of hand before I ever entered the church. I remembered sitting beside Mama, always as close as I could get to those wonderful stained glass windows I admired so much. I still remember the patterns in the glass and the words engraved in the little plaque under the window sill, "In memory of Thelma Barrett, our loving grandmother." Clyde Barrett was one of Walt's closest friends and a deacon. He was also a pall bearer at Mama's funeral. The stained glass windows here are tall and skinny and made in shades of blue and purple, not like the big, multicolored windows at home in Texas.

The sermon began with the reading of the scripture text, John 15:16, *"Ye have not chosen me, but I have chosen you, and ordained you, that ye should go and bring forth fruit, and that your fruit should remain: that whatsoever ye shall ask of the Father in my name, he may give it you."*

Those words penetrated my soul like a sword. It was the scripture Mama and I had memorized together on the afternoon I was baptized all those years ago. She cried tears of joy that day … the first real joy I'd seen in her eyes since Daddy died. After the baptism she gave me Daddy's bible. Today was the first time since I left Texas that I had heard them.

The words from the pulpit that day continued to penetrate me. It was as if I were the only person in the room. There was both comfort and shame in those words as I grappled with how Mama would have wanted me to live my life … and how I had rejected prayer itself in my defiance of His continued involvement in my life. Only once was I briefly distracted from the pulpit message as Laura put her hand in mine and I looked directly into her eyes and — for the first time since Mama's death — felt truly blessed.

After the service Charlie and Terri meet with Pastor Bernard in a small room with two of the elders for a time of prayer … a different prayer than I had prayed for Mama those last days before she died.

Charlie's prayers had already been answered. Out of the habits of my old rebellious attitude I couldn't help but ask that old, nagging question … Why hadn't my prayers for Mama been answered? Without warning Laura's stinging words echoed in my head, "It's not about you, Andy!" In the light of what I'd heard today, I immediately felt small and selfish again, she was right. I needed to put this behind me and celebrate the answered prayers of reconciliation for Terri and Charlie before us now. In a way, they were my prayers too, because I had lived with the pain of Charlie's separation from Terri over the years as well, and it was over now. It was the answer to a prayer that I had never audibly uttered. But my very participation in their relationship had caused countless prayers to go up from others connected to me through my involvement in this. I could see now that a good portion of my own life had been lived as a kind of prayer leading to this moment even as I had refused to acknowledge the Lord's presence in my life. The answer to this lived, yet unspoken prayer was finally a resounding "Yes!"

In this we can rejoice ... and today, that is enough.

Johnny's Legacy

April 12, 1990 … Platteville

Johnny has almost everything packed for the move to Denver. For the past two months he's been going through more than twenty years of living in this old house. In a few days the volunteers from the church and the Center will be here to take it all to the new house in Denver. The only things left to pack are his bed, a few toiletry items, and his Mother's old writing desk and chair. He'll be carrying those things in his own truck.

He knows he'll need to clear the desk out before he takes it, but he hasn't had the heart to go through it since she died five years ago. It is the only thing left in the house that still contains her undisturbed memories. The lid stuck a little when he opened it. He took the key from the blue velvet box and unlocked the drawer. Inside he found a Schaeffer's fountain pen, a bottle of blue-black ink, and some aging parchment stationery. When he opened the drawer fully, he found two bundles of letters, each tied with blue satin ribbon. They had never been sealed, addressed or mailed. He untied the first bundle and removed the top letter from the envelope.

September 5, 1947

Dearest Wally,
I can't count the number of times I've tried to write you in these two years. Even now, I don't know if I can finish it, but you

deserve to know why I left Brownsville.

*After that night we were together on the
lake, I felt so guilty the morning after, that
I knew I couldn't trust myself alone with
you again, so I turned you away for the
next few weeks. After a while I heard that
you were seeing someone else. I couldn't
blame anyone but myself for that because
you had to assume that I didn't want to
see you anymore. When I saw you out with
Shirley that night I couldn't bring myself to
face you and give you the ring back. Out of
frustration I left home and came to stay with
my grandmother here in Denver.*

*I hadn't planned to stay here, but
circumstances changed and I decided to
stay. What I mean to say is that by the time
I found out that I was going to be a mother
I knew that you and Shirley were already
married, and I knew I couldn't ruin your
future together by telling you then, so I kept
silent. Please forgive me for not telling you
...*

The letter was unfinished. Wally had to be the Walter
Johnson Andy had written occasionally. The ring must
have been from him.

Johnny remembered his conflicts with Mother about
her flat refusal to tell him who his father was. Those
conflicts always ended in some form of rebellion from
him ... late nights with dangerous friends, reckless
escapades which could easily have turned fatal, and the
marijuana she'd found in his room not long before he
joined the Marines. But now he understood her adamant

refusal and her decision to raise him alone rather than destroy Walt's fledgling marriage.

The other envelopes stared at him from the desk. Johnny felt as if he was intruding, but they would not be refused their audience. Each letter revealed more about Mother's struggles as a single parent than she could ever have told him. They were a kind of diary, a way for her to share Johnny's successes, failures and accomplishments with Wally over the years. She signed some of them, but mostly just poured out her heart through the trials and blessings ... in silence ... alone. As he continued to read, Johnny felt her tears of regret, joy, fear and hope between her hand-written lines. Those letters were her Ebenezer stones.

One particular letter haunted him,

September 5, 1970

Dear Wally,

As I write this, I'm nearing Dallas on a bus. I need to tell you about Johnny. He's coming home from Viet Nam. They called me last night at Nora's house in Brownsville and told me that Johnny has been seriously wounded and is now being transported to the West Coast for intensive treatment. He's lost part of his leg and has other massive injuries after a land mine went off near him. They say he'll be discharged from the Marines after his surgeries are completed in a few months. The last of his surgeries can be done in Denver.

I can't imagine what the Lord's purpose in these horrible circumstances might be, but I'm struggling to trust Him in this. In fact, this is the most difficult time I've ever had keeping my faith alive. I wish you could be here to walk through this with me, but it was my decision to keep Johnny separated from you and I must continue to bear this alone. At least Johnny's alive. They tell me that others who were there with him on that mission did not make it home at all.

It is a blessing to know that my niece, Nora, is connected with you there through the church and that her son Andy is in your Sunday school class. At least my prayers for that little family have been answered through you. Andy has a special quality about him, even now after his father's tragic death. He loves to hear about Moses. Sometimes he asks me to read Exodus to him. I continue to pray that you will mentor him as you are now. I just wish I could be there to witness that, but Johnny needs me now and I must go to him. I only hope and pray that we will learn to live together in peace now. Our last time together before he enlisted was unbearable.

I wish I could embrace you tonight and feel your strength, know your faith as I struggle with Johnny's uncertain future ...

— another unfinished letter. Johnny found himself re-reading and remembering those first days after Viet Nam and the pain he had brought her with his poisonous attitude and stinging words. Those words had brought tears to her eyes, and now to his. He was dumbfounded by the paradox exposed in these letters. He had to have time to absorb the idea of a living, breathing father, the revelations about his relationship to his Mother, and the crisis of faith she'd gone through on his behalf after Viet Nam. He couldn't read any more letters right now.

It was all too much for Johnny, especially with his rapidly approaching wedding. In another four days Gloria would be his new bride and they'd be on their honeymoon almost twenty years after his debilitating wounds in Viet Nam. Their love had grown steadily over the fourteen years since their first meeting, but he'd always pushed the possibility of acting on it away as an impossible dream. At age forty-five he had all but given up on finding a life's companion, but Gloria, at age twenty-nine, had not allowed him to say no. It was Gloria who had been the aggressor the past year or so by making it painfully obvious that she wanted to not only spend their lives together, but give Jeremy the father he needed as well. Johnny had watched her grow up from that frightened fifteen year old mother-to-be into a radiant, energetic young woman. Gloria and Johnny together had taken the Center for Hope forward into a new era after his mother's death. The Center was now an adequately funded, state-wide organization coordinating the efforts of over a hundred churches in encouraging the "right to life" over "choice."

Johnny needed to sleep now. The day's revelations had taken a toll on his limited energies. But sleep would not come as he agonized over whether he should reveal his mother's secrets five years after her death. Should he contact Walter Johnson to let him know he was his father? Or, should her secrets remain locked away? Just after midnight Johnny re-tied the bundles as he had found them, placed them back in the drawer and locked them away.

2 p.m. the following Saturday

Pacing nervously in the dressing room of the church, I wait for the wedding to start. I'd met Johnny for the first time fourteen years ago in the Denver bus station, only a couple of miles away. I could never have imagined that I'd be standing here today as Johnny's best man. And I'd never have imagined that the bride would be that shy mother-to-be we'd picked up that day in Cheyenne to take to Denver.

Jeremy was so excited and nervous about giving his mother away during the ceremony that he'd asked me to straighten his bow tie three times in the last fifteen minutes. It was the first time either of us had ever worn a tuxedo, and he was self-conscious about his freckles. I was just self-conscious about the bow-tie.

Laura comes in a few minutes later to give us each a last minute approval. As she pins his boutonniere on, she straightens his tie one more time and gives him an assuring wink. He blushes and looks up at me again. I give him the thumbs up just as the music starts and we exit the dressing room.

Final Revelations

Seventeen years later ... June 12, 2007

About two years ago Laura and I moved from Grand Junction to Denver and I began my new job in a Denver high-rise office building as a mid-level manager. With the increase in my salary, Laura decided to take a substantial pay cut and work exclusively for the Center for Hope with Gloria and Johnny.

Today as I look out the 12th floor window of my office, I see police rushing to the scene about two blocks away. It's after 4:30, so I decide to leave for home. The elevator is almost full and we stop two more times on the way to the ground floor. I think about my job in Grand Junction at the farm equipment company. There were no elevators, no crowds, and I had a brief thought about taking Laura back out there again to get away from the big city crowds. But it was only a brief thought that faded when I remembered how happy Laura is here working at the Center. She is a natural there and comes home almost every day with a new story about how the Lord is at work in another young mother-to-be.

Those thoughts evaporate as we reach the ground floor and I move toward the revolving door to exit the building. I can hear more sirens as I walk two more blocks toward my car and turn the corner. The ambulance is now in full view and I can see them working on someone lying on the curb. The police are already interviewing bystanders and they are barricading the sidewalk with crime scene tape. I continue to walk toward my car on the opposite side of the street. Paramedics work frantically on the victim as one of the two girls the police are interviewing collapses.

They put her on a stretcher just as the paramedics slump in exhausted disappointment, and stop working on the man. They cover his face as his blood continues to cover the curb. When the paramedics stand I get a better look and see the man's shoes … my knees turn to jello and I sit on the curb in denial. After a few minutes I stand and cross the street toward the police line. The policeman tries to hold me back, but I insist and tell him that I think the victim is the man who helped raise me. He lifts the tape and allows me through. I speak briefly with the paramedic and ask him to uncover the victim's face. My worst fears are realized … it's Johnny.

I realize that the van across the street belongs to the Center for Hope, and Johnny must have been driving them somewhere. After the police interview, I speak to the girl still standing and get a description of how this happened. Her name is Rita and she has recovered enough to tell me that her ex-boyfriend is the killer and the police are after him now. I speak with the police and tell them I need to be the one who tells Johnny's wife, Gloria.

I'm still in shock when I get to my car. The twenty minute drive to Johnny's house seems to take hours. I struggle for the words and try to rehearse different phrases, but nothing works. I park in the driveway and sit in silence, still searching for the words.

It's the hardest thing I've ever done, this walk to Gloria's door. I still have no idea how to tell her what's happened. I hear her inside vacuuming and wait until the noise stops before I reach to ring the doorbell. Again I stop, my hand shaking. I still don't know the words. How do I tell her that Johnny's dead? How do I tell Gloria that the life they've built together for seventeen years is over? I turn and face the street hoping to build courage, but all I see is his rake and wheel barrow parked next to the tree. The unopened bag of grass seed waits for him to return at the end of the day.

I remember the conversation Johnny and I had years ago, the day before their wedding. He'd had doubts about their sixteen year age difference and asked me if he was cheating Gloria and Jeremy by strapping them to a handicapped man his age. I remember his answer came in the form of an enthusiastic fourteen-year-old Jeremy showing up, asking him if it would be okay if he called him "Dad" before the adoption was really final. Johnny told him it was fine and Jeremy hugged him and ran straight to his mom yelling at the top of his lungs "HE SAID IT'S OKAY MOM, DAD SAID IT'S OKAY!"

Johnny looked back at me after that and said, "I guess I got my answer." It was the happiest I'd ever seen Johnny. Over the years since their wedding I've seen that same delight time and time again on all three of their faces ... and now Johnny was gone. I turned again to face the door just as Gloria opened it.

"Hi Andy. I saw you through the window. Is everything all right?"

I looked at her and couldn't hold back the tears as I hugged her and told her about Johnny's heroic death while protecting the lives of those two girls. She couldn't speak through her tears as we sat in the living room.

Jeremy, now 31 years old, is no longer the skinny nervous young boy. Gloria needs his strength. He and Laura arrive a few minutes later, coming straight from the Center. Gloria buries her face in Jeremy's strong chest and sobs. After a while Laura and I leave them to their private grieving and drive home in silence. When we pull into our driveway, she turns directly toward me and says, "We're alone now, Andy. It's okay to let go. I know you loved Johnny like a brother."

When I turn toward her I can see her tears beginning to form. We sit there for a few minutes in each other's arms remembering Johnny and asking ourselves why this had to happen to a man so dedicated to others. Sleep came slowly for both of us as we both struggled to free our minds from the loss of him.

I finally gave up trying to sleep and slipped quietly out of the room when I heard the slow, regular breathing of Laura's sleep. My chair in the living room seemed a better choice for me now. The clock on the mantle read 2:15. I stared out the window toward the mountains. The view out our west-facing picture window reminded me of the panorama Bronson and I had enjoyed from the top of that boulder in Platteville.

They're all gone now, Bronson, Aunt Margaret and now Johnny. I couldn't imagine where I might be now if Aunt Margaret and Johnny hadn't taken me in that winter. And Bronson, that wonderful old dog made life bearable by listening to every word I said to him about Mama and Daddy and how God had let me down. He understood. He listened. He didn't judge me. He knew what it meant to be alone on the road, not knowing what the future holds.

My thoughts drift back to those early days in Platteville as I watch clouds drift by a distant, high mountain ridge in the moonlight … I can almost hear Johnny calling Bronson into the back yard so we can leave for Sunday school … I remember yelling "goodbye Bronson, goodbye boy! We'll be back after church!"

I wake slightly, but only briefly as my mind continues to drift, distorting past and present … Johnny's driving to church … he turns the wrong way and we head up the mountain. The snow is slippery under the tires as we climb higher and higher. The road ends at the bottom of a cliff. I need Bronson! I struggle to stand on the icy rocks at the base of the cliff. I look back downhill toward the truck and see it sliding down the hill. Johnny's bloody head rests on the steering wheel and a trail of blood colors the snow between the ruts. Aunt Margaret stands behind a nearby boulder silently watching as the truck slides faster and then rolls end-over-end down the mountain into oblivion.

A blast of wind knocks me to my knees on the rocks. The wind continues to fan the flames on a bush above me as a voice from the bush engulfs everything, "Are you here for confession?" The words penetrate to the bone ... I deliberately turn away and discover a door in the cliff ... I sense there is peace on the other side, and approach. Through the opening I see a shadow and hear Mama's voice, "I heard your prayers for me, Andy. Jesus knows you. He's always known you ..." When I cross through the door, she's gone and I feel the heat from the flames. The penetrating voice returns, "You did not choose me, but I chose you and appointed you." The heat from the bush sucks the life from the air. I fall to my knees again on the rocks and try to reply, but cannot speak ...

A soft touch on my cheek startles me awake ... "It's okay, Honey! You were trembling and you're soaked with sweat. You must have been having a nightmare."

I stand, trembling inside, and face the window. The bright morning sun lights the same ridgeline where the clouds floated in the moonlight last night. My throat is as dry as my night shirt is drenched with sweat.

"Are you alright, Andy?" Laura asks as she steps in front of me, wiping my brow with a cold, damp cloth.

"Yeah, Honey. I'm okay now." I reach down and give her a kiss before I go upstairs to take a shower. She grabs my hands and turns me back toward her just as I turn away.

"I love you, Andy. Do you need to talk about last night?"

"Not right now. I need some time to think."

"I'll have breakfast ready when you come back down."

I finally turn and go upstairs as Laura watches from the living room door.

After breakfast we leave for Gloria's house again.

That afternoon as we were looking at their wedding album, Gloria smiled at me and said, "I really loved him you know. We had a deep, enduring, romantic love that came from within. He doubted that at first because of our age difference, but he came to know it over the years. We both knew that our marriage was a gift from God that we could never have anticipated, an intimacy of body and soul ... we completed each other. The Lord gave us seventeen years together. What a gift Johnny was. After a few minutes Jeremy sat on the couch beside her and wiped the tears from her eyes.

"He died doing the Lord's work Mom ... and he was my Dad. He'd want us to lean on the Lord now and remember that we'll see him again in glory."

Then Jeremy looked back at me and said, "At Margaret's funeral you told me that I should *'Remember the way she was when we were together ... to remember her smile, and the way she made me laugh.'* It helped me through that tough time then, and I've been remembering Dad that same way today ... the way he took me fishing and laughed on the way home about not catching anything ... the way he couldn't take his eyes off Mom when she was cooking dinner, or just walking in the door. You knew he adored her. And because of your words Andy, I have years of memories of him to treasure."

Then he turned back toward Gloria and said. "Those memories are Dad's gift to us Mom ... God's gift to us. I want to thank the Lord for Dad's life and connection to all of us. Andy, you've known Dad longer than anyone here. He talked about you all the time. One of my sweetest memories of Dad was to hear him pray for you and Laura every night over dinner just before he blessed the food. Would you lead us in prayer for Dad, Andy? It would mean a lot to Mom and me"

Laura squeezed my hand. Then she put her arm around my waist as if to reassure me that she understood my uneasiness. Last night's dream flashed through my mind and strangely, I remembered the last part of the scripture that boomed from the burning bush. "... that you should go and bear fruit and that your fruit should abide, so that whatever you ask the Father in my name, he may give it to you." Those words and Laura's reassuring touch brought an unexpected confidence and I relaxed into the words ...

"Father we all have been blessed by this man you placed among us. He shared his love with all of us without reservation. We all thank you for Johnny. Thousands of other lives have also been blessed by your work through him and Aunt Margaret. We pray now specifically for Gloria and Jeremy in their grief. We pray that his continuing memory will bring you glory over the course of their lives. Hold them in your hand during this time of grief and loss, and help them find your comfort, even through this tragic circumstance. Give us all the strength and grace to forgive the man who caused his death, for we know that in that forgiveness we are also forgiven. Be with us all as we celebrate Johnny's life tomorrow and lay him to rest in your everlasting peace and presence.

And Lord, it has been a long time since I spoke with

you in earnest. Forgive me for my decades of sinful rebellion and doubt, and restore me to the faith to which we have been called. I stand here before my brothers and sisters in this room with a contrite heart and ask your forgiveness for my rebellion. I also ask for the prayers of my brothers and sisters here in my restoration to faith. You placed Jeremy here today to ask me directly to pray for Johnny. That open, direct request broke my decades of silence to you. I now see your unbounded grace and protective hand in my life since Mama and Daddy's death. Only a loving God could have put Laura in my life to keep me connected with you daily, whether I realized it or not. And only You could have guided me here to Aunt Margaret and Johnny in the winter of my young life. Today I am finally able to put my selfish agenda behind me and remember Mama in the joyous moments we had together instead of blaming you for her life cut short. I know now that she is free of the physical pain she suffered on this earth in those final months, and I look forward to seeing her again in glory along with Johnny and Aunt Margaret. Forgive me, Lord. Change my life. Restore my soul. After a long time in the desert I now long for your continued presence."

When I paused just before saying "Amen," Jeremy took up the prayer, then Gloria, and finally Laura. They all joined in support of my confession and individually gave thanks for Johnny's life.

As Laura and I left the house I felt an unaccustomed peace. Even the stars in the Denver sky looked brighter. It was as if a veil had finally been lifted for me, and I could now completely join Laura in the clear, pure Colorado air. I continued to unburden my soul that night to Laura in the privacy of our home, with conversation more intimate than any physical contact could ever be. I learned of her constant prayers over the years. She also spoke about the blessing of witnessing Terri and Charlie's reconciliation and the hope that I would see the hand of God working through me in their lives ... and she had felt the change in me during the sermon the following day at their church.

Johnny's funeral the next day was at the same church where Aunt Margaret had been remembered. The crowd was even larger for Johnny and with the high public profile his murder had received, the television stations were poised outside. As a result, private donations to the Center for Hope, large and small, increased ten-fold, at least for a while.

Two weeks later ...

Johnny's study seems empty now as Gloria enters. This was his quiet place, his only respite from the rigors of life when he needed quiet and rest. In the past couple of years he had spent more time here. His wounds had taken their toll over the years, and at 62 he had become more fragile than most men. But here, in this room he had found strength again through the word of God and the view out his window toward those glorious mountains to the west beyond the trees. At night, just before going to sleep he'd often spoken of the subtle changes in the season, the purity of the snow, or a bird he'd seen through he window. Stories from the window had often been their version of "pillow talk" to quiet their souls before sleep. Gloria sat in his favorite chair and absorbed the view through the window. After a few seconds she heard a woodpecker in the tree and watched quietly as he worked his way around one particular limb. Johnny had loved the sound of the woodpeckers ... she felt a new, but strangely familiar peace about his death in those rhythms.

The layer of dust on the old writing desk in the corner was silent witness to the fact that Johnny hadn't opened it in years. He'd told Gloria that it had belonged to Margaret, and that Andy should probably inherit it someday. Gloria decided to dust and polish it before calling Andy to come for it. Johnny had never invited her to explore the desk and she decided to honor that and pass it on to Andy untouched, except for the polish she had just lovingly applied. That evening she called Andy to tell him about Johnny's wishes that he inherit his Aunt Margaret's unopened desk.

July 4, 2007

Laura and I arrive at Gloria's house around noon to celebrate the day with Gloria and Jeremy. We drive the pickup because we'll be taking Aunt Margaret's writing desk home with us.

At the end of the day Jeremy and I enter Johnny's study to move the desk to my truck, unopened. I sit briefly at the desk and remember Aunt Margaret writing here, always uncharacteristically somber. I discover the drawer is locked and speculate briefly about what may be inside before carrying it to the truck. The next morning I rise shortly after dawn to a quiet house while Laura still sleeps. Aunt Margaret's desk stands silently by the window and I remember the mystery of the locked drawer.

I open the desk and explore the compartments above the writing surface. After a few minutes I discover a small blue velvet box with a boy's high-school senior ring and key inside. As I open the drawer, I discover the

two bundles of letters and begin to read, "Dear Wally
…"

Laura respected my privacy for the rest of the
morning, disturbing me only to bring me a cup of coffee
as I continued to read. She could sense it was a private
time for me, a time of healing and revelation.

That afternoon I told her about the letters and we
both realized that without the connection between Aunt
Margaret and Walt on that night in Brownsville over
sixty years ago, Johnny would never have been born.
In Aunt Margaret's private letters, the plan for our lives
and countless others had been revealed. And, without
Mama's death, in God's perfect timing, we would never
have begun our lives together in a sin-filled club named
the "Midnight Roundup." Suddenly my old anger about
unanswered prayer was revealed for the petty selfishness
it really was … the Lord had been patiently at work
through all of it, shaping not only my life, but the lives
of those connected to me from Brownsville to Colorado.
Walt and Aunt Margaret's one night of indiscretion had
been used by the Lord as a springboard for changing
many lives for the better, including mine.

Aunt Margaret had been so careful to keep these
letters private to prevent damaging the lives of others
over the years. We carefully considered and prayed about
whether to tell Walt about the contents of the letters. We
knew Walt was not in good health and that in his last
letter he had told us that Shirley was gone now.

We prayed together again as we packed and
addressed the box of letters … prayers with Laura seem
familiar now.

Brownsville, Texas - August 12, 2007 10 a.m.

Walt greets the mailman on the front porch and they exchange a few brief words. After all, he's been Walt's regular mailman for the past ten years. In the bundle of mail he finds an envelope addressed to his wife Shirley. It's been over two years since she passed away and he still receives mail addressed to her once in a while. It's just an advertising flyer, but he runs his fingers across her name on the label and decides not to toss it in the trash just yet. In a few minutes the postman stops back by and brings Walt a small square box he'd neglected to give him earlier.

It's from Andy and Laura. He hasn't heard from them in a while and speculates about what they might have sent. He pours himself a cup of coffee before he sits at the kitchen table to open the box. There is a letter just under the lid on top of the packing.

Dear Walt,

Tragedy struck two months ago. I was walking through Denver on my way home and heard sirens. When I turned a corner I could see blood along the curb beneath the paramedics working frantically on a man lying at the edge of the sidewalk. A small crowd had gathered and the police were holding them back from the drama unfolding before them.

I crossed the narrow street to avoid the confusion, continuing my walk toward the lot where I had parked. But a haunting pall came over me when I saw the shoes of the man on the sidewalk.

I knew those shoes!

I stopped.

I froze.

I listened.

The police were taking statements from two young women on the street as the life-blood dripped over the curb and the paramedics suddenly slumped in horrible disappointment and exhaustion. They covered his face.

The police continued to talk to those two young ladies. One of them was sitting on the step at the back of the ambulance. She was pregnant and obviously distressed, but it was the other girl the paramedics turned to help as she collapsed. Her name was Rita.

Earlier that day Rita had an argument with her former boyfriend, the father of her baby. He had insisted that Rita have an abortion and she flatly refused. She told him about the counseling she'd received at the Center and how they'd arranged to provide a safe place for her to stay until the baby was born. In anger, he had returned to her apartment later in the day, and encountered Johnny and the other girl as they were moving Rita to her new temporary home. An argument ensued and Johnny stepped in front of him as he flew into a rage and lunged at Rita with a large knife. Johnny, handicapped as he was, used his military training to overcome him and send him packing. But Johnny was more seriously injured than they realized at first and he collapsed on the sidewalk within a minute or two. He died there in front of Rita and Linda.

Johnny gave his life to protect those girls. For the second time in his life, he had sacrificed his personal safety for others. In Viet Nam he earned the Silver Star, but that day in Denver he obtained an even greater glory. He is finally at peace with his Lord and Savior.

There is more to the story though, much more. As you already know, Johnny and Aunt Margaret were a saving grace in my life at a time when I was lost and alone. When Johnny died, he left me his mother's writing desk. Inside I found the letters you have now in the package we sent you. Those letters are a kind of diary, a chronological accounting of the life Aunt Margaret and Johnny lived. The letters were written, but never mailed to Johnny's father who never knew about his son. Aunt Margaret had chosen not to contact him because she knew it could destroy his fledgling marriage. She made a conscious choice to raise Johnny alone with all the attendant hardships a single mother knows.

As hard as this has been for me, Johnny's death has finally enabled me to pray in earnest again for the first time since Mama's funeral. In this horrible tragedy I have regained my thirst for Jesus.

It is also plain to me now that Johnny's ultimate sacrifice has touched hundreds of other lives through the public revelation of how he and Aunt Margaret lived and dedicated their entire lives in the service of others. I was certainly one of those whose life was enriched by their sacrifice.

But that is not the final chapter. Johnny, the man who so willingly sacrificed his life for others in life-and-death encounters, was your son.

I am sending these letters to you in the hope that you will understand the profound purpose of that loving, but human encounter you and Aunt Margaret experienced in Brownsville that night in 1945.

Paradoxically, through that encounter your lives have richly blessed thousands of others, including mine.

Your "once-again" prayerful brother in Christ,
Andy

Walt looked at the open box before him on the kitchen table and once again remembered that night with Maggie in 1945. He lifted the two ribbon-bound bundles from the packing and speculated about those decades together they had missed ... and Johnny's sacrificial life and death. He sat for a long time, alone with those letters, absorbing Maggie's tear-stained words. For the first time in his life he was able to see the Lord's purpose in Maggie's sudden disappearance and the need for their abbreviated relationship ... and he wept, smiled, and sometimes laughed as Maggie shared their lives with him through that old Schaeffer pen. Eventually he dozed off at the table into a strange, warm world of hope and light ... and he could see Maggie on the other side of a meadow holding the hand of a young boy as she walked toward him ... on holy ground.

The next morning his daughter found him, sitting peacefully at his kitchen table, his head resting beside a small box ... his forehead cold, his breathing silenced. The Schaeffer fountain pen was still in his hand beside an unfinished letter with only the opening words:

"Dear Maggie ..."

Story's End

Post Script

"Dear Walt" was not premeditated!

Quite the contrary … after hearing an extraordinary Sunday morning portrayal of Moses' exile to Midian, unrelenting words invaded my thoughts, demanding to be heard, until I set them down on paper. Even so, I still cannot explain the insistence of those beginning words that I write them in a letter to someone named "Walt" that very Sunday afternoon.

There is no one person named Walt in my conscious memory of any particular consequence, and therein may lie the attraction of the name … that "Walt" is not associated with a specific person, but instead represents a composite of lives that have consistently steered me in this particular direction, even during the times I was in my own Midian desert.

I did not set out to write a novel. In fact, as I wrote the first few pages, I was hoping I could develop it into my first real short story. But as the characters took on their respective lives and relationships, they required the same thorough development and inclusion as the text of the Dear Walt letter that very first Sunday. The plot took shape and extended through its own energy, due in part to Pastor Dan's continuing multi-Sunday treatise on the early days of Moses.

I simply could not dismiss the compelling parallels of Moses' flight from Egypt because it was "a place he could no longer live" in his self-imposed exile, to Andy's bus journey to Denver and his first days in Platteville. For Moses, Midian offered refuge from the immediate storms of life, as Platteville had for Andy. But over time, Midian was also the place where God prepared Moses for his eventual calling by transforming him into a shepherd, the same occupation which Jesus himself claims in the New Testament. Unwittingly, Andy was trained, much like a shepherd, to deal with difficult situations in other people's lives as well, all the while kicking and screaming against God, and repeatedly dismissing the call to earnest prayer in the burning bush dreams.

In today's society many of us have taken similar journeys away from "places where we can no longer live." I know I have. My journey lasted three and a half decades. Sometimes our journeys are initiated by difficult family circumstances, or an overwhelming urge to express newfound independence as we grow into adulthood. In other cases we may feel hurt or slighted by a church or other untenable religious connection and rebel, as surely as Andy did, against God himself because of it. But if we are truly called by God, he will eventually find us in our everyday circumstance and confront us with our own burning bush experience, often in the middle of life threatening circumstance or our own self-constructed mess. The challenge is to understand in our own burning bush moment that we are standing on holy ground and have no choice but to acknowledge that we were never really in charge of our lives in the first place. The comfort in that moment comes only when we surrender control to Him and realize that with God there are no limits on healing.

Instead of turning away from the burning bush, perhaps we should seek it out.

 **Native Texan R.D. Frazier** grew up in North Texas, but has spent most of his adult life in the Houston suburban area with his wife of nearly 30 years. After a two-year enlistment with the Marine Corps, he worked professionally as a photographer early in his career. He also spent several months working in western Colorado -- where he eventually set much of the plot of *'Dear Walt.'*

However, facing the challenging economic instability of the energy crisis in the early 1980s, he developed a newfound enthusiasm for technology, and made the switch to computers and publishing. He currently works as a print-and-web graphic designer, develops websites commercially, and spends much of his 'off-work' time writing.

Today, reflecting back on the decades after his own teenage rebellion against the church, Ron now understands and appreciates the painful ... yet necessary ... revelation of God's grace in his life. Revelation that laid him bare and exposed him once again to God's keeping presence. At age 51, facing a life-threatening heart condition, he came face to face with his own immortality and slowly began his journey back to the God who had always been faithful to him.

Much like Andy in *'Dear Walt,'* Ron crawled through turbulence and chaos of a life lived without walking with the Lord -- much like Andy's, his own long journey brought him home, and he is no longer "in a place he could no longer live."

'Dear Walt' is his first novel, and while the plot is based in Colorado, both the fictional characters and plot actually grew out of his return to the faith of his early years after a 35-year absence.

You are invited to visit our companion web site, **DearWalt.com** for extra information about the book and how it evolved from "possibly a short story" to a reality. There you'll find tidbits about the author's choice of Colorado as the location, as well as details about the cover photograph (taken by the author).

And, while most fictional characters don't actually communicate via email, Andy is definitely the exception, and you may send him an email via our online form. We also have interactive comment forms at the bottom of most entries on the web site, where you can interact with the author, editor, staff, and other web site visitors.

Of course **DearWalt.com** is also a convenient place to order extra copies of the book for giveaways, Christmas, and birthday presents. We also recommend other books and make them available for purchase at our Dear Walt online bookstore.

Be sure to watch for upcoming books by R.D. Frazier and read special "previews" from the manuscript-in-process before the books actually become available. He already has another book under way, entitled ***"Welcome to Ricochet!"***

Sneak Preview

Jack had no idea as he drove down the back roads of West Texas that he was about to experience a revolutionary lifestyle change. Little did he know when he heard those words, "Welcome to Ricochet!" that he was about to be swept into a madcap world. As R.D. Frazier blends elements of small-town tradition with the glitzy venue of city life, his lead character, Jack, takes on a chutzpah of his own while he's temporarily stuck in Ricochet, Texas, amid characters who make his life take unexpected turns ... a town of 1023 residents ... that's not even on the map!